DOMINATED BY DESIRE

THE DESIRE SERIES BOOK 1

BARBARA DONLON BRADLEY

DOMINATED BY DESIRE
Copyright © 2022 by Barbara Donlon Bradley

ISBN: 979-8-88653-110-7

Published by Satin Romance
An Imprint of Melange Books, LLC
White Bear Lake, MN 55110
www.satinromance.com

Published in the United States of America.

Cover Design by Ashley Redbird Designs

ONE

Heather stood next to her commander, going over everything she had learned about Vespian society so far. He wanted to be sure she was ready for her next assignment. She found the idea of guarding the ambassador a bit boring, but she'd done this before. It shouldn't be a long one. The man was only to be on Earth for a few days.

Her first glimpse of the Vespian ambassador caught her off guard. She wasn't sure what she expected, but it wasn't seeing him coming in like some sort of rock star. Shirt missing, exposing tight, sculpted abs, along with well-muscled shoulders and arms. He was the stuff of most women's wet dreams and he dressed the part.

"That is the ambassador?" She couldn't keep the shock out of her voice. His jet-black hair held a bit of a blue shine, and he kept running his fingers through the collar-length thick locks like he wanted to draw attention to it. He was tall too. Had to be over seven feet, even for her six-foot-three frame that was tall.

"I know it isn't what you expect but, he is doing this for charity." Her commander's voice was laced with a touch of laughter. "From what I hear he was talked into this. They wanted him to be one of the dates for this auction. That he refused."

All she could do was stare. The women surrounding him were practically throwing themselves at him, reaching to touch whatever they could. Giggles and groans filled the air as hands made contact with his muscled arms and legs.

How was she going to work with him now that she had seen this? She wasn't sure if she could, with *this* flashing in her mind all the time.

Those women able to touch him tried to pull him toward them. Luckily, he had anchored himself well and had plenty of protection to keep them at bay. She was sure he reveled in the attention. He had a smile that could melt a polar ice cap.

"If it's all right with you, sir, I'll wait for this to end elsewhere." She didn't want to see any more. If she was to treat him with any kind of professionalism, it would be smart for her to find another place to wait inside the embassy.

"That's fine. This shouldn't take very long."

Heather turned around and climbed the steps to the large double doors. Her title of ice princess fit her well at this moment. Most women would enjoy watching this display, but it just made her uncomfortable.

Unable to stop herself, she turned one last time to watch the spectacle and found him staring right at her. Everything disappeared during that moment. Nothing else existed but the two of them connecting through the throng of the crowd. The moment she realized she was starting to attract attention she broke eye contact and walked into the building.

What had just happened?

Her heart beat hard in her chest. No one ever affected her. That was one of the reasons she was brought in. Where all the other women had ended up sleeping with the man, she would be immune.

She needed something to calm herself down.

Meditation normally worked for her, but she needed

DOMINATED BY DESIRE

some place quiet and empty. She found just about every room occupied. She nodded and smiled as she entered and then left different rooms.

Eventually, she did find a quiet corridor. All she needed was a small alcove and a few minutes. She heard several sets of footsteps and sighed. Not this time. She turned back to find herself face to face with the ambassador and a small entourage.

Being this close to him set her body on fire. His gaze trapped her, heating her from the inside out. Training kept her from crumbling at his feet.

"Sorry, mistress, but this is the ambassador's wing. No one is allowed down it but him and his most trusted guards."

The man's voice was pleasant, but she found she couldn't look at anyone but the ambassador. She found herself drowning in his eyes. They were a golden tone with a deep amber ring around the edge. She had never seen anything like it.

Tearing her gaze from his, she blinked a couple times before she could focus on the man who spoke to her. "I am sorry. Guess I got a little lost."

"Of course." The man bowed to her. "One of these men will take you to your room."

"Thank you." She wiped her hands on her pants, a nervous gesture she had, and followed the man down the hall. It took every ounce of will power to not turn around to look at the ambassador again.

"And who is that?" Storm found the petite woman intriguing. She had such expressive eyes.

"She has been assigned to help you with the treaty."

"Really?" He looked over his shoulder to watch her turn

5

the corner. "I thought this race decided I was too difficult to work with. Their women can't fight the pheromones I exude and the men all want to kill me. Didn't they say there was no one able to do this?"

"Yes sir, but she's been tested against your pheromones and fared better than anyone else. Plus, she has security training to protect you and their humans. You know these humans have wanted one of their own with you from the beginning. It was a compromise that the elders approved."

"That little thing is going to protect me?" If the elders approved, he wouldn't fight it, but he couldn't see it. Besides, it would be interesting to see if she could do her job as well as they said.

"She comes highly recommended. One of the planet's best."

"We shall see."

Heather dressed for the formal meal. She checked her uniform in the mirror to make sure everything was in place. This assignment would isolate her from everyone she knew. Normally she would welcome it, but she feared she wouldn't fare any better than those who had tried before her. The one thing she had been able to do before this meal was meditate. It had helped. She had been able to center herself and regain composure. She should be able to face the ambassador with poise now.

One more adjustment and she headed to the main hall where the meal would take place. She entered through the doors and took in her surroundings.

The dining hall bustled with waiters and servers greeting people and taking them to their proper seats. Taking a few calming breaths, she stepped into the room and waited her turn. It didn't take too long before she was seated next to her commander.

"You sure I'm right for the job?" After her reaction to the ambassador earlier, she didn't feel as confident in herself as her superiors seemed to be.

"Yes. You passed all the tests, and you are the best in security. He emits a natural pheromone that makes people either throw themselves at him or passionately hate him. You showed you were immune to it so that makes you the perfect candidate."

She sure didn't feel like she was immune.

The room quieted as they prepared to introduce the ambassador to the crowd. Women sighed and tried to leave their seats to get closer to him. Men either had a big dopey grin or looked like they could kill him.

"This is what I need to protect him from? Just keep him locked up." She kept her voice soft as she leaned toward her commander.

"That's why you're perfect for this," his voice just as soft. "You see the big picture. You know we can't lock him up, but understand he needs to be kept from other people. It's just too dangerous to have him wander around."

"Yes, sir." She felt the ambassador's gaze on her. And as much as she wanted to melt at his feet like the rest of the women, she was better than that. Using all her training, she schooled her features and looked back. She had a job to do and nothing would deter her.

He gave her a smile that melted any resolve she had. There was no way she would be able to do this job. Time to get out before she got into trouble. "Sir, I'm not sure about this."

"Admiral Barrington hand-picked you."

That made her pause. The admiral had been there for her since she was at the academy.

"Look, I understand," said her commander. "He's got a personality that pushes the best of us."

"You don't seem to be affected."

"I'm under sedation." He showed her a small patch resting on his wrist under his jacket. "Everyone at this table is, except for you. You are our only hope if we want to be allies with this planet."

If she felt something from being in the same room with him and she wasn't sedated, just how bad was it for everyone else? She watched as the ambassador took his seat. A loud gong sounded and the waiters started to deliver their food. The appetizers arrived first. "I don't see how I am the only person for the job. There has to be someone else."

"Lieutenant, you can argue with me all you want. I didn't make this decision. The Admiral did. You've been assigned. End of discussion."

"Sorry, sir." She took a couple of bites. "It's just I'm not sure I'm as immune as everyone thinks."

"You'll be fine." He picked up the glass in front of him and downed it. Heather noticed the sheen of sweat on his brow. Even medicated, he was having problems. "You're feeling the effect of the pheromone. Nothing like everyone else in this room, but we knew you'd feel it a little. And every Vespian has it. It's part of the race. That's one of the reasons we can't go to their planet and they picked one of the men they felt wouldn't cause a war. His pheromones don't have the strength that other visitors from their planet have had."

"Why do we want them as allies?" She knew the answer, but the grain they had to offer seemed insignificant in the face of the problems they had to deal with just gaining them as allies.

"You know that grain would allow us to end hunger here, but it won't grow on Earth. They can grow as much as we need and are willing to give it to us, but we have to prove ourselves."

The appetizer was replaced with a salad.

"And I'm the one to do that? Are you sure they went through my record? I haven't been the model soldier."

"I know that, but you were the one chosen, so you do your duty and help the planet." He speared a piece of lettuce with his fork.

Dinner went by pretty quickly. She did notice the air circulation was working overtime. Keeping the room clean so emotions were kept at a decent level.

She was grateful she could speak to her commander so candidly. It allowed her to voice her concerns without making a fool of herself. So now she had to protect the man as well as figure out what the planet had to do to prove itself. She should have read the fine print before she accepted this assignment.

Once the meal was done, they were led to another room for dancing and mingling.

"It's time for me to leave. You've already seen your room, right? Is there anything you need from me before I go?"

"Take me with you?" She half-joked. "I'm not sure who my main contact is here. Normally we would have a meeting, so I would know who I am to deal with. Why haven't we done that?"

"Another concession. You will meet the people you will deal with tonight. So have fun but stay sharp. Alcohol probably intensifies the problem." He took his coat from one of the servants and headed toward the door.

She turned to the ballroom, scanning the area for anything out of the ordinary. As she started to do a second sweep, she found her view blocked by a broad pair of shoulders.

"Care to dance?"

What a wonderfully deep voice. She looked up to find the

ambassador standing in front of her. Much taller than the average human, he towered above her.

How did he do that? He was across the room only seconds ago. She did her best to ignore him. "I should be watching the crowd, Ambassador."

"True, but dancing will allow you to study the whole group without looking like you're doing some sort of study." He stood beside her and started to look around with her.

She knew her job better than that and knew she wasn't looking obvious until he joined her. "No one noticed me until you came over here."

He smiled at her slight rebuff. Offering her his hand, he didn't give her a chance to say no again. Heather placed her hand in his, hoping this wouldn't be a mistake on her part.

The warmth of his hand penetrated and heated her blood. If she was immune, she felt for the women who weren't. Every time he looked at her or touched her she felt it to her toes. Her body hummed at his close proximity. How was she going to do her job?

She needed to clear her mind. One calming breath and she turned her focus from the man who held her in his arms to their surroundings and the people who seemed hyper-focused on him.

One woman caught her attention. She kept lifting her head to see him. She was able to slip from her partner and was headed right for them.

"Um, we need to move. Let me lead." She took control of their steps, maneuvering them out of the way. It didn't take long before the woman was gathered by a few of the guards standing nearby and pulled out of danger.

"You have sharp eyes."

"Thanks." She saw a flash of silver. "Duck."

He dipped her deep. Pressing their bodies together. She could feel the hardness of his thighs against hers. The angle he held her at allowed her to feel his member at her apex. It sent sparks of desire through her. Something she didn't expect.

She watched a small dagger fly close but over their bodies. He reached his hand up and stopped the blade in mid-flight. With a slight flourish, he tucked it into her jacket pocket.

His employees went to work subduing the man who threw it and led him out of the room like it was all in a day's work. Her partner seemed to enjoy their intimacy because he hadn't straightened yet.

"Do you mind?" She tried to act indignant, but it was taking all her energy to keep her wits about her.

He straightened, taking her with him. "Just wanted to be sure the danger had passed."

She doubted that but remained silent. Her body screamed when it wasn't near his. Instinct was to snuggle up to him, to feel his warmth once again. It took all her willpower to keep her feet moving.

She could do this. All she had to do was to focus and not on him. She picked a safe location to bring her calm back to center. A couple of deep breaths and she felt in control once again.

"You okay?"

"I'm fine, Ambassador." She looked up at him, working hard on keeping her emotions under control.

"Don't call me that." A frown creased his handsome face as he moved her with the music.

"What?" Those damn eyes got the best of her. So clear and sharp, she wanted to stare into them for hours.

"Ambassador."

"Sorry, but we never had a meeting, remember?" She didn't mean to sound snippy, but she couldn't keep it out of her voice. "No one happened to mention your name in passing."

"Ah, well, that makes sense. My name is too hard for most humans to pronounce."

Then why was he giving her such a hard time?

"But I have a simplified version that works for me and should be easy for you to say." He smiled at her. "Call me Storm."

"Yes, sir."

"No sir, either, not from you."

"Okay, Storm." She wasn't sure what to think. Why would he care what she called him? They barely knew each other. "Can we take a break? I'm starting to get evil looks from the women wanting to fawn all over you."

"Of course." He kept a hold of her hand, leading her to where his people stood. "This is Heather."

They nodded. He didn't need to say anymore. They knew who she was. She had been hired to keep the man safe, yet she didn't know anyone in his entourage. How was she supposed to do her job without the proper information?

"You going to introduce me to everyone? Or I am supposed to guess as I work with each of them?" Somehow, she had lost control of the situation.

"Watching you guess might be fun." He grinned as he wrapped an arm around her to make the proper introductions. Not one name could she repeat.

Why did he feel a need to touch her when it seemed that the women nearby were becoming jealous of her? She could feel it building around them. Someone might have to protect her if he kept this up, but his grip was strong and she didn't want to make a scene.

"Question. Do each of you have a simple version of your names or I'm going to have to come up with ones I can say and remember?"

"We all have simpler names you should be able to say, mistress. Mine is Fridon."

"Thank goodness."

An older man brought them drinks, bringing her attention back to Storm. She thanked the server as she took hers.

"Why did you thank him?" asked Storm.

"Because it's the polite thing to do." She wished she could move and put a little space between them, but he still had his arm around her and she wasn't sure how to break his hold without seeming rude.

"But it's his job." His curiosity was evident.

"True, but we all want to be told we're doing a good job from time to time. Thanking him lets him know I appreciate what he does for a living." She found it interesting that his question was so genuine.

"Interesting. Our people accept their position and do their job without question."

She scratched her head, wondering how to explain it better. It had to be something he was familiar with. A grin covered her face when she came up with the perfect subject. "When you are intimate with a woman do you show your appreciation, or do you just expect her to understand because she was doing her job?"

"When I am intimate with a woman I always show my appreciation with my partner. I do that during the act." He said it softly, his face very close to her ear.

Okay, that was the wrong subject matter. She felt it all the way to her toes. Fear had her stepping away from him, breaking his hold on her. Being rude wasn't part of her worry. Him being too close was.

It didn't seem to faze him. Storm just stepped next to her and wrapped his arm around her once again. And that was the way the rest of the evening went. When she found an opportunity to move away from him, he found a way to come back into contact with her. Her whole being was in a heightened state of arousal. It took all her strength not to jump on him and beg him to have his way with her there with everyone watching.

When the evening finally came to an end, she practically dashed to her room and headed straight for the shower. It was going to be long and cold and hopefully would help with her libido.

Storm sat on the couch in his suite, contemplating the evening.

"You pushed her hard, sir. Why?"

"I'm not sure, Fridon." He leaned forward as he spoke. "I don't need protection and we know that, but for some reason the elders decided I needed to have it. Out of all the candidates they had, they picked her. Why?"

"We've been raised to never question them, sir. You know that." The young man got up and poured himself a glass of water. "Want some?"

"No. I need a clear head." Water had an alcoholic effect on his race.

"So why did you push so hard?" Fridon sat across from Storm.

"I wanted to see what would happen if she was hit with the full force of our pheromones. I knew it could have caused a little trouble, but our air system would remove a lot of it as long as I didn't walk through the crowd."

"And what did you learn?" The elders assigned Fridon to keep an eye on Storm. For some reason, they had a special interest in the human and him.

"That she is very strong. I could feel her desire, yet she refused to act on it. A weaker woman wouldn't have been able to resist."

"You want her." He said it matter-of-factly. Storm never turned down a bed partner, and this was the first time he had walked away without one. Any of the women there tonight would have accommodated him.

"What?" He sat back. Was it that obvious? "No, but she has piqued my interest."

"So she has passed your test?"

"Yes."

"I wonder how she passed the elders' one."

He hadn't thought about why they picked her. Now he had to worry about that. Sleep wasn't going to come easy to him.

Heather found it difficult to sleep. Three cold showers later, and she still hadn't gotten her libido under control. She had thought about calling her commander and quitting but ended up jumping back into the shower. Meditation had worked a little yet not enough to relax her for sleep.

She paced her room, wondering what would work. Perhaps if she snuck down to the kitchen she could get a hot toddy of some sort to quiet her nerves and allow her to sleep. Her simple nightgown covered her well enough so she left the matching robe behind.

Barefoot, she tiptoed down the hall from her room to the central section of the house. Most of the help had gone to bed, so she shouldn't run into anyone along the way. As she turned another corner she heard a faint noise. Her sixth sense kicked in and told her something was wrong. She needed a place to hide until whatever she sensed had gone past and she could follow them. A small alcove beckoned and she slipped inside. Steel strong arms wrapped around her waist as a large hand covered her mouth.

No one could ever hold her. She proceeded to fight whoever had her and found herself flipped around and staring into the golden eyes of Storm. What was he doing here?

He dragged her into a small door in the alcove and

pushed it gently closed. The confined space intensified the feelings she had been trying to banish. Her nipples got hard just because he held her.

Storm slid one of his legs between hers, pulling her up onto it so they could see eye to eye. The nightgown she wore rode up on her, leaving her core naked against the soft cloth she now rested against. She opened her mouth to protest and realized her mistake too late.

His head dipped toward hers, his mouth covering her lips as his tongue invaded. He cradled her head in his hand, angling it to give him better access to her.

She tried to hold back. Wanted to break the kiss altogether, but her willpower deserted her in the onslaught of the passion flaring between them. Everything screamed for more. She fell into the desire swirling through her, giving as much as he would take.

He deepened the kiss, his hands leaving her waist and head to slide up under the gown, touching the fevered flesh beneath.

She felt them on her buttocks, then slide up her back and around to her breasts. The pebbled tips ached for more as he caressed them. He shifted her, her legs wrapping around him to maintain the contact. Now she could press her core against the hardened length of him. Her whole being was on fire.

It affected him as much as her because she felt the tremor race through him.

Just as fast as it started it stopped. She found herself on her feet as the door opened and several guards faced them.

"Everything all right, sir?"

"Yes." His voice came out deeper than normal. He cleared his throat and spoke again. "We ducked in here when the intruders drew close. Did you get them?"

"Yes, sir. We found them just outside of this area. Looks like they turned on each other, as we found them all fighting when we arrived. They've been moved to security to be questioned whenever you're ready."

"Good. I'll be there in a few minutes." He gently touched her shoulder. "Do you wish to join the interrogation?"

She nodded. Talking was out of the question. She wondered if the guards could see her disheveled look and swollen lips. If they did, they showed no reaction.

Storm offered her his hand, which she took and they followed the men to the security section.

"You might not like the way we do things around here, but it is our way," he said.

He had kept his distance from her, allowing her to regain some control. What had gotten into her? She never behaved like this before. Most men who showed her any attention learned quickly she didn't want it. Yet with Storm, she practically threw herself at him. What was wrong with her?

Keeping her gaze averted, she swore she noticed the two wet marks on his clothes. One on his thigh and the other over his groin. Their clothing was the self-cleaning type all the other planets used, wasn't it? Heat filled her cheeks. Imagined or not, she did that to him. What must he think of her?

Relief filled her when they entered the security section. Something to draw her focus.

Two of the guards stepped into the room. One held a strange looking weapon.

"Tell us why you invaded the ambassador's home."

The four men just stared at them.

"Do you know what this is?" the guard with the weapon asked. "It's from Vespia." He turned it on a low setting, pressing it against the stomach of one of the intruders, causing him to crumple to the ground. He turned it up a notch and aimed it at the next man.

"We know nothing." His answer wasn't what they wanted to hear. The guard pressed it against the neck of the second man, causing him to cry out in pain before crumpling as well. A large burn mark showed on his throat.

"It is designed to help with our animals. We can use it on the lightest setting." He pointed to the first man on the floor. "To keep them from wandering. The highest setting kills." He moved it to the top notch and sliced through a table sitting in the room. "Clean and precise. Now, why are you here?"

Sweat broke out on the brow of the third one. "I didn't get paid enough to die."

"Shut up," said one of the other two. "How do you know they won't kill you after you talk?"

"I'd rather die at their hands than his." He looked up at the guards, fear dancing in his eyes. "We were hired to get the woman. We don't know why, just following orders."

She looked at Storm. "Woman?"

"You."

"Me? Why?"

"That is the question, isn't it?"

TWO

The next morning, Storm stood in front of the monitor, speaking to the head of the Vespian council.

"We understand there was a break in last night. That's not like you. What distracted you?"

"Nothing, Anseri." Except a little wisp of a woman with white blonde hair and bright violet eyes. She had a tough exterior but was so soft if you knew where to touch. He had enjoyed their little interlude. "We caught them before any damage could be done."

"What did they want?"

"That new diplomat you're thrusting on me." He figured someone had already told them everything that happened, so he wasn't sure why they were asking him to repeat the information, but he was going to let them know he wasn't happy about it.

"We were afraid of that. Someone doesn't want our planets to unite, but we've come up with a solution. All trade agreements will be done on our planet."

"Anseri." He felt his brow crease. "You know that can't be done. We don't allow outsiders on our planet."

"She won't be an outsider as your mate, will she?"

"You want me to bond with her for a treaty?" His anger started to boil. He couldn't believe what they were asking of him. No Vespian had been forced to mate with an outsider. It went against their rules. Why would they suddenly ignore that?

"One day you will rule this council. Can you think of a better way to complete this treaty? Did you forget how your grandfather was bonded?"

"No, Anseri." His grandfather had been promised to one of the council's daughters, but then was attracted to an outsider during a dignitary mission and threw everything away for that woman. It helped bring that race and their people to their side during a bloody war the Vespians ultimately won. One they might not have if his grandfather hadn't taken that woman for a mate.

"We need them. These people from Earth hold the key to our future." She paused for a moment. "That is all I can tell you."

"Yes, Anseri." He kept his anger over the situation under control. The soldier in him knew he had to follow orders, but the man hated being told what to do. Heather struck him the same way. He wondered how his little human was going to take this. She couldn't be very happy about it either. "Who is telling her?"

"I believe she is speaking to her people right now. She'll be instructed to meet you in your quarters when she finishes with her communiqué."

Now all he had to do was wait.

"Excuse me?" She thought her ears were playing tricks on her.

"What part didn't you understand?"

"I am to marry him?" She couldn't believe this. "Sir, I wasn't trained to be a dignitary. I was trained to work in the science field before I went into security."

"Correction, Lieutenant. You scored high in the science area and wanted that to be your field, but your innate abilities in security put you there." His voice held no anger, but he rarely called her by her rank. Only when he wasn't pleased with her. "The Vespian council was the one who picked you out of all the other people up for this security detail, and as part of the negotiations, they wish to bring our planets together through marriage. I'm sorry you're not happy about it, but you will follow orders. Understood?"

"Yes, sir." She kept her features schooled, but inside she was in turmoil. Marriage? To a man who made her blood boil? This just wasn't fair.

"They will be sending a Vespian protocol specialist here to work with you. Once the marriage has taken place, you will finish negotiations on Vespia." Before she could protest again, he continued. "Someone has been assigned to train you in that as well. You are to meet with the ambassador after we're finished, then wait for the Earth diplomat who will train you. He should be there in an hour."

She turned off her screen and plopped into a chair. Screaming wouldn't help, although it would make her feel better. How was she going to face him? It was as if everyone knew about the steamy kiss and decided the kiss was a good measure for marriage.

Running through her mantra a couple of times, she stood and headed out the door. Might as well get this over with.

The moment the men outside his large double doors saw her, they opened them and stepped aside.

"I see news travels fast here." She stepped into his room for the first time.

"Most of my people have too much time on their hands."

He glared at the two of them before the doors closed. "What were you told?"

He seemed almost nervous over how she would react. He should be as mad as she was. Why was he taking it so well?

"Not much. I'm to be trained by my government, then your government and then we're off to Vespia to finish the negotiations. Did I forget anything?" She snapped her fingers. "Oh, yeah, we're supposed to be married."

He grinned. "You seem to be taking it well."

"Oh, believe me I want to scream, then throw something, but I've been trained to be better than that."

"I can take you someplace where you can do those things."

"Thanks, but I have to meet a diplomatic trainer in about an hour, and I'll want more time than the hour offered right now." She looked about the huge suite, amazed at how white it was. White walls, white furniture, so sterile. "Vespians not into color?"

He looked around. "I'd rather earth tones, but this is what your people interpreted from what we sent them."

"Someone didn't get the right memo." She found the huge bed that must have been specially made for his seven-foot four-inch frame, but that brought back memories of their kiss and she wasn't ready to confront that yet. She turned to find him inches from her.

"There is a ceremony intended mates go through." His gold eyes searched her face.

"We have a simple ritual too." She sure hoped his would be simple. "The man normally gives his bride-to-be a diamond ring."

"It is my planet's wish to have the ceremony happen now." He continued talking like she hadn't said anything. She just loved being ignored. Kicking something sure would make her feel better.

Storm gestured to a man hovering in the background. She

sensed him back there but hadn't paid much attention to him because Storm hadn't.

He was dressed in strange garb, carrying a small leather book that looked centuries old. The little man stopped in front of them and waited. Two others came out, wearing the same strange clothes. One carried a chalice and the other a weird looking leather strap. The items rested on a bit of cloth.

"And what do *you* wish?" It came out a little sarcastic, but she couldn't help herself. She had lost control of the whole thing and had no clue how to get it back.

He hesitated for a moment. She could tell he was choosing his words carefully. "Like you, I am a soldier and have been trained to follow orders. Is that not what you're doing?"

He had a point. Storm knelt and gestured for her to do the same.

The little man spoke in a strange language she could only guess was Vespian. He gestured over their heads as he spoke, sprinkling an iridescent powder over them. Next, he took the chalice from his assistant and offered it first to Storm, who took a drink, then to her.

She held it and looked at Storm. She should be fighting this. Why wasn't she? Her hesitation put a worried look on his face. They were both caught up in something neither had control over, and he was right. She was only following orders. The marriage would probably be annulled the moment the treaty was signed.

Lifting the cup, she took a sip, finding the liquid bitter to the taste. She couldn't help making a face as she swallowed it. Whatever was in the liquid made her head buzz a little. Next the man took the leather strap and said a few more strange words. Taking her left hand and Storm's right he wrapped the strap around each, speaking his odd little language before tying the ends.

She started feeling lightheaded. Her world spun then went dark.

"These humans are a little weak, aren't they?"

Storm had been quick enough to catch her the moment she passed out. He turned to glare at the little man. "You sure your potion wasn't a little too strong?"

"Sure it was." He pointed to the soft, thin leather slowly seeping into their wrists. "Didn't think she should know the details of this ritual."

"She will be part of our world now. Would you keep secrets from me?"

"Of course not. But secrecy is our way and you know it." The Vespian religious leader shuffled to the door. "The bond will be complete once the cord has disappeared. She will probably think this marriage can be reversed once the treaty has been signed. You will have to convince her to accept it."

"Why her?"

"She is your destiny. Treat her well."

"I promise." Being careful of the leather, he picked her up and placed her on the couch. He had thought about placing her on his bed for a moment or two, but knew he needed to take this one step at a time.

He was bonded. Storm couldn't believe it. When he learned they wanted the bonding ceremony this soon he tried to get out of it again. The argument he had with the elders and their religious leader didn't work. It came down to two things. One, the elders had their own reason for wanting this human as his mate and two, he could never win an argument with a man who had visions. Heather was seen in a vision as his mate. That was all it took for them to make the decision. He had always trusted their decisions before, so he put his and her fate in the hope they were right again.

Once the leather had been absorbed thoroughly, he woke her. "You alright?"

Her eyes fluttered open. "Yeah. What was in that drink?"

"No one knows." He helped her sit up.

She rubbed her wrist. Did she still feel it on her?

"It sure packed a punch." She sat up when she realized where she was and what had just transpired. "I need to be meeting that stupid trainer."

"You could skip it for the day." He was amazed at how she snapped to the task at hand, but she had no idea what she had been through. "I'm not sure how long the wine will sit in your system. It could make you groggy for a while."

"I'm fine." She pushed herself to her feet only to land right back on the couch. She looked up at him and grinned. "Okay, maybe it still has a little bit of an effect, but I can do this. It will probably only be a 'what do you know, so I know what to teach' lesson anyway."

The diplomat they sent was a young man barely out of training. She was sure of it. Great, she needed someone to show her the ropes, and they sent her a bookworm.

He set his pad on a nearby table and shook hands with her. Something happened during that handshake because she felt a slight flush and his whole demeanor changed. He cleared his throat. "Right, so I have my notes right here."

He picked up his pad and proceeded to read from it, but he kept looking at her. She wasn't sure why, but it made her uneasy. Once he had covered what he knew of her assignment, he set the pad down and took her hand. "So what do you need to know?"

"Um, isn't that why you're here?" She pulled her hand out of his grasp and moved so that there was some furniture between them.

"Did you know you have the prettiest eyes?"

Something was definitely wrong. Men found her attractive, but she never had one go this overboard. "Excuse me, maybe we should reschedule."

"No, no." He cleared his throat. "I'm quite capable of doing this."

She crossed to the air unit and turned it on high. It seemed to calm him down for a moment, but it didn't last long. Pretty soon, he was chasing her around the room. Spouting how much he loved and wanted her and how he would die for her.

"You need to get a hold of yourself." He was acting like all those women who chased after Storm.

"I only want to hold you." He lunged for her.

She really didn't want to hurt him, but she knew she needed to subdue him now before matters got out of hand. She stepped to the side as he lunged, making him miss her completely and land on the floor with a thud. She grabbed him by both arms and, bracing her foot on his neck, she pulled them hard behind his back. "Don't move or I'll dislocate your shoulders."

Storm took that moment to come charging into the room like an enraged bull.

She looked at Storm with fire in her eyes. "What the hell was in that drink?"

THREE

"Did he hurt you?" Storm had sensed something wrong with her and raced to get here. He feared he'd have to tear the man off her but found she had it all under control. She stood over him with one foot on his head, pinning his arms behind him.

"Do I look hurt?" She glared at him, controlling the man at her feet with very little effort.

No. She looked glorious. And very angry.

Several guards came in and secured the young man before leading him out.

"What was in that drink?" she asked again.

"Nothing that would cause that." At least he didn't think it would.

"You sure? Maybe it's your wine that causes all the women to go gaga over you, and now that I've had some from your planet it's caused the same effect." She sat in a chair, clearly upset by the whole affair. "He was fine until he shook my hand."

"I don't have to touch anyone to cause that reaction." He felt for her. He had been living with it all his life. This was a first for her. One he didn't think would happen. "I'll see what I can find about this, but I recommend you stay away from people until we can figure out how to counteract it." She just nodded. Perhaps his gift would lift her spirits. "I have something for you."

"What?" Her tone was flat.

"When you mentioned the ritual of this planet I thought it would be a nice gesture for me to follow it since you went along with ours." He pulled out a small box. "I'm not sure if it is the right thing, but the man at the store said this was traditionally what all brides wanted."

She took the box and looked at it before looking at him. He watched as several emotions flitted across her face. "There's another part to the ritual. You are to get on one knee and place it on the ring finger on my left hand."

He did as she asked. Pulling the ring from its velvet confines, he slipped it onto her finger. It looked good on her hand. His way of marking her as taken. There was an instant gratification in that.

"It's beautiful." She flexed her fingers. "Did you get the biggest rock in the place?"

"No. Was I supposed to?" He took her hand in his to see where he could have gone wrong. The moment he touched her, he realized what the man went through. A desire quick and powerful sliced through him. It took him over. All he could think of was having her.

"What?" She looked in his eyes and saw it. Hers widened in fear. "Not you too. All you did was touch me."

She pulled her hand out of his and dashed from the room.

She wasn't sure where she was running to, but she knew she needed to put some distance between them. Maybe it would help. Just before he tackled her to the floor, she knew he was right behind her. She wasn't sure what alerted her, but she braced for it.

He took the brunt of the fall, cushioning her landing with his body. Then he rolled her over so he was on top and he knew she couldn't get away. She tried to get out of his grasp, but he would have none of it. Grabbing both hands, he pinned them between them.

"Now. What was the point of that?"

"Putting distance between us so you could think clearly?" She tried to wiggle free, but he had her pinned too well. She wasn't going anywhere.

"Not sure if that would work, but there is something you need to know about my people. It doesn't look good to see a man's bondmate running away from him. Speaks badly of the relationship." He dipped his head, capturing her lips with his.

She felt the deep, drugging kiss to her bones. Nerve endings screamed for more. Her brain screamed for her to gain control before it was too late. But he was in control. His lips covered hers. His tongue filled her mouth, begging hers to dance with it. Heather found herself losing the battle as strong desire seeped into her. He finally broke the kiss and lifted his head enough to look into her eyes.

She could see the raw passion burning there. If she wasn't careful, he would take her right then and there and they had a crowd of people building around them. "And how does it look for the man to ravish his bondmate out in public?"

"No one would think twice of it on my planet."

He kissed her again. This one a little longer and deeper. It had her gasping for air. She was going to lose this battle. He must have noticed the fear she fought to keep out of her eyes, because his whole demeanor changed. How he was able to fight what had taken over him, she didn't know, but was grateful.

"But we're not on my planet and those around me seem to forget that." He got up and offered her a hand.

She took it, waiting for the strange reaction to take him over again.

He wrapped an arm around her shoulders and steered her toward his chambers. Those who had surrounded them wouldn't meet her gaze, which suited her fine. She wasn't sure if she could hold her head high after that. Her knees felt weak.

"Before you touched the young man, he didn't seem to be attracted to you?"

His question brought her back to what had happened before the kiss. Two kisses and she was putty in his hands. What kind of diplomat was she? "I didn't notice anything out of the ordinary. But I was too busy thinking they sent me someone fresh out of the academy instead of someone seasoned in the field to pay any attention to anything."

"Then maybe it wasn't you." He walked into his room with her and headed to the bathroom. Opening a drawer, he pulled out a small machine and ran it over her palm. Through the violet light, residue on her hand could be seen. He had the same residue on his from helping her up earlier and possibly when he slipped the ring on her finger. Another machine took a small sample of the residue and ran it for diagnosis.

"He put something on your hand all right. It seems to be a love potion."

The intercom beeped at that moment. "Sir, call coming in for Heather. It's her commander."

They reentered the main room so she could answer the link. It seemed strange that he would be calling her right after this.

Her commander appeared on the screen. "Lieutenant, why did the embassy turn away the man I sent?"

"Because we just had another incident, sir. We thought

we let in the man you sent, but it turned out to be a decoy."

"Anyone hurt?"

"No, sir." She wanted to say only her pride, but instead she remained professional. "You want to show me a picture of the man who was supposed to be here?" The image of a middle-aged man popped up. She turned to look at Storm. "See? That's what I expected. I should have figured something was wrong the moment I saw him."

"Who?" asked her commander.

"Do you still have him here?" asked Heather.

Storm nodded.

She turned back to her commanding officer. "We'll send a picture of the young man we have in custody in a few minutes. Let me know if he shows up in any of our databases. For now though, it looks like we're going to have to cut off visitations. Any training done should be done via comlink. We have some work to do here. I'll contact you later." She severed the link and turned back to Storm.

"I have known that man all my career. I trust him." She sat down in an overstuffed white chair. "But as tight as both sides have been with security, how did anyone know I was staying here? How did they know I needed someone to train me as a dignitary that fast? There has to be a spy somewhere in the ranks."

Storm walked back to the bathroom and came out with another tool. This one removed all the residue from their hands.

"Thanks, was afraid I wouldn't be able to shake hands with people there for a while." She stood and started to pace. "When did your people tell you about the marriage?"

"About the same time yours told you."

"So you always carry around the little guy in the funny clothes?"

"No. He requested to come on this mission." He smiled at her when he realized what she was thinking. "Very astute, but he has visions we never question. He is innocent in all this."

"You really need to be careful where you aim that thing. No wonder women try to tear off your clothes." He tilted his head at her, not quite sure what she was talking about. "That smile is deadly."

"Does it make you want to tear off my clothes?" He brightened the smile just for her.

And so much more, but she wasn't about to let him know that. He made a move to grab her, which she dodged, or so she thought. Instead, she found herself pinned under him once again.

"Now, where were we?"

"Discussing who could be after you."

"You mean you." He nibbled on her ear.

"Us then." She felt sensations rocket through her blood. She arched against him, trying to dislodge him, but just made matters worse. He settled himself between her legs and continued to nibble on her ear and the side of her neck. Now all she could think of was his hardening length right where she wanted it. When he moved against her, sparks shot through her veins from the contact.

She felt like she was on fire. Focusing on the conversation wasn't working. At the moment all she could focus on was where his lips were, sucking on a bit of her neck, making her insides clench.

"You taste so good." Pulling her hands up above her head, he pinned them with one of his while he worked on her uniform with the other. "I want to taste more."

He made short work of the seals on the top, revealing her skin to the cool air. She arched her back again when she felt the heat of his mouth on her flesh. A sigh escaped her when his lips closed on one of her breasts.

She was so focused on the sensations she didn't realize his hands hadn't stopped on her top and had removed the rest of their clothing. There was nothing between them now. She could feel the little hairs on his legs when he shifted them against hers. Could feel his member pulse against her thigh.

His lips made an upward trek to her lips. He captured her mouth with his as he entered her. Her body shuddered as he filled her. Her muscles tightened around him. An orgasm, quick and sure, overcame her.

"Good lord, woman." His breath came out like a pant. He rested his forehead against hers as he fought for control.

"Shh, there's more where that came from." Where did that come from? She should have told him it had been too long and her body was betraying her, but her lips wouldn't move. Her body did. It knew what to do to keep the sensations going, and it wasn't about to stop him from causing the delicious waves of desire crashing through her. She wrapped her legs around him, giving him better access. He moved inside her, causing a delicious friction she wanted more of. He pressed his lips against her throat, nibbling on the spot that got a strong reaction from her earlier.

She felt her muscles tighten again. Her body had a vise grip on him. His intake of breath let her know that grip affected him. He picked up his tempo, sliding in and out of her faster. It pushed them both closer to the edge.

His lips latched onto her neck as he drove deeper into her. She felt teeth scrape against her skin as everything tightened in her. The most powerful orgasm she had ever felt had its hold on her. The vibration started gently and as it built in intensity it took over. From her toes to the tips of her hair, her body started to hum. Then everything splintered around her. She lost track of her surroundings as lights exploded behind her closed eyes. It was an out-of-body experience for her.

When she finally became aware again, she found Storm snuggled against her.

"I see you're back." His breath tickled her collarbone.

"Sorry. Never had that happen before."

"I'll add that to my list."

"What list?"

"That you are very quiet when you're intimate. Mind-blowing orgasms are out-of-body experiences." He sat up and scooped her up into his arms. "And quite boneless afterward."

He carried her to the bed and gently laid her down. In seconds, he joined her, pulling her into his embrace before pulling the covers over them.

Her only thought was she was going to be so fired over this.

She arched her back as she opened her eyes. That was some dream. Focusing on the room, she sat up fast. This wasn't her room.

It hadn't been a dream. She moved to get up.

"Where are you going?" She turned to find him lying beside her. Had he been waiting for her to wake up? He had that heart-stopping smile on his face. Wrapping the covers in his hand, he started to pull them off her, revealing all of her to his predatory gaze.

What had she done?

"As much as I'd like to spend the rest of the day right here where we can get to know each other better..." His gaze roamed over her, igniting her desire with just a look. "There is a series of medical tests you must go through before we leave for Vespia. I have been told the doctors want to get started on them now."

She climbed out of bed, trying to keep her dignity, and padded over to her clothes. Picking up her pants, she held them out to him. "How did you get these off me?"

"Vespian secret." He watched her with that same predatory smile.

She pulled the pants on, then her top, shaking her head. Vespian secret or not she couldn't believe she had shown no control with him. Just because she was to marry the man didn't mean she was supposed to fall into bed with him the first chance she got. Then she realized they never even made it to the bed and felt her cheeks heat up a bit.

Heather dressed and hoped it helped her gain better control of her emotions. When she looked at Storm, he was fully clothed too. He escorted her to the doctors, before heading off. It figured he'd leave her now. She hated doctors.

"Could you step into this archway?"

She did as they asked, waiting for the thing to turn on.

"Thank you." The head doctor gestured for her to step out.

"That's it?" She didn't see any lights flashing or hear any type of noise.

"That's it. We'll give the results to Storm when we're finished."

Now the questions would begin. Again.

She sat at a small table in the hall near the kitchen, sipping coffee. It didn't take him long to find her. So what would his first question be?

"Your results are back and the doctors would like to speak to us."

So there will be a whole panel of people asking questions. Pretty normal. She could almost bank on what their first question would be. Heather followed Storm back to the main med lab. She found herself looking at the large scanner again. They had nothing so advanced on Earth. There were large devices like that. She had spent plenty of time inside them, but they took a lot longer to do the job.

"I don't know." She answered the unspoken question she got just about every time someone scanned her for the first time.

Storm looked at her. "You don't know what?"

She stepped up to her image and manipulated it so that it showed the small of her back. Lodged at the base of her spine was a small metal cylinder. "I don't know what it is or where it came from. It's been there for as long as I can remember. The technology is more advanced than Earth's, so the doctors were afraid to remove it. It's some sort of suppression device."

He looked at the doctors who nodded in agreement. "What about your parents? They had to know where it came from."

"I'm an orphan. They found me in a patch of heather when I was about four, hence my name. Became a ward of the government. They raised me. A lot of children were raised that way. Families who couldn't feed their families offered their offspring to the government who would raise them and train them." How many times through the years had she repeated this? Now everyone would start treating her strangely. Just like before. She brushed her short hair behind one ear.

"We'd like to study it a little more." One of the doctors looked at Storm for permission. "If you wouldn't mind a little surgery."

"Surgery isn't necessary." She placed her hand on the small of her back and brought the cylinder forward. "It slides in and out of my skin pretty easily."

"Have you ever been far from it?" Storm watched her. Probably looking for something strange to happen. That was what the doctors all did. Made her feel like a specimen in a Petri dish.

"Not really. Every once in a while a new doctor joins the medical staff and wants to study it themself, thinking they were smarter than the doctor before them, but once they realized they'd never figure out what it does, they were afraid to go too far with it. It has a very loud alarm if it is moved too far from its home."

"Will you step through our equipment again?" It took only seconds. But she knew it would affect her for a lifetime.

They didn't keep her cylinder long. Once they were through, she slipped it back where it belonged. She straightened her blouse. "Anything else?"

"No, we will call you when we have more results."

"Good." Time to go get her things together. This was about the time she normally found herself under a microscope, and she hated the feeling.

"So, what is it?' asked Storm. He stared at the image floating on the screen.

"Pretty much what she said it was. It suppresses her abnormalities. Makes her read normal for human." He pulled up her image before they removed the cylinder. "If you look at her readings here, you'll see she stays in the normal range. But when I bring up the image after she removed it most of those readings are off the scale."

Storm looked at the readings. So she wasn't human, but her readings weren't quite Vespian either. It looked like a combination of the two. He studied it a little more. "This almost looks like ancient blood."

"We were thinking the same thing, but we need to run more tests."

"I get the impression she has been through too many already. Can you keep them to a minimum?"

"We can try. We have plenty of samples to work with for now."

"Good. No need to make her endure anything she doesn't need to." He turned to the doctor. "You really think she's full-blooded ancient?

"Since we've never met one alive before, we're not sure

what to think. We are sure of one thing. She is very precious."

He had already figured that out. The device shifted on the screen so he could see it from any angle. It didn't seem to be anything harmful. She could remove it and do without it with ease. "So if you remove the device, she'll just be more enhanced? Is that a bad thing?"

"We're not sure. This technology is a bit beyond ours as well. It does keep her readings where they should be and hides things like your mark. It keeps her protected from prying eyes."

"What?" He looked where the doctor pointed to the screen. There, on the side of her neck, was a small image. When did he do that? Then he thought about it. He had focused on the side of her throat while they had been intimate. Without realizing it, he'd marked her as his. That might cause some trouble later, but what was done was done. "And there is no harm to her?"

"It was designed to protect her. Keep her hidden from something." He pressed a button and a small section flashed. "That is the alarm section she spoke of."

"We just don't know what it's keeping her safe from."

"No, sir, but as long as it stays within her, she should be fine." The doctor cleared the screen. "We'll continue to monitor the device and study it."

"Good." He headed back toward his room when he sensed her. Anger boiled in her. He hesitated long enough to figure out where she was. She was in her room, which was now empty. Now he understood the anger.

Something whizzed by his head the moment he entered the vacant room.

"Where's my shit?"

"Where it belongs." She was beautiful when she was angry. Her pale skin had a slight flush to it, just like it did right after they had been intimate.

That stopped her for a moment. "It belongs here."

He shook his head as he walked toward her. Her leery look warned him to be careful, but she didn't frighten him in the least. Wrapping his arms around her from behind, he pinned her arms to her sides before lifting her off the ground and carrying her down the hall. She continued to struggle, so he flipped her and threw her over his shoulder. "Stop struggling."

"Not 'til you put me down."

He slapped her on her buttocks as he continued to his room. He wasn't sure how many staff he passed, but he didn't care. He was enjoying every minute. Her anger did nothing but fire him up. "I'll put you down when I'm good and ready."

He walked into his room and dropped her unceremoniously onto his bed.

Her items were stacked neatly beside it. She seemed shocked to see them there. She was quiet for only a moment before she jumped off the bed and continued with her tirade. "How dare you move my things!" The anger she felt hid a hurt deep inside her.

"How dare I?" He crowded her up against the wall. Time to end this before she got out of hand. "You forget where you are? Who you belong to?"

"I belong to no one." There was that hurt look again.

"You are mine." He dipped his head and nibbled on the spot where he had left his mark. She didn't understand what it meant yet, so he had to be lenient, but she needed to know there were times when she shouldn't argue with him.

He grabbed her uniform top and tore it off her, then he did the same with her trousers. His clothing came next. In seconds, he was inside her. Proving she was his to take whenever he wanted.

He held her in place with his weight and height. Using one hand, he lifted her chin so she would look him in the eyes. Such a myriad of emotions there. The hurt was still there but fading fast. It was being replaced by shock and a touch of desire. No man had ever possessed her like this before, and he found a strange satisfaction at being the first.

He pressed against her, pushing himself deeper into her. Those wonderfully expressive eyes took on a hunger as the desire took over. Her legs locked around his waist to help keep him in place.

"You shall be with no one else but me." He pounded into her, her slick sheath taking him in again and again. It felt so good.

"And you?" Her voice came out deep and seductive as her muscles tightened against him. Her head dropped to his shoulder as a ripple of pleasure raced through her. That ripple affected him too.

"I want no one but you." He knew he was close. Then he felt her muscles lock onto him with a grip that forced him to shake to keep control.

With her, it started as a tremble before she exploded all around him. The power of her orgasm came close to taking him with her. That had never happened before. But he knew it was her.

Since he met her he found he always wanted her. He walked around with a constant erection, fantasizing about when and where he would take her. No other woman had ever had this effect on him, and he was going to enjoy it for as long as it lasted.

"And if I argue with you?" She lifted her head and looked into his eyes again. They glowed with satisfaction. Everything else had been burned away by her orgasm.

"I know how to win." His lips captured hers and he started moving once again. Her body was like a fine instrument that he had a natural feel for. It took only a few strokes for her to grip him with all her might once again. He felt her orgasm grab her, causing her to shudder all around him. That shudder sent him over the edge. He didn't try to fight it.

He listened to their ragged breathing afterward. "This is the only way to fight."

"So why did you move my things?" Her voice low. The hurt was back.

"It made sense. You weren't going to be using your room anymore. This is your room now. I want you here with me." He kept her pinned against the wall. He liked having this kind of control. "Why were you so mad at me?"

"Because every time people learned about my little added addition, they normally shunned me." She could have hidden that from him but chose not to. He was proud of her bravery.

"After the sex we've had? Oh, honey, it's going to take a hell of a lot more than that to scare me off." He ground his hips against her, drawing a sharp intake of breath when he hit the right spot. "You are far too addicting for me to give up now."

The intercom beeped.

He said something under his breath before releasing her. He crossed to the screen and activated it. "What?"

"The Vespian protocol instructor is here."

"So fast?" Heather commented. She dashed to her things, trying to find something to wear.

"You can relax. The instructor has seen everything."

"Well, I sure don't want me naked to be added to his list." She held up her tattered uniform up and shook her head.

"It's a her and she is very discrete."

"Know her well?" She found a top and pulled it over her head. Now she rummaged through her things to find something for the bottom half. Just as she pulled a pair of pants on, the door opened.

"Heather. I'd like you to meet my sister."

FOUR

"Your sister?" She looked at the woman with interest. Something he didn't want. Of all the protocol experts, they had to send her. She'd be undermining his authority at every turn. "Younger or older?"

"Younger, unfortunately, by a minute and a half," his sister answered. "Mom said I did come out first, but he would have none of that and pulled me back in so he could be born first."

"Oh, that does sound like him." Heather gave him a knowing smile.

He watched the interchange between them. Heather was delighted to have someone who knew him to talk to.

His sister, on the other hand, didn't miss a thing. He watched as she took in their disheveled state. Heather's items lay scattered about the floor in her mad dash to cover herself.

The fact that her things were in his room in the first place probably gave her a lot to think about, but she must have been informed that they were to mate.

He had thought about greeting his sister naked, as he had

in the past but not knowing how Heather would react made him dress.

He wondered what the council had told his sister before she arrived. He wanted to know the real reason she was here. "Sister, you never come to just visit."

"I am here to train your future mate." She smiled at him, then turned her attention to Heather. "We can start our lessons now if you wish."

"Of course." She glanced at Storm before turning her attention back to his sister. "Where do you wish to start? I have read all the security files your planet sent over."

"How about what my brother has taught you?" She gestured for Heather to follow her. "We can walk in the gardens as we talk."

"I'd rather you stay indoors." Storm thought his sister would take his words as overprotective, but he needed to think about Heather's safety first. She might not be aware of the attempts on Heather yet. Besides, if they went out into the garden, he couldn't hear what they said.

"There is a beautiful library that should work," Heather recommended.

"That's fine." She linked arms with Heather and, with one last look at her brother, she focused her attention back on Heather. "Lead the way."

That look dared him to follow. He knew he'd have to rely on the security cameras to see what sort of mischief his sister would be up to.

Heather had never been very good at small talk so she remained quiet as they walked.

"You seem to know your way well. How long have you been here?" His sister had a nice voice. A bit like her brother's, but higher pitched.

"Thirty-two hours. I memorized the blueprints before I got here."

"My brother moves fast." The comment hung between the two of them.

"You talking about the marriage?" Heather glanced at her before heading down the corridor that held the library. She had the same jet-colored hair and golden eyes, but her ring was a green color. "Not his doing. Our governments brewed this one up."

"Really?" She didn't sound convinced, but it didn't matter. Heather wasn't there to please the woman, just learn from her.

"Here we are." She pulled the double doors toward her to open them. "I'm sure you have a thousand questions, so ask away."

"All in good time, Heather." She gave her a friendly smile. "My brother has been here several times, so he knows a lot about your planet, but this is my first time here."

"Feel free to access the database anytime you wish."

"I always find databases to be boring. I'd rather hear it from you. What do you do for fun?"

Heather just looked at her. She did her duty. Nothing else really intrigued her. When her associates went out for recreation, she stayed behind. It was all a bit frivolous to her. Hence the title of ice princess. "Fun? I guess stay home and read."

"Hmm." She looked about for a few moments before sitting down in an overstuffed chair. She studied Heather. "You must have a thousand questions too. Care to ask any?"

She did, but her training had taught her to never question. Answers came as they were needed. "I'm sure they will be answered along the way."

"Well, then let's get started. Since you haven't had a lot of time around our race and most of what you have learned firsthand is from my brother, I'd like to know what your impression of us is."

Should she go with the politically correct or the truth? "From what I have seen from your brother and the staff, there seem to be two kinds of people. Those from a working-class and those from a privileged class."

"A lot of people get that, but that's because our race, as a whole, has very dominant males. My brother being one of them. Everyone works, they all serve in the military for a while. Some stay in the service. Others have callings, like musicians and artists. The privileged roles come with a price."

"Like having to marry a total stranger?" She didn't like the way the conversation was going. Instead of sitting down, she wandered about the room. Anything to help keep her focused.

"Yes. Or not being able to stay in the service even if it is your desire. Everyone sacrifices for the good of the whole."

"You must be talking about yourself." Heather looked over at her.

"Very astute." She watched Heather pace. "You seem to be a little agitated. Perhaps we should go outside. My brother isn't here to stop us."

"It's not really a good idea." Heather sat down in another overstuffed chair. "There have been several incidents, and I seem to be the main target."

"Why?"

"That is the question. Until we can answer that, I'm going to be stuck here." With a man who made her blood boil and had her body screaming for more.

"Sounds like fun."

Even now she felt her desire spiraling out of control, and he wasn't even in the room. She needed to get a grip. Focus on something to help center her, not think about the incredibly sexy, yet pushy man who dominated her thoughts.

"You okay?"

"I'm fine." Heather smiled. She wanted to shout no, your brother is driving me insane. "So how do the women put up with such pushy men?"

"We have our moments too. You'll see that. The only thing I can say is push back. The men can be quite obnoxious, but they want their women to stand up for themselves."

"Pretty sure that won't be a problem." Heather stood up again. She turned to the doors. Something called to her. She felt it deep inside. This was crazy.

Heather turned back to Storm's sister and found her watching her intently. "Am I to call you Storm's sister the entire time you're here, or do you have a name?"

"My name is hard for you to pronounce."

"Yeah, that seems to be pretty common with Vespian names. Do you have a simplified version like your brother?" Heather sat down again.

The doors opened at that moment and Storm walked in. She felt relief the moment she saw him. Out of the corner of her eye, she saw his sister switch her gaze from her to Storm. Maybe his sister would focus on him instead of her.

"I know you women wanted some time to yourselves, but I just received a communiqué from home. The elders are coming here. As protocol instructor, you need to make sure we have everything ready for them. The leader of this planet will be here as well for a banquet tomorrow evening."

"Our commander-in-chief? I must get my dress uniform." Heather jumped up out of her chair, only to find her arm caught in Storm's grip.

"Dress uniform? I would think you would want to impress my people since you will be living among us." He didn't look angry, just serious.

"I am a member of this planet's military. I have my own

protocol to fulfill." She was just as serious. She might be leaving Earth, but she still needed to show her allegiance to it. "I am expected to show my planet's leader the respect he deserves."

"And my leaders deserve the same respect."

He was right. How was she going to do this? She wasn't sure how to please both of them. "When are we to greet them?"

"Your leader will be here in the early afternoon. My leaders will arrive several hours later."

"That will work."

He tilted his head at her.

"I can dress according to my protocol when the commander-in-chief arrives and then be able to change and greet your people properly. Will that work for you?" She sure hoped it would.

He gave her a nod and released her arm. His focus then turned to his sister. He didn't like the intense look she gave them. "Enjoying the view?"

"Very much." She gave them a big smile. "I was sent with a gift for your future mate. May I give it to her?"

"Of course."

She stood and walked to the door. It didn't take her long before she returned with a small box for Heather. "Press the button on the top."

Heather placed the box on the coffee table in front of her and pressed the button suggested. She watched in amazement as it opened up to reveal several yards of material. Picking it up, she found a beautiful long dress. High collar, low neckline, full, long sleeves. At least it would cover her. She had seen some of the images of dress wear from her security tapes and the women of the race exposed a lot more than this dress did. "Wedding gown?"

"Formal dress for you to wear." Storm touched the material.

"Great." Now she knew she had to make sure she stuck to her plan. She couldn't upset either side.

"Heather, do you mind if I speak to my brother? Alone?"

"Not at all." Heather needed a little time to herself. Everything was happening too fast. She darted out of the library before he could stop her. Not an easy feat.

"Why did you send her away?"

"You're smitten." She sat back in her chair and smiled.

"What? Don't be silly." He wondered what she suspected.

"I have never seen you do that before."

"I don't know what you're talking about." But he did. He did treat Heather differently. His excuse was she didn't understand their ways, so he had to be more lenient.

"Please." She stood. "You let her decide how to balance the protocol of both planets. In the past, when confronted by something like this you didn't allow anyone a choice. It was your way or else."

"She isn't from our planet."

"Never stopped you before."

"Why are you here, sister?" He needed to change the subject before she overstepped her boundaries.

"I was sent by the leaders to teach your mate how to fit into our society."

"Then do that and stay out of my personal life."

Heather hadn't gotten very far before she felt a slight headache. They had plagued her from time to time in the past, and it was normally caused when the cylinder had been removed. She walked into the central medical area and found one of the doctors working on a screen.

"Mistress? Are you all right?"

"I'm fine. I seem to be suffering from another one of my headaches."

"Another one?' He ran a hand scanner over her.

"I get them when the device is removed. I'm hoping you might have something to get rid of it?" She ran her fingers through her hair. She kept it short because of military protocol. The moment it touched her collar, she would set the computer to shorten it. Would this be something else she'd have to change?

"Let's try this." He pressed a small hypo against her neck.

She felt relief instantly. "Thank you."

"Please let us know if you continue to have these headaches."

"I will." She gave him a smile. "It's normal for me, so there's nothing for you to worry about."

The doctor didn't look convinced but nodded.

She left the room and headed to the kitchen. Going back to her room was out of the question since she didn't have one anymore and going to Storm's room alone just didn't feel right. Heather refused to wander the halls. She knew Storm would come looking for her sooner or later. Besides, a cup of coffee would help steady her nerves and give her a chance to try to keep her thoughts from wandering. Why was she worried about her hair anyway?

It was all his fault. Being around him made her lose all concentration.

If she wanted to be evil, she could try to hide from him, but he seemed to know where she was and she wasn't sure if she was ready to push him that hard yet. How would he punish her if she did?

"Wandering the halls?"

His deep voice flowed over her like honey.

"Thought you were talking to your sister."

"She annoys me."

Heather couldn't help but grin. "Really? I thought nothing got to you."

"You do." He pulled her into his embrace. "I find I don't want to be without you for too long."

"I still think there was something in that wine."

He wrapped his arm around her. "Promise. Nothing out of the ordinary. I did have it checked."

"Dinner is ready." One of the servants stepped up to them.

"Hungry?"

Not really, but if they had a lot of schedule working to do, she probably should put something in her stomach. "What is on the agenda for this evening?"

His gaze started at the top of her head and worked its way down to her feet before he looked her in the eyes. That heart-melting smile spread across his face. "You need to eat."

She sat amongst her items, trying to figure out where her medals were. Ignoring him was hard, but she needed to be sure she was dressed properly and his staring at her the whole time just made matters worse. Plus, Storm seemed to be cross with her because she was taking so long.

"Are you done, yet?" He had his arms crossed over his chest as he stood over her.

"And tomorrow you won't be the same way?" She grinned when she found the velvet box she had been looking for. She handed the box to him as he helped her to her feet. "You're sure your people know how to do this?"

"They will not ruin your uniform. Promise." He opened the door for one of the servants to enter.

She nodded as she placed her uniform into their arms, they gave her a slight bow before exiting the room.

"Why don't you try on the dress? Just in case it needs to be altered." He pointed to the gown lying on the bed.

"You're right." She picked up the dress and started toward the bathroom.

"Where are you going?"

"To change?" She wasn't quite sure she understood his question.

"Change here." He gestured about the room.

"Right." She gave him a disbelieving look. "I'll never get the dress on."

"I'll be on my best behavior."

She looked at him. Was this his way of showing her she should trust him? If she were to continue to the bathroom, could she hurt the budding relationship they were building? Her modesty was ingrained but the man had been intimate with her twice now. Was there a need for it? "And are you going to keep your hands to yourself?"

"Like I said, I'll be on my best behavior." He didn't promise her a thing but gave her that bone-melting smile.

"You're terrible." She laughed. His libido did seem to have a mind of its own, but she needed to show she did trust him. "You know two can play at this game."

"Really?" He perked up a bit.

"I have been thwarting men for years." She stepped back from him. "You don't have a chance."

"That sounds like a challenge." His eyes lit up at the thought.

Maybe taunting him wasn't the smartest thing she could have done. She pulled the dress over her head, removing her other outfit as the dress slid down her body. She had learned how to do this during different assignments. Came in handy from time to time. The top came off without a hitch, but a large pair of hands stopped the progress of the dress and she couldn't reach her pants.

"You're cheating?" he sounded astonished.

"Really? Where are your hands?" She slipped her arms through the sleeves of the dress. He unhooked her pants and pulled them down her hips. The dress followed, keeping his hands at bay.

The low neckline allowed her to wiggle into the dress without having to release the seams. Once on, it fit like a glove but she found a problem. The material across her breasts was too skimpy. One false move and she'd be popping out.

Storm batted her hands away from the material when she tried to fix it and arranged it so it covered what she wanted but exposed what he wanted to see. Taking her hand, he led her to a nearby mirror. "You look beautiful."

She stared at the image looking back at her. "That can't be me."

His hands slipped beneath the top of her dress, gently cupping her. "Do you feel that?"

"Yes." All he had to do was touch her and her libido came to life. Her heart was beating double time from a simple caress.

"Then you know it's you." He bent his head to nibble on her neck. She tilted her head so he could have total access to that side.

His lips pressed against her throat before nipping against the same soft skin. He blazed a trail down the tender flesh until he hit her shoulder and the material of the dress. "As much as I'd like to just rip the dress from you, I don't think my leaders would appreciate the gesture. You need to take it off before I take it off you."

"But you just said you wouldn't rip it off me."

"So you want to see how gentle I can be with you? That dress is coming off. It blocks my view too much." He ran the tips of his fingers across her exposed skin, causing little goosebumps to rise up in the path. "Let's see how far I get before I turn into a wild man."

Shivers went down her spine as he walked behind her. She felt the gentle pressure of his fingers against the magnetic seal that held the dress together, then the tips of his fingers brushing her skin as he slid them through the seam to the bottom of her spine.

"I do like the view from here." His words soft, right next to her ear.

She looked down and saw why. She was completely exposed to him. He dipped his hands into the bodice to pay a little homage to her breasts before going lower. When one of his hands closed over her mound, she felt her body clench. His fingers separated the soft folds and explored, drawing a few sounds from her.

"Really?" She could feel his grin against her throat. "So I need to explore here a little more to see what sort of sounds I can elicit from you?"

"Storm." She touched her cheeks because she could feel them heating up.

"I have embarrassed you."

"I'm just not used to such talk." She didn't think he'd be so tuned in to what she thought or felt. It was nice having a partner who cared that much. "Maybe we should remove the dress? Wasn't that the main goal?"

"Was it?" He moved back around and grasped the cuff of the sleeve. Giving it a tug, he pulled it down one arm. "I thought it was not to damage the dress before I have my way with you."

"You do have a one-track mind."

"When it comes to you, I seem to." He helped her step out of the dress and clasped his hands together. "Now where were we?"

"What about the dress?"

"Someone will be along to get it." His eyes lit up. "I know. Let's take a bath."

"What?" Confusion overcame her. When did they talk about taking a bath?

"I have read that the bathtub can be a great place to be intimate."

"If you have one big enough." He must have been planning this one for a while.

He smiled and grabbed her hand. He half dragged her out onto a balcony. "Is that big enough?"

"Not a bathtub. It's a hot tub."

"And what is the difference?" He pulled his shirt off before shedding his pants.

"Um, you don't use soap?" She wasn't sure herself. They had always been a waste of time to her. Of course, the only people who ever invited her to one were men, and she felt the confined space was just asking for trouble. Just like now. "Don't you have tubs on Vespia?"

"We use sonic waves to clean the body." Storm picked her up and dropped her into the water before he hopped over the edge to join her. "Interesting sensation."

"Jets." She wasn't sure what to say or to do, but Storm had a gleam in his eyes that said he knew exactly what he wanted to do to her. And there really was no escape. Before she could move a muscle, he had crowded her into one corner of the tub.

"And what is a jet?" He went down on his knees in front of her so they would be closer to the same height.

"The thing that makes the water swirl." She felt his fingers at her mound again. When they brushed against sensitive flesh, she sucked in her breath.

"I see." His lips captured hers, his tongue searching, touching the recesses of her mouth, making her forget anything but the sensations he was causing.

They started to build in her, and she could feel her body tighten and move as he worked his magic with his fingers.

Then everything exploded. She heard two words but wasn't sure who said them.

"Oh, God."

"I'm truly sorry, sir."

"This had better be good." Storm growled at the interruption. Keeping Heather shielded from view, he turned toward the shaking young man near the edge of the hot tub.

"There's a communiqué from the elders." The frightened man kept his eyes down. "They said it couldn't wait."

So did she say oh God because of the orgasm, or did he say it because of the interruption?

Storm climbed out of the tub and walked over to another screen. One she hadn't noticed before this. Weren't they also security cameras? Then she realized she was going to be seen by the council. There were only two choices, either sink as low as possible so the cameras wouldn't pick her up or get out before they were on the screen. She opted for scrambling out. The only piece of clothing she could find to wear was Storm's shirt so she slipped it on. Then she found the towels.

She tried to stay out of view as she toweled off, but it was not to be. Although they spoke Vespian and she didn't understand the language, she did get the implications when Storm came over and brought her to the screen.

What now?

"Is that your mate?"

"Who else would I be with?" Storm wanted to reach through the screen and throttle the elder smiling at him.

"There's a whole planet of women there. Just because you have to mate with her doesn't mean you have to have anything to do with her." She seemed pleased to see him with Heather.

"Yes, Anseri."

"Can she understand us?"

"No, Anseri. I haven't been given clearance to add our language to her universal translator."

"You have it now. Please make sure it is in place before we arrive." She shifted in her seat. "She sure is a pretty little thing and from the looks of things you wasted no time in enjoying her company."

"Yes, Anseri." He put his arm around her. It was not the smartest thing he could have done because of what the elder might read into it, but he felt a need to show his protection. He wasn't happy about the focus this elder was giving to Heather. It normally meant she wanted something.

"You received the dress?"

"Yes, Anseri."

"Good. And your family crest?"

"It's safe at home." Why did they want the family crest?

"It should have been in the box with the dress. We wish her to wear it."

"Can I ask why? There have now been two incidents. Do you not feel she is wearing a big enough target already?"

"I am aware of what has happened there. This time, we will have all our security to protect her. If it happens again, then we will have to assume it's someone from our people and take the proper measures." The elder stopped talking for a moment while an aide whispered in her ear. "If it is someone from her planet, then it should stop once we have her in our custody."

He hoped so. It was bad enough he always had to be aware of assassination attempts. Having to worry about attempts on her life too would compound the problem.

FIVE

Once the screen went blank, he turned to Heather. She stood there wearing his shirt, trying to be patient but wondering what she was supposed to do now. Even new to the Vespian way, she knew to expect something.

"It seems we missed something in the package." He headed back into the room. Gown and box had been removed. Storm walked to the doors and pulled them open. "Bring me the person who removed the box."

They started scurrying around, which helped his anger abate a bit. Heather must have walked up behind him because he found her tugging at his arm. "Bit grumpy, are we?"

"Not with you." He looked at the way the material wrapped around her frame, giving him little peeks of a thigh or a breast from time to time. His body hardened. "I do like this look for you."

"I can tell."

He grabbed her, pulled her close, and rubbed himself against her. "Then you know you need to fix this."

Then someone cleared their throat.

"Understand you were bellowing earlier." His sister stood in front of them, grinning from ear to ear. Taking in everything. "I have the crest. I wouldn't dare leave it in a box to be accidentally thrown away."

"What? Are you listening in on my conversations with the elders?" He spoke to her in Vespian, probably the last time he would be able to. If she was listening in, then she knew Heather's translator needed to be upgraded and that would be her job.

She walked around them and sauntered into the room. Switching to English, she spoke to Storm. "I think you should get dressed, brother, while I speak to Heather."

He growled under his breath but let go of Heather and did as she asked. "Tiko, you are a pain sometimes."

"Tiko?" Heather spoke up. "That I can pronounce."

He grinned. His sister deserved it.

"I have a gift for you." Storm's sister handed her a wrapped-up cloth, not commenting on his little pet name for her. He noticed she didn't give his mate permission to use Tiko, but she didn't deny her either.

"What is it?" Heather undid the binds before unfolding the cloth to reveal the family seal now mounted on a chain. She ran her fingers over it gently. "It's beautiful."

He always thought so. It was the tree of life from their planet, surrounded by the key elements to keep life going. Her caress showed him she respected it as much as he did.

"But I can't wear this."

"You have to," Storm and his sister said it in unison.

"Don't tell me that's what the call was about. They want me to wear this." She slipped the chain around her neck. It fell right at the juncture where the bodice stopped on the dress. "At least I now understand why the top was cut so low."

"What top?" asked Storm's sister.

"The dress."

"Ah." She pulled a small device out of her pocket. "I am also supposed to load our language to your translator."

"It can be uploaded from..." Heather stopped. They were very cautious and probably didn't trust the equipment. "And you can't do it that way because of security reasons."

"You do catch on fast." His sister smiled at her. "Where is your translator?"

"Behind my left ear." She pulled her hair back to show the access point for her to use. Storm also noticed the faintest sign of his mark. He knew his sister spotted it too because of the look she gave him.

"I'll need you to lie down."

Heather nodded and stretched out on the couch.

After Storm's sister set everything up to download, she grabbed her brother by the arm and dragged him out of earshot. "Are you crazy?"

"Couldn't help myself." He shrugged. The damage was done, no reason to be upset now.

"She's not supposed to have that mark until after the mating ceremony." She glanced at Heather. "In fact, she shouldn't have been able to receive it. Have you two bonded already?"

"Uncle came with me. Something about wanting to see what was out there before he finished his term as religious leader. You know he's the one person none of us can say no to."

"So that is why you've gone along with this." She reached out to his left arm and felt the invisible bond around his wrist. "I couldn't figure out why you didn't fight this whole thing. What did he tell you?"

"She's my destiny."

"This will disappear once the mating ceremony happens." She let go of his wrist. "Have you told her about it?"

"Told me about what?" She picked up the device Storm's sister had placed on her shoulder and sat up.

"Say my name."

"Tiko." Heather then laughed as the translator told her what the nickname really meant. "Storm, making me think Tiko was a name I could use was wrong. Unless you want me to call you a dung heap for the rest of your life."

"I'd rather you not." She stepped up and removed the downloader. "You should be able to understand anyone now. There might be a few old dialects that can cause a little trouble, but overall you should be able to converse with anyone from our planet."

"Thank you." She folded her hands into her lap. "Now you two can't talk about me and keep me in the dark."

"True." His sister smiled. "In the morning, we'll go over protocol for the banquet. There's quite a bit you're going to need to know. In the meantime why don't you ask my brother about our marriage ceremony? I'm sure there's a lot he can tell you about it."

"Why did that sound like a dare?" Heather asked after his sister left.

"Because it was." His fingers started to work on the front of the shirt. "Now, where were we?"

"Oh, no you don't." She batted his hands away. "I have a feeling you don't think I'm going to like this, so you're trying to distract me."

He sighed but didn't stop trying to get the shirt off her. He just might commit murder by the end of the day. "You know how modest you are?"

"I'm no more modest than the next human."

He could argue that point but decided it would only make matters worse. If his sister hadn't said anything, he would have had more time before having to explain. Maybe it was better to get it out in the open now. Give her time to accept it. "And you've made a comment or two about my lack of modesty."

She nodded.

"Our whole society is that way. Where you cover up when in public, we don't have to. What you consider private and should be kept in the bedroom we celebrate, whenever and wherever we want to." He finally got the shirt off her and smiled at the treasure he had revealed. "Our wedding ceremony is a reflection of that. We wear capes, or maybe you call them robes. Nothing on underneath. Our religious figure says a few words and then the ceremony begins."

"I'm not sure I understand."

"That's why I'm going to show you the ceremony that way you won't have any confusion." He touched her face. "It's a sacred and beautiful ceremony to us. Just let me gather a few things first and you'll see what I'm talking about."

He stepped away from her, enjoying the view once again. "And don't cover up. I like you that way."

The bed had a sheet he could use for the cape. As he went to pull it off the bed, he noticed his closet doors were open. Hanging in them were two capes that would work perfectly. He found it odd they were there since he didn't pack anything like that but didn't question. The desire to do this now overwhelmed him. "I'm not sure where these came from, but they will do."

He slipped one over her shoulders, then donned the other one himself. "Now we need to find a special place."

"At the embassy?"

"I know just the spot." Taking her hand, he had her following him, racing down several halls and out into the night. They dashed across the grass to a wooded area that would conceal them from prying eyes.

"Now." He turned her toward him and took both of her hands in his. "Our religious leader would stand nearby. Not always where the couple could see him. It's the same for the guests. This moment is about the couple and no one else."

"Then why have it witnessed like this?"

"It's part of our tradition." He saw the fear in her eyes. "That is why we're doing this now. Just the two of us. I don't want you to fear what we find beautiful and sacred."

"And if I can't go through with it?"

"I'll never make you do something you don't want to." He'd have to find a way, but for now he needed her calm enough to go through the trial run. Perhaps if he could get her to see how glorious it was, he could make her forget about anything else.

"So what happens after the guy says his piece?" She was frightened. He could hear it in her voice and felt it in the beat of her pulse.

"I open my arms with the cape and you do the same. Then step in and wrap your arms around me." She moved fast, but the heat of her body against his was what he wanted anyway. He wrapped his cloak about her and eased her to the ground.

"And now?"

"We share our need for each other." He didn't give her a chance to protest. First, he captured her lips as he released the ties at her throat so he could have access. There was something about the soft tissue there that drew him. His fingers deftly worked at the folds of her mound, causing her to arch against him. When he felt her slick and wet, he entered her.

Heather's legs wrapped around him, her hips already moving. Each time he entered her, he felt like he was home. Her muscles tightened around him, drawing a moan from him.

"Now you repeat after me."

"What?" She was so caught up in the sensations

enveloping them both, she had forgotten about the ceremony. "Oh. Right."

"You are my heart, my soul. There will be no other. I will protect you, care for you, give you the passion you deserve. Make you as happy as I can for the rest of my days."

She repeated the words. Her voice sultry, and caught up in the throes of passion, but her eyes were clear and bright, and looking at him. Then a tremor passed through her and she lost contact with him. Her orgasm took her hard and fast and pulled him along with her. The grip her muscles had on him was exquisite, tightening ever so slightly until he found it hard to think.

His world splintered around him.

"You know this could get addictive." She came close to purring.

"Glad you see it my way." He wanted to shout his joy at her reaction. "So when I grab you in the hallway and drag you into some dark corner to have my way with you, there will be no argument?"

"I—"

He covered her mouth with his so she couldn't say anything else.

The next morning he sat with her, drinking coffee. "I do like this beverage."

"You don't have coffee on Vespia?" She gave him a mock look of horror. "Can't go if you don't have my coffee."

"Really?" He loved the way the white gown she wore that first night clung to all the right places. "And if I were to throw you over my shoulder and force you onto the ship?"

"I'll be obnoxious and fight you all the way." She took a sip of her coffee. "It's the coffee that keeps me human."

He rose from his chair, came up behind her and slipped

one hand inside her gown. "As long as you still get on the ship you can be as obnoxious as you want."

"Like you?" She looked up at him, leaning her head against his arm.

Something changed between them last night. She was more comfortable with him and his advances. He'd like to think she was more comfortable with the upcoming ceremony, but he wouldn't know for sure until they talked about it.

His sister came slamming into the room. "Are you two out of your minds?"

"What are you talking about?" Heather was the first one to speak.

"Last night. The mating ceremony?" She was angry. She stared at his arm still inside Heather's nightgown. "Can you please focus?"

"We are." Heather pulled his hand out of her top since he hadn't removed it himself. "You brought up the ceremony and your brother wanted to show me what was involved. So we, um, did a dry run."

"I wouldn't say it was dry."

She blushed a pretty shade of pink at his words.

"And where did you get the capes?" Storm's sister stared at him.

"They were in my closet." He wasn't quite sure what she was so angry about. "I don't know how they got there, but they came in handy."

"I do." Heather took another sip of her coffee.

"They were mom and dad's in case you didn't, wait, you know who left them?" His sister turned her attention to Heather.

"Yeah." She set her cup down. "The strange little man who did that other ceremony. The chalice and the rope were resting on those capes. He must have left them behind after the ceremony."

"You two have no clue what happened last night, do you?" She looked at him, then looked at Heather. "He was there last night."

"Who was where?" Heather didn't get the implications, but he did.

"In the woods. I watched him bless your union."

"What were you doing there?" Storm had wanted last night to be special between him and Heather, now he was learning it was more than that.

"I saw the two of you running across the lawn last night and knew what was on your mind. I had to be sure you were going to be safe."

He glared at her.

"Don't give me that. I've seen the way you become hyper-focused on something and this time it's Heather. You weren't thinking about safety, just privacy. Someone had to watch your back."

"So you were our witness." He looked at Heather, realizing she was truly his.

"Yes."

"I'm not sure I understand."

"We had the real ceremony last night."

"What?" She looked from Storm to his sister. "But I thought there were certain things that had to happen."

"True, and they did happen. Our religious leader was there to proceed over the ceremony." He knelt beside her chair, watching her reaction.

"But we were alone."

"We thought we were alone." He touched her face softly. "We've fulfilled the obligation of the mating vows."

"Does that mean I don't have to go through something so intimate with an audience?"

"Is that all you can think of?" Storm's sister slammed her hand on the table. "You broke protocol!"

"How?" He stood and glowered at his sister. "If he was there, then he approved. How was that breaking protocol?"

She got flustered because she didn't have an answer. "Your mate and I need to go over what will happen tonight."

Heather stood. "Let me get changed."

"I haven't seen a mark." Storm still couldn't believe the ceremony had happened.

"That's because you are as blind as they come." She punched him in the chest. "It's right where I hit you."

He walked to a mirror and noticed the small mark just below his right nipple. "How about that."

"What mark?"

"Did he leave that out? The mating ritual marks the couple. You both have the same mark." She took Heather by the arm and brought her to the same mirror. First, she pointed to Storm's chest, then to the left side of her neck.

"And what does the mark mean?"

"That you're my mate." He pulled her into his embrace. "And my sister needs to show you the respect of being my mate."

"I have." She looked hurt by his words.

"Ignore his gruffness. He's just upset you interrupted him before he got a chance to repeat last night." Heather grabbed some clothes and changed.

"Not going to dart into the bathroom?" asked Storm. Yesterday she wanted to try the dress on in another room and today her modesty seemed to be gone.

"Why? Everybody here has seen it all already." Heather changed while she spoke. "There is a lot that needs to be done before everyone gets here. I know your people are making sure your leaders are made comfortable, but since I'm the only human in this building, I must do the same."

She started toward the door. They opened just as she reached them, which stopped her for a second. It was one thing to have a computer open doors aboard ship, but to have people do it unnerved her. "Don't think I'll ever get used to this."

"She moves pretty quickly, so you might want to keep up." He wanted to laugh as his sister scrambled out the door.

"Do you take everything in stride like this?"

Heather wanted to beat her. Of course she didn't take everything in stride, but what could she do? "Like what? My life being turned upside down by not one but two Vespians?"

"And how do you handle things when massive mistakes happen?"

"You make the best of it." Heather rubbed her head. The beginnings of a headache starting. "I was nothing more than an unknown human who worked for our government three days ago. My assignment was to protect the ambassador of Vespia. Then my assignment changed. Now I'm married to the ambassador, who seems to have a jealous girlfriend or two."

"What makes you say that?"

"Why else would anyone want to target me? I am nothing." Heather took a right turn toward the kitchens. The head chef bowed to her as she entered. "A lieutenant in the UCE military. Not big brass, not some sort of special agent. Just someone from security who happened to pique the interest of a bunch of dignitaries. Now I have to contend with this. Making sure two worlds are happy and treated evenly. I also have to come home with a treaty that works for both worlds. I didn't ask for any of this."

"How may I help you, mistress?" the head chef had stepped up the moment she walked into the room.

"I need to know what you have planned for the leader of the UCE."

"UCE?"

"United Countries of Earth. It's not pretty, but it works," Heather explained.

"We were sent a list of foods to prepare for him as well as our leaders. This is what we came up with to keep both sides happy and not have two separate menus." He handed her a card that showed what would be served.

"Perfect. If you treat them differently, they could take offense." She looked it over before handing it back. "Thank you."

"Welcome, Mistress."

"And the seating arrangements? Has that been done yet?"

"Yes, Mistress. They are waiting for your approval in the main hall."

Heather walked out of the kitchen and headed to the rooms where the leaders would be able to freshen up and rest if they wished. She walked into one room and started shouting. "Who is in charge of these rooms?"

A timid young woman stepped forward. "I am, Mistress. Is there something wrong?"

"I'm sorry that I shouted, but I didn't see you and have learned it is the best way to get people to move around here. Could you make sure you have the exact same flowers in each room? If you have anything different, it could cause trouble."

"Of course."

"Now, what did I need to know about the dinner tonight?" Heather asked herself out loud. She snapped her fingers and headed to the other rooms with his sister in tow. "You haven't said a whole lot since we started."

"I need your undivided attention for our protocol." She smiled.

"You've got it." Heather spoke to the young woman she had talked to earlier for a moment or two, then signaled for her sister-in-law to follow her. "We can talk on our way to the hall."

"Good. Perhaps we could go out into the gardens afterwards? I'm sure they will be used this evening as well."

"Trying to piss him off, are you? Sure. It shouldn't take him too long to reach us." The doors to the main hall opened, so she got to see how everything was being set up. She did make a few changes but overall was happy with the way things were going.

"Now, why would I want to anger my brother?" asked Storm's sister.

"Still mad because he broke protocol." She walked out into the gardens to watch as lights were being strung to help illuminate it for later that evening. A few more directions to a few servants standing by and she faced her sister-in-law. "So how much do you want to bet he'll be down here in less than a minute?"

"You know him well in a short period of time."

Heather gestured to her body. "Favorite new toy."

She laughed. "We can cover this one thing while we wait. You know about our marriage ritual. What did Storm tell you about our people?"

"That you don't have the same view of modesty we do."

"True. You will find people on our planet in any state of dress. For this meeting, they will dress to accommodate your race, but we have these servants labeled as pleasurers. They are there to give pleasure anywhere and anytime."

"You mean sexual pleasure?" Heather blanched at her nod. "But my people won't understand that."

"They have been told to be very discrete and will only stick to our guests. Humans are off limits."

"Thank you for that." Heather felt better. "It would be very hard to explain. Don't get me wrong, we like to consider ourselves very open, but that is just pushing the limits a bit."

"You need to be aware."

"Me?" She pointed to a place where the flowers didn't match the rest of the decor.

"You are now considered Vespian and you will be approached."

"But I don't want that." Heather had enough to deal with and Storm would probably kill the first man who looked at her sideways.

"Which is why I need to show you how to turn them down."

"Protocol."

"That's my job."

"Can't I just take them down?" she made a little slash in the air. "Might help me get some of my frustrations out."

"Thought that was my brother's job."

"Different type of frustration." Heather looked at the door. Storm should be showing up any moment now.

"A simple gesture will do the trick." She made a simple slash with her hand.

"That's it?" Heather repeated it.

"Yes. Right hand, palm down, index and middle finger extended."

"I sure hope I don't need to use this." She did the gesture once more.

"Hopefully not, but you're ready just in case."

Storm came through the doors with a frown on his face.

"How about that, and I have a second to spare." Heather winked at her mate's sister as she stood to greet him.

Heather stood next to Storm in her formal dress uniform, realizing this would be the last time she wore it. The commander-in-chief looked pleased to see it on her.

"Lieutenant, I half expected you to be wearing Vespian garb."

"That will be this evening, sir. At dinner." She gave him a formal salute.

He nodded, returning the salute.

They spoke for a few minutes about the treaty and what was expected of her before she was released to change clothes.

Storm took him to the side and started talking his ear off, giving her time to get dressed for the meal that evening.

Her hair had been brushed and pulled back from her face. Her skin was perfumed and pampered. She felt like royalty. The dress still exposed more than she wished and she would love to use something to cover up a little more but was afraid she'd upset someone. She suspected the dress was made that way on purpose because there between her breasts rested Storm's family crest, obvious for all to see.

Now all she had to do was wait for Storm to come get her and the waiting was the most difficult. Her uniforms were so much easier to deal with, blending in the background was more her style.

She rubbed her head. The headache was back, and she hadn't had time to go by the medical center. Heather wondered if she had enough time to sneak down there real quick when the doors opened and Storm strode in.

Her heart skipped a beat. He wore clothing close to the dress she wore. Form-fitting, showing off his muscles, he looked wonderful. The family crest emblazoned on the material.

"We don't look like much of a target, do we?" she asked.

"I know, and I hate putting you in this much danger."

"I'm used to being shot at." She tried to fluff the fabric barely covering her once more. "It's the weird looks and the rules that will get the best of me tonight."

He offered her his arm. "Are you ready?"

"And if I said no?" She took his arm.

"I'd have to drag you out there in my usual style." He placed his other hand on top of hers.

"That's what I thought, and having your people see this end…" She touched her butt then her face. "Before they see this end, is not what I had in mind."

"They will respect you no matter what."

"We'll see." She took a deep breath as they walked through the doors and down the hall.

"Have you grown? You're not hitting me in my navel anymore."

"I'm six foot three! And wearing four-inch heels." She lifted one foot to show the shoe off. "Something I'm not used to so I just might break my neck in the process."

"You might be tall for a human, but when the average height for Vespian women is six foot eight, you will be considered petite."

"Even in four-inch heels?"

"You plan on wearing them all the time?" There was a glint in his eye she recognized. The man had a one-track mind.

"Probably not." She rubbed her head. The dull throb had blossomed into a real pain. "Can we stop by the medlab?"

"Problem?"

"My headache is still bothering me." She gave him a soft smile. "Not to worry. The removal of the device has given me headaches for up to a week, so this isn't anything out of the ordinary."

"You're sure?"

"Yes."

She had spent hours with her mate's sister, learning the ins and outs of what she should and shouldn't do. Standing in a receiving line for several hours in four-inch heels should have been on the top of the list. They were comfortable enough, but she kept fearing that she would lose her balance and fall flat on her face. Thank goodness she was surrounded, with Storm was to her left and his sister was to her right.

Heather nodded and smiled, remembering to keep her hands to herself. Trying to remember everything had her afraid to do anything. She found either Storm or his sister would prompt her when she made a minor misstep, so she hadn't made a fool of herself yet.

She did a mental jump for joy when she saw the end of the line. Now maybe she could get a chance to relax for a second. It took several toasts and one rather lengthy speech by the head elder and the commander-in-chief before Heather finally got to sit down.

Drinks were poured and people started talking amongst themselves. She found many looking at her. Not used to being the center of attention she wanted it to stop. She tightened her grip on Storm's hand.

"Problem?" Storm placed his other hand on top of Heather's.

"Sorry." She released her death grip and gave him an apologetic smile. "Just not used to all this attention. Why couldn't we get a table in the back somewhere?"

"Because this way, we both have to be on our best behavior. If we were in the back, I'd find a way to get out of here so we could be alone." He gave her a quick kiss. "And we're a target, remember?" He touched the crest resting between her breasts, which sent shivers through her when he trailed his fingers against the soft tissue exposed there.

"How can I forget when I have everyone staring at me like I'm a specimen on display at the zoo?"

"I can give them a different reason to stare if you wish." He gave her a wink as he ran a finger down her throat.

It brought a blush to her cheeks and a comment from his sister. "Do we have to separate you two?"

"I am talking to Heather, not you." He gave his sister a cold stare before he turned his focus solely to his mate.

A bowl of fruit was placed in front of Heather who stared at it in shock.

"Good Lord, they brought the biggest cut of all the fruits." She looked at Storm's sister. "Thought you said to pick the smallest one."

"All you have to do is offer Storm a piece. He knows what to do."

"With my mouth?" Heather found the idea a bit intimate for her in such a public setting.

"With your mouth."

She found him staring at her mouth intently, just waiting to swoop in and take his prize. With nervous fingers, she pulled out a smallish chunk of pineapple and stuck it between her teeth. The moment she tilted her head up toward his, his lips were on hers. Storm sucked the fruit from between her lips, chomped it once, and swallowed before he swept his tongue into her mouth.

The sweetness of the fruit still lingered, adding to the heady sensation of their tongues dancing together. She forgot they were in a crowd with thousands of eyes on them. His hand caressed her jaw, then her throat.

Someone cleared their throat.

Storm broke the kiss, but his breathing was labored like hers and he rested his forehead against hers, trying to gain control.

Heather was grateful he was having as much trouble with his composure as she was. She didn't want the kiss to end.

"If you two could behave yourselves for a moment they'll serve the food." Storm's sister shook her head. "At least the audience liked it."

"Is your sister always this annoying?" Heather found she could breathe normally now.

"Yes." He gave her another quick but heated kiss. "We'll pick this up later."

"Whose idea was it to do the fruit thing anyway?" She cut a glance to her mate's sister, who suddenly tried to look very innocent.

"Blame the elders. It was their request."

The rest of the meal was pretty tame. Heather found it hard to eat with so many focusing on her and Storm. Once the plates were cleared, Storm stood and offered her his arm.

"You going to deny me the chance to get to know your mate?" a soft female voice sounded to his right.

"Of course not." He turned to Heather. "This is the leader of our society and my mother, Anseri."

"Mother? You couldn't have mentioned that a little earlier?" Heather gripped his arm hard. She felt like crawling into a hole somewhere after the way she had made comments about this leader to both Storm and his sister.

"Come. Sit. I'd like to get to know you better."

"Yes, Ma'am." Heather sank into the seat Storm had just vacated.

"So formal." She picked up her glass. "You can call me, Mother."

"Yes, Ma'am." Heather felt the blood drain from her face. What did she know? What should she admit to? No one prepared her for this.

"Why are you so frightened?" She placed her hand on Heather's left wrist. "So I see the rumors are true."

"I'm not sure I understand." What did she do now?

"You and Storm have gone through the mating ceremony."

"Oh, that." That mating ceremony seemed to be the main topic of conversation with these people. First his sister and now his mother. "Yes, we've already been reprimanded once, but in our defense your son was trying to prepare me for the real one. How were we to know that strange little man would be there?"

"That strange little man is my brother."

"Oh." Heather felt her shoulders hunch a bit. "I'm really making a mess of this, aren't I?"

"You're doing fine. You're honest and I like that. You aren't trying too hard to get in my good graces. That's always good." She picked up her glass and toasted her son who stood a few feet in front of the dais watching them. "And my son seems quite smitten with you."

"I'm the newest toy that he can't get enough of."

"Really?" She smiled at that one. "Is the new toy complaining?"

How could she answer that? "No. Just being honest again."

"Then let's change the subject, shall we?" She touched Heather's arm again, drawing her gaze. "I'm sure you have questions? Like why you were picked for this assignment over other candidates?"

"It had crossed my mind." And was a question she never thought she'd get an answer to.

"We had several criteria. One of course was the candidate had to be female and in a certain age bracket. That took about half the candidates out. Another thing we looked at was military training. That was a must."

"Why?" So far everything made perfect sense.

"When you were told you were to marry my son, what did you do?"

"Filed a complaint."

"But you did what was expected of you, correct?" The woman smiled at her comment.

"Of course. It's my duty." Heather understood what she meant.

"That thinned the list down more." She took another sip

of her drink. "Now let me ask if you realized that you probably will never step foot on Earth again once you leave with us."

"Hadn't really given it much thought."

"Exactly." She smiled. "Another criteria. You are an orphan. No family ties to keep you here. We will be all the family you'll need. We also wanted someone who knew how to defend herself. Our race is an aggressive one and a timid woman wouldn't fit into our society. I have read your dossier. You stand up for your beliefs."

Sometimes at the cost of something else.

"There was one more thing. Children."

Heather knew this was coming. She couldn't have children. She was sterile.

SIX

"We know you're sterile." She placed her hand on Heather's again. "So is my son. I feared if the woman chosen for him was fertile and found out they would never have children, she might stray to have that child."

"How would they stray? He keeps a very short leash." Heather looked at Storm who hadn't moved since they started talking. She didn't mean it the way it came out, but his mother didn't seem to be fazed by her comment. "Besides, Storm explained that Vespians can have more than one partner and still be mated."

"True, but my son is very loyal. He wouldn't want to share something so precious to him." His mom chuckled. "Look at him. He seems so forlorn there."

"One more question and we can put him out of his misery." Heather watched him fidget while he waited for them to finish talking. "Why didn't he tell me his mother was the leader of the planet?"

"He has been trained to only give out information when he feels it is pertinent."

"The need to know basis." Heather nodded, understanding the military way. "But it would have been nice having a little notice."

"Did you feel a little broadsided?"

Heather nodded.

"He also might have thought it would have overwhelmed you."

"I'm not a child." She probably sounded a little petulant, but she couldn't help it.

"True, but our society is so different from yours. You have only scratched the surface." The moment she finished her sentence Storm joined them.

Heather hadn't seen him move. She felt the heat of his hand on her elbow as he helped her to her feet and steered her away from his mother. How had he known the audience was over? Did she miss some subtle hint?

"So, did the two of you have a good talk?" His voice held a hint of something she had never heard from him before. Was that a touch of fear?

"We sure did." She gave him her brightest smile. "Thank you for telling me she is your mother before I met her. It really made it easy for me."

"Oh, that." He gave her an apologetic smile. "Guess it slipped my mind."

"Sure it did." She walked beside him, thinking about all she had learned. Her silence must have worried him.

"You mad?"

"No." She patted his arm. She was adjusting to his way of thinking quickly. Part of her understood why he did it. She could have bolted at any moment with everything that had happened in the last forty-eight hours. He didn't want to say the one thing that would send her over the edge. "Just thinking. Your mother explained how I was chosen to be your wife. I can see the logic, yet I feel there was something she wanted to tell me but felt she couldn't."

"Mother comes across that way sometimes. It comes with

the job." He wrapped his arm around her. "Would you care to get some fresh air?"

"That would be great, but this place is pretty packed." She looked up at him. "Don't expect to find some little out of the way corner."

"Even if I had it guarded just in case we could sneak away?" He stole a quick kiss, then got them as far as the doors before someone called him. He growled at the intrusion. "Wait right here. I promise I won't be long."

She was amazed he left her alone. No sister to babysit or guards surrounding her like she was something delicate. It was kind of nice. Enjoying the fresh air, she stepped out onto the patio, hoping to feel the breeze stir her hair. She hadn't been allowed any leisure time in days.

As she kept to herself, enjoying the quiet moment, she found a young man kneeling at her feet. One of the pleasurers. How he found her, she wasn't sure. Her sister-in-law had passed the word she didn't want to be approached, and all had obeyed, but this one.

It took her a second or two to remember the proper gesture for no. She used the signal and tried to step away, but he blocked her way again. She sighed. He wasn't going to take no for an answer. Why did she have to get the one who didn't get the memo?

"Does the word no not register for you or do you want a beating?" Perhaps the words would penetrate where the proper gestures wouldn't. She moved once again, but this time when he blocked her he grabbed her and tried to drag her to a secluded spot. In seconds, he was a heap at her feet. One palm to the nose broke it, allowing blood to gush everywhere, and then she finished defending herself with a knee to the groin. That should end any other thoughts of trying to molest her.

"No means no." His groan brought security. Where were

they when all this was transpiring? "Get him out of here before Storm sees him."

She dusted her hands and sought to fix her dress, which had gotten a little out of shape in the scuffle, but she realized she couldn't do it without a mirror.

There was a restroom right inside the doors, so she slipped in without too many people seeing her. There were several women at the mirrors, but they cleared the area when they realized who she was. Royalty had its perks.

She tried to fix the dress but found she needed more than two hands. The bodice had shifted and the only way to get it back where it belonged was to undo the dress and move it, and she couldn't reach the magnetized seam. Asking another patron was out of the question. There'd be too much talk, but she couldn't go out with half of her exposed.

Peeking out the door, she looked for someone she knew and realized she really only had three choices, and two of them would probably get her into more trouble. Luckily, Storm's sister happened to be nearby and spotted her. Heather signaled her over.

"I heard you were in here." She stepped into the bathroom and allowed the door to close behind her. "Everything all right?"

"Yes, it's just my dress seems to be a little off kilter." She dropped her hand so she could see her predicament.

"What happened?" She stepped up behind Heather and released the dress enough to put everything back where it belonged. "My brother wouldn't leave you like this."

"No, he wouldn't." She checked herself in the mirror, making sure everything was where it should be. "One of your pleasuring servants wouldn't take no for an answer. Now he's sporting a broken nose and speaking a few octaves higher."

"Good for you." She closed the seam of the dress and

stepped back. "Have you told my brother? He won't be happy."

"I'm not going to ruin his evening because of one stupid man." She pulled the bodice up, hoping it would look like it did when he left her. Fluffing the lace, she decided it would have to do. "I'm sure security will alert him anyway. Until then, he doesn't need to know. Now, I can sense him lurking right outside the door. We have to make this look good."

They came out giggling and whispering to each other.

Storm stood there with his arms crossed. "What are you two up to?"

"What makes you think we're up to something?" asked Heather as she linked arms with him. She wanted to act normal but was afraid he saw right through them.

"Because my sister is involved. I got in more trouble as a child because of her." He looked down at her. "What happened to your dress?"

"I told you one of them was bound to pop out and you weren't there to put it back, so I had to do it myself." She tried to sound nonchalant.

"If you had just waited for me, I would have done a better job." He took a hold of her bodice and pulled. Everything fell into place. "Looks like they got a little scraped up in the process too."

He could be clueless about so many things, but when it came to her body, he was like a hawk. How was she going to get out of this?

"I see the two of you have finally been given some freedom." The new voice made Heather turn around. Perhaps she would be the out Heather needed.

Heather had noticed the woman before. Her tight black dress exposed more than it covered. Storm seemed oblivious as he smiled at the woman. He wrapped his arm around Heather possessively. "Thank you, yes."

"Come, there are a few people you need to be introduced

to." Storm's sister pulled Heather out of his hold and hurried her away.

"That was rude." Heather pulled herself free from her grip.

"Yeah, well, you don't want to get caught up with her."

"Why?"

"Old family. Lots of ties. Thought she would be where you are someday." She grabbed Heather by the arm and dragged her a few more feet before Heather pulled out of her grip again.

"We just went through a lot to get these puppies back where they belong. Cut it out." She pulled at the material around her breasts to make sure they would stay in place. "So that's an old girlfriend. Wondered when they'd start showing up."

"What? No. They never really dated or anything. Storm might have had a dalliance here and there, but never anyone serious."

"Then why are you dragging me away like she was?"

"Because Vespian women can be quite cruel when they want to, and you don't deserve that tonight. My brother can handle her and send her on her way."

"And you think we humans aren't cruel? I have been on the wrong end of many a comment that would hurt a weaker person." Heather lifted her dress to move. "Did you close this right? I feel like there is a whole lot more material all of the sudden."

She stepped behind Heather and tried to get the back of the dress to work. "The magnets have stopped working. Someone demagnetized them." She grabbed the back of the dress to keep Heather from spilling out all over.

"You've got to be kidding." Could it get any worse?

"Nope." She looked over Heather's shoulder. "Storm is coming."

"Of course he is." She put on her best smile and waited.

"Ladies?"

"Storm." They said it at the same time.

"What seems to be the problem?"

"Little glitch with the dress. No big deal. We can fix it." Heather started to back up, hoping Storm's sister would move with her. They didn't get too far before Storm stopped them and made her turn around. The back of her dress gaped open where his sister wasn't holding it.

At that point head of security showed up. Heather hung her head. This wasn't going her way at all.

"Let's go." He pointed for Heather and his sister to go first.

"If you don't need me." His sister started to let go of Heather's dress.

"Oh, no. You're coming. You are always in the center of trouble." He grabbed the back of the dress as well. "Besides, if you were to let go now my mate would be mortified and I can't have that."

It was a long walk to the security center. Heather felt like a fool with the two of them holding onto the back of her dress for dear life.

Storm saw the half-naked man with a bloody nose and turned to his sister. "You want to explain this?"

She pointed to Heather.

"Traitor." Heather held her dress in place. "He wouldn't take no for an answer."

"These people are trained to please, not harass."

"So you don't believe me?" More than anything, that pissed her off. Keeping a death grip on her dress, she stepped up to him and jabbed him in the chest. "You haven't let me out of your sight because you think I'm so fragile, yet when I am left alone and attacked this is the way you're going to handle it? Not the smartest move you could have made."

She heard a snicker behind her. Whipping around, she

found two very straight faces. One belonged to his sister. "Thought not."

"Are you arguing with me?"

She saw the intense gaze and remembered what happened the last time she argued with him. It sent little slivers of desire through her, but she realized she was close to overstepping her boundaries. "I am vigorously inserting my opinion."

Storm didn't show any reaction for a moment, then he laughed and pulled her into his embrace. "You are glorious when you're 'vigorously inserting your opinion.'"

"Um, sir." The guard stepped up to a view screen and brought up the image of her being approached by the man in the cell. "She is telling the truth."

She looked at the screen, grateful they had caught it on tape, yet pissed off that he had to see it before he believed her.

As Storm watched the scene unfold, she realized why his name fit him so well. His eyes darkened, his brows furrowed, like a storm he was ready to strike. The angry glare he gave the man had the guy quaking in his cell.

"We found these items on his person."

Storm picked up each of the items and looked at them. One of the items he threw to his sister while he stared a hole into the man who was looking very nervous in the cell. "You came here to harm my future wife?" He used the human's words instead of calling her his mate.

Heather heard the device hum as Storm's sister ran it up the magnet. In seconds, the dress was back together, but she was still having issues. Holding the dress in place, she stepped up to Storm and placed a hand on his arm. "I think I inflicted my share of damage."

He noticed the broken nose. "True, but that isn't that much for what he could have done."

She wanted to kick him for still thinking of her as a

fragile flower. "One, I can protect myself and two have you noticed what he is grabbing? Doesn't matter what planet you are from when you get hit there you are worth nothing." She turned her back to them and tried to get the dress to sit right. She gave up when she couldn't get it to do what she wanted. "He should be glad I had this dress on or he could have gotten a stiletto in the gonads. That would have put him in the hospital."

"Keep him for me to deal with later." He slipped an arm around Heather and escorted her out of the room. "You shouldn't have been in that situation in the first place."

She wanted to say if he hadn't left her this wouldn't have happened but knew it went beyond this. She stopped him in the hall. "You can't watch over me all the time."

"You mean like this?" He looked down at her dress. Her rosy tips peeked up at him. His hands brushed against her skin as he adjusted the material to get everything back into place.

It took him seconds to fix what she hadn't been able to do since she kicked the man's ass. It just wasn't right.

"I'm serious. I've been through a lot more than a man trying to molest me. If you don't believe I can protect myself how is anyone else going to believe it?" She smoothed the material as much as she could. It was beyond repair by this point. "This poor dress has seen too much action. It looks like we've been at it all night."

"I can rectify that." He scooped her up in his arms.

"Mom wants you."

"Didn't I dismiss you?" Storm turned to growl at his sister.

"Don't care. You are wanted on the dais now. No excuses." She fought a smile that wanted to explode onto her face. "The council has another surprise for you."

"Oh goody. This day hasn't had enough of those." Heather tapped him on the shoulder so he would put her down. Storm stole a quick kiss before he lowered her so she could stand on her own.

They walked into the main hall to find everyone staring at them.

"Did something pop out again?" Heather asked in a soft voice.

Storm looked down. "Everything is right where it should be." He escorted her to their seats. "You wished to speak to us?"

"Heather's leader wished to speak."

Storm turned to look at her and she shrugged. "I have no idea."

She just hoped whatever it was wouldn't be too embarrassing. The Vespians had a lot more technology than they did. There wasn't a whole lot Earth could offer.

She listened as he went on and on about the treaty and how the joining of her and Storm would bring both worlds together. She just kept waiting for the big surprise.

"As we watch these two together we see everything we hope to accomplish with our treaty. As the commander-in-chief of this planet, I have hoped to contribute to the nuptials in some way. I have learned that our lieutenant doesn't have anyone to give her away at the human ceremony, so I am volunteering."

He gave her a big smile. All she could do was smile back.

How many times were they going to be married?

SEVEN

"You okay?" Storm placed a hand on her arm.

"Yep." She gave him a bright smile. One that didn't go to her eyes. "Need some fresh air."

"He's not done talking."

"Great." She sat there wondering what else would be expected of her. A wedding took months, even years to plan for some brides and she would have hours or days. Her mind buzzed with all the things she would have to do.

So was it going to be the long white gown or the military wedding? That part was up for grabs. She continued to listen, hoping he would stop soon when she caught military and formal. Wonderful. Just what she wanted. That meant a lot of explaining to Storm who probably saw their military as something he could wipe out in one day.

A toast was offered and she lifted her glass as expected. But her mind went into overdrive. So much to do. "Has he mentioned a date?"

"Two days from now." He looked at her with concern. "You sure you're okay?"

"Two days. I have two days to pull this off." She pinched her nose. "I'm going to need an army."

"Perhaps you're right and we should go out for a bit of fresh air." Storm stood and offered her his hand. He led her out into the gardens. "Why did what your leader said upset you so much?"

"A military wedding entails a lot more than a regular wedding. If I could have worn a regular bridal gown, I could have gotten it done. But we're talking formal military wedding gown. They have to be special ordered months in advance. I have to have my medals, be fitted, get permission to have the wedding." She felt a little giddy. "But since the commander-in-chief is walking me down the aisle, I guess I don't have to worry about the last part and we know where the medals are."

"Take a deep breath."

She looked up at him. "Do you know what *elope* means?"

"Yes, and I think we've already done that." He hugged her. "I have never seen you like this."

"How long have we really known each other?"

"True, but we've been through a lifetime of emotions in just a few days and nothing up until this has ruffled you."

"You're right." She sat on the marble bench in the little alcove he had secured for them. "I think tonight I have been through them all. Fear, when I learned that your mother was the leader of your race and she wanted to talk to me. Laughter when I watched as you waited for us to finish talking. You were like a child waiting for that bit of candy you had been promised. Anger, when that little weasel of a man made me wish I was somewhere else. Frustration when I couldn't get that damn dress to fit right. Sadness when I realized I have spent thirty years of my life on this planet and I wouldn't miss any of it. And joy, because I have the rest of my life to spend with you."

"Perhaps I need to take your mind off things for a moment." He drew her into his lap.

"And someone will come around that corner wanting one

of us in about a minute or two." She wrapped her arms around him. "Just how fast can you do this?"

"Not that fast." He held her tight. "You do realize that it doesn't matter. I can keep people at bay as long as you need me to."

"I just want this evening to be over, so there will be no more surprises. I've had my share, thank you very much."

"Say the word and I'll drag you to our room where no one can interrupt us."

She leaned her head against his chest. She felt his heartbeat strong and steady against her cheek. "This is very comforting."

"I hate interrupting you two."

"No, you don't," Heather groused at Storm's sister. "I think you like it, Toki. Gives you a chance to annoy your brother. But guess what, you're annoying me too."

"Toki? Oh, that does fit her." Storm grinned at his sister. She now had a new nickname. Heather didn't realize she had figured out his sister's simpler name she was just emphasizing the wrong vowel. He would explain it to Heather later, but for now his sister deserved to be called pain.

Heather had been mulling a name for his sister in her head for a while and kept coming back to pain in Vespian. It fit the way she felt at the moment and was a word she could pronounce.

"I truly am sorry." She smiled at them both. "But you're required to dance."

"Vespian dancing or Earth dancing?" Heather wasn't sure if she could make her way through the intricate steps she had been taught.

"Not sure about that one." She turned her back to them. "All I know is that you must attend."

"Can I throttle her when we're done?" She stood and looked at him.

"Does that mean I can hold her down?" He stood and took her hand.

"Sure does."

The evening finally winded down and they were allowed to go back to their room. Heather peeled the dress off and pulled on her gown. She sat cross-legged on the bed with a small electronic pad in her grip. "When we wake in the morning, don't remind me what I have to do. Give me those few moments of freedom before the world comes crashing in around me."

"Should I remind you that my mother is coming to visit first thing in the morning?" Storm stared at the small pad in her hand before he undressed and climbed into bed beside her.

"Please don't. That just might make me go crazy. As it is, I need to figure out where to start in the morning." She pressed a few keys and plopped back onto the bed. "This is going to be impossible."

Storm pulled the pad from her.

"But I have so much to do." She watched the pad until he sat it on the nightstand on his side of the bed. The only way she was going to get it was to crawl over him, and he could tell she was contemplating it. Time to distract her.

He rolled over on top of her. "And it can wait 'til the morning." He hooked a finger around the strap of her gown and pulled it off one shoulder. "What you need to do is unwind."

"You like pinning me like this, don't you?"

"You're much softer than the bed." He lowered his head to nibble on her throat.

"True, but haven't you wondered what it would be like if I ever led this little dance of ours?"

"Are you complaining?" He pulled up to look at her. "I have made sure you have been satisfied every time. Sometimes more than once."

"I know that."

The faint hint of a blush filled her cheeks. He enjoyed that he could do that to her.

"But that's not what I'm talking about." Heather looked up at him.

"Then explain yourself."

"How about I show you?" She smiled at him as she rolled him under her. In one swift motion, she lowered herself onto his shaft. Her body shuddered as he filled her. The delicious invasion had her tilting her head back and closing her eyes. Once she felt she could focus on him again she opened her eyes and looked at him. "Now, what were you asking?"

He grinned as he moved beneath her. "I see there are some benefits from you being here."

She didn't realize how much access he had to her body even in the gown, until she felt his hands roam from her breasts to her mound.

Her gown fluttered to the floor.

"Don't know why you even try to cover up. I'd rather not have my view blocked." His fingers searched until they found her button.

"Sometimes guessing what is underneath—" She closed her eyes, pausing while she fought for control. "Oh, my, can be more arousing than seeing it." Heather thought she would be in control by being on top, but he still knew how to make her body hum for him. His hands knew where to touch to heighten her desire. She moved faster against him. Her muscles squeezed him as she slid up and down. She felt it build inside. This orgasm started slow, like a soft vibration, then built to a point where she couldn't think. Everything around her shattered.

Storm took control of her hips, pumping into her as hard

as he could. He arched into her once more before he hit his release. Her world splintered a second time, as muscles constricted and her body clenched. Colors exploded behind closed lids. The orgasm sent her on a ride that made her whole body boneless. She draped herself against him, a soft smile on her face.

Storm brushed a few strands of hair out of her face. Finally, she found a little peace in all the madness they had been through. She had been so overwhelmed she couldn't think straight. When she should be enjoying the beginning of their lives together, she was stressing about every little thing. He wanted to lighten her load but didn't know how.

And why did that one man push her the way he did? His goal was to hurt her, but that went against the pleasurer's creed. They were there to please, and that was all. Pleasing Heather would have been a coop, he understood that, but if she said no, she said no and all of them knew to back off.

He didn't understand why all the attacks were focused on her. Tomorrow, he'd have her life dissected. Try to figure out why they'd be after her. Right now, he wanted to enjoy the way she trusted him so much she fell asleep with him still inside her.

He stretched as he closed the last file he had read on her life. There was nothing out of the ordinary. She had been exemplary as a student. Received just about every medal possible for a woman her age. Gotten in her share of fights, been thrown in the brig a time or two for standing up for what she believed in. The perfect woman, as far as he was concerned.

So why was she suddenly the center of some sort of

controversy? It came back to him. She had been fine until he stepped into her life. How had they coming into contact with each other become a catalyst though?

He heard movement behind him.

"You awake?"

"Umhmmm." She worked her way to the edge of the bed. "What are you doing?"

"Trying to figure out why you've become such a target." He stood up and walked to the bed. "It just doesn't make sense."

"Personally, I think it's too early for us to even think about that." She sat up. "When is your mother arriving?"

"About two hours."

She flopped back on the bed. "Good."

"Come on lazy bones, time to take a shower."

"Smart move." She slid out of bed and padded to the bathroom. "Are we getting married for like the twentieth time?"

"It seems like it." He followed her in, not sure if she was awake or asleep. He turned on the water and helped her in before following her. "You with me this morning?"

She tilted her face up so the water would flow over her body. He decided not to say anything else. This morning might be all about her. He grabbed a soft cleaning sponge and filled it with soap. Then he gently started rubbing it against her back. Once he had lathered her back, he worked on her buttocks, legs and worked his way around to his favorite part of her body. He gently cleansed her arms, then her stomach, before rubbing the cloth across her breasts. She came alive then, stealing the cloth from him, giving him a wicked smile.

"Your turn." She took the cloth and washed his back, spending a little more time at his derriere before cleaning his legs. Her mouth followed the trail of the cloth, having him hard and ready in seconds. The moment her lips closed around his member he knew what she was up to.

He pulled her to her feet, and pressing her back into the tiles, he buried himself deep inside her. "We will get to the stage where we explore each other thoroughly, but right now I'm about ready to explode, and foreplay is more than I can handle."

He pulled out and drove back in. "I want you in so many ways right now I can't count."

She tilted her hips so he could go deeper. "One time I will get my way."

"I promise. Perhaps on the way to Vespia. We won't have to come out of the room for the entire flight." He felt her shudder and knew she was close. "We could experiment with anything you want."

"Really?" Her breath hitched and her muscles tightened against him. He started moving faster, pumping in and out as fast as she would allow.

He felt the vise grip she had on him as she went over the edge. It wasn't long before he followed her there, free-falling with her. Happy with her for not holding back.

She rested against him. "Anyway, we can just call today a sick day?"

"Unfortunately, no." he wished he could keep her to himself so they could explore each other to their heart's desire. "My mother might understand but wouldn't agree. She'd be as annoying as my sister."

"Is that possible?"

He laughed as he lifted her out of the shower. "Go on, get dressed. You might want a little in your stomach before she arrives. With mother you never know what she is going to do."

Heather dressed in something simple. She took a couple pieces of fruit and nibbled on them as she worked her way through the night before. "Why me?"

"Haven't figured that out yet."

"Me either. I haven't been involved in anything out of the ordinary. Other than you. Your sister told me last night that you didn't really have anyone you were truly serious about that might be jealous, except the woman in black last night."

"Sora? She is from one of the original families. But we were never really promised to each other. Mother didn't approve of her." He brushed a stray hair from her face. "You didn't have a boyfriend I need to be aware of?"

"I shunned any male who might have had a little interest and news like that travels fast. Doubt anyone would even remember I exist."

The doors swung open to allow his mother to come in. "Morning, children." She gave Storm a quick kiss on the cheek as well as Heather. "So how are we feeling this morning?"

"About the same." Heather offered her a cup of coffee, which she poured when she got approval.

"So what have you two been talking about?"

"Why I seem to be the center of attention." Heather sat the cup down before she parked herself. "It doesn't really make sense."

"True, but there are a lot of people who would love to be in either of your positions." Storm's mother picked up the cup Heather had left for her. "You will wield a lot of power."

"Really? I wanted last night to end several hours before it did but didn't get my way. Where's the power in that?" Heather picked up her cup. "Felt a little helpless."

"You're still new to this." Anseri smiled as she took a sip of her coffee. "I'm assuming you've gone through each other's files."

"He's gone through mine, but I haven't had time to return the favor yet." She took a sip before gesturing with her coffee cup. "Have a wedding to plan."

"Yes. I wanted to talk to you two about that. We have

already spoken to your commander. We're afraid a public display like that might put you two in more jeopardy."

Heather gave her a bright smile. "So you talked him out of it? I don't have to try to plan a wedding that should take a year to get right in two days?"

"Sorry, dear, the wedding will go off as planned, it will just be all done by hologram." She patted her hand. "As far as your dress is concerned, we can create whatever you need with the computer aboard our ship. Just give Storm the specs and it will be done. Everything else will be done by the head office. Whatever that means."

"Lots of red tape." Heather stood. "Any way I can speak to my commander?"

"Yes. Your commander-in-chief did expect you to talk to him. I believe he's waiting on one of the comlinks."

"What?" She dashed to the screen but had no clue how it worked. "Little help here."

Storm walked over and activated the screen. The commander popped right up.

"Lieutenant."

"Sir." She gave a salute, then stood at attention.

"At ease. I wanted to speak to you about this wedding."

"Yes, sir." Mentally, she wanted to stab him a few times but knew he'd be the only one getting his way today. She went into a relaxed military stance.

"I wasn't sure it was a good idea to make the wedding military, but the Vespian leader informed me it would be a nice gesture. The wedding will be broadcast on both planets and she felt the Vespian people would understand the formality if it was military. She also informed me that they will take care of everything, including your uniform." He spoke off-screen for a moment. "The data they need has been transmitted."

"Thank you, sir."

"I will see you in two days, Lieutenant."

"Yes, sir." She relaxed when the screen went blank.

"I noticed you didn't mention the hologram to him," commented Storm's mother.

"No, Ma'am, I didn't. Wasn't sure if he knew and if I was aware of something he wasn't he would become suspicious and complicate an already very complicated situation." She sat down next to her coffee again, wishing it was something stronger. The next two days were going to be hell. "I'm pretty sure my plate is a little too full right now."

"Mother," Storm leaned down to speak softly in his mother's ear. "Don't you think you're putting her under a lot of duress? Perhaps—"

"She will deal with worse being your mate," she answered just as softly. "Let's see how she handles it."

"I can hear you." She needed a way to burn off her frustration. A good workout would do that. "Excuse me."

"Where are you going?" asked Storm.

"To exercise." She went to her things and pulled out one of her workout uniforms.

"I'll help you get all the exercise you need." He gave her a smile.

"I mean, I need to burn off a little frustration."

"I know how to make you forget everything but the moment." He took a step toward her, his smile never dimming.

"No, I mean I need to punch something." The man had a one-track mind and in front of his mother. Heather wished he would just play nice and let her go, but she had a feeling he wasn't letting her out of his sight.

"Didn't know you like it rough." This time, he had gotten close enough to wrap his arms around her. "I'll have to make a note of it."

"Storm. I need a break. I need to do something other than sit in this room all day wondering when you're going to pounce on me."

"Perhaps you should train her in some of our combat exercises. I'm sure that will help her mind and body relax."

They stood in a gym. Heather wondered what she'd be learning. The room was void of people, so she wouldn't put anything past him.

"I'd like to see what you can do." He wore soft flowing trousers cinched at the waist.

"Okay." Heather found the fact that he was shirtless a little distracting. "You really don't fight fair, do you?"

"You could remove your shirt as well."

She thought about it for a second or two, but modesty won out. "What would you like me to do?"

"You know what I'd like to do." He wiggled his eyebrows at her.

"I mean here." He was really starting to infuriate her.

"I mean anywhere."

She pinched her nose in frustration. "You're supposed to be training me?"

"I've been trying, but you keep fighting me."

"Ha, ha." That was all she could take. She charged at him and just as she would have made contact she found her feet pulled out from under her and she landed on her back with Storm right on top of her.

"Anger is never a reason to attack." He pressed a soft kiss against her lips. "Now, every time you land on your back I get to kiss you. Each one deeper and more sensual. If you can get me on my back, I'll remove an article of clothing."

"You only have the one."

"I know." He helped her to her feet.

"There's only one problem with your offer." He gave her an innocent look. "You win either way."

"I know." He took a stance and signaled for her to try

again. "And if I beat you too many times, you will start losing articles of clothing too."

"You really don't fight fair."

"When it comes to you, I can't. If I were to fight fair, I wouldn't get my way and we both enjoy it when I get my way."

She needed to prove herself to this man. Although she had been hired to protect him, she hadn't been able to do her job. He had kept her secluded and under his protection most of the time.

He would be expecting her to just charge him, so she would use that as a ploy. As she moved at him, he started to move toward her and took that energy to propel her behind him. She planted herself, and as he turned toward her, she gave him a sidekick to the chest. As her foot made contact, she found it in a vise grip which put her in motion again. She wasn't sure how he did it, but in the seconds it took for them to land, he had pulled her up and twisted so that she landed on her back once again.

"Not bad." He lowered his mouth to hers, swirling his tongue into hers. It sent sparks all through her when he continued the onslaught like the kiss would never end. Her body moved under him, wanting more. He broke the kiss but didn't let her go. "You do have some skills."

"Thanks. I think." She looked up into his golden eyes, watching with awe how they changed colors with his arousal. One kiss did that? What would two do?

He helped her to her feet once more.

Now what should she do? The last ploy didn't work. He seemed to be able to anticipate anything she tried. Then she smiled.

"Oh, you think you can best me?" He smiled back.

"My best weapon is my body." She took a step toward him. "Isn't it?"

"I like it."

He reached out to grab her, and she slid to the floor. His momentum kept him moving in one direction, which gave her a chance to get behind him once again, and she pinned him to the ground a moment before he flipped them over, pinning her beneath him once again.

"I'd call that a tie." He gave her another deep, long drugging kiss that left them both a little breathless.

"I did pin you."

"Yes, you did, yet look where you are once again." He brushed a few stray hairs out of her face. "Under me. So ultimately I win."

"How is that fair?"

"Because we both must remove our clothing." He ran his tongue along her neck, causing her to arch against him. "After all, it was a tie." His hands started to work on the seam that held her garment together, releasing her breasts to his lips. "Then I can bury myself deep within you and we can experience the joy we do every time our bodies connect like that."

His teeth grazed one of the exposed tips, causing her to suck in her breath. "I'm surprised you have been able to keep up with me." His fingers continued down the seam of her outfit, dipping and playing whenever he felt like it. It had her writhing beneath him. "Vespians have voracious appetites and other humans haven't been able to withstand the demand."

"Are you telling me you've put women in the hospital over your sexual appetite?" She felt him surge into her. When did he remove his pants? How did she keep missing these things?

"Maybe." He started moving inside her. The deliciousness of him sliding in and out of her grabbed most of her attention. She could understand why those women were willing to be with him so badly, because every time he touched her she wanted him. It didn't matter if they had just finished making love.

"You feel so good." He arched up to look at her face. "You don't know how well your body grips me, holds me tight inside."

His words just made her muscles tighten a little more. He stroked in and out, causing her breath to hitch a little. She was getting close.

"Promise me it will always be like this." Her body clenched around him as her orgasm took her. So powerful it left her breathless. "Each time gets bigger. One of these days I'm going to supernova."

"As long as it's with me, I have no problem." He moved inside her. "But we're not done, so you still have your chance."

"You are insatiable." She wrapped her legs high on his waist.

"Are you complaining?" he pulled out and just hovered for a second.

"Are you kidding?" A sigh escaped her when he surged back in. "I seem to be just like you. I do have one question, though."

"And what is that?" He started moving faster inside her.

"Do you have an aversion to beds? As many times as we have made love, I can't remember it ever being on a bed."

He laughed.

EIGHT

Heather stood near the main room in her wedding uniform. She clutched her flowers, hoping it would all be over soon. She was amazed, though. Somehow, they pulled it off. The commander-in-chief stood next to her, waiting for the cue to walk her down the aisle.

She wondered how Storm was doing. He had rarely seen her since their exercise yesterday morning. Between trying to make sure the gown was properly made and communicating with Earth to get everything coordinated properly, she didn't have time for him.

His mother made matters worse when she kicked him out of the room for the night. Somehow she had found out it was bad luck for the groom to see his bride in her gown before the wedding, and she took matters into her own hands. Heather's heart broke at the sad look on his face when his mother closed the door on him.

She was sure he would be all over her the moment he got a chance, and she wanted him to help her forget everything she had been through the last forty-eight hours, so she hoped it would happen soon.

The music started and her commander-in-chief offered his arm. "You ready?"

She nodded.

The room she stepped into wasn't really that big, but the images on the screen made it look like a beautiful garden. She noticed they moved about the room to give those who were watching the illusion that they were walking down a path covered with petals.

Storm stood there waiting for her. It was probably the first time she saw just a touch of fear in his eyes. For some reason, this ceremony did it to a lot of men. He wore an elegant black tuxedo with a simple white shirt. Her heart swelled at the sight of him. He was the most handsome man she had ever seen and to know he would go through this for her made her heart beat a little harder.

When did she fall in love with him? Or was it all the sex talking? She wondered why she hadn't really fought any of this. Storm was a wonderful lover, but how did she end up here so fast? It didn't make sense.

That first kiss in the closet set forth a series of events she couldn't have dreamed up in her best fantasies, but she was living it. Tied to a man she never thought she would be attracted to.

She had been alone all her life, not quite fitting in. Now she felt whole. He filled a gap in her life she had never thought would be filled. Fate had moved her in a direction she never expected.

She took Storm's hand, and the ceremony began. Since she didn't belong to any particular religious denomination, they brought in a military clergyman to give them a nonde-nominational ceremony. Something simple.

Once the vows were said, she felt a weight lifted from her shoulders. No more obligations to fulfill. She looked at Storm. At least none she was aware of.

When the clergyman gave Storm permission to kiss her,

he grabbed her like she was a lifeline and claimed her lips. It took the clergy clearing his throat for them to break apart.

"Are we done?" he asked softly.

"All we have to do is walk down the aisle as husband and wife." She found herself scooped up in his arms as he ran away with her. She heard someone say we're clear in the background as the room grid went blank. "You can put me down now."

"I know. Mother said I couldn't take off with you the moment it was over. Something about a formal dinner with your commander-in-chief along with some of your co-workers." He almost pouted as he explained what would happen next.

"And I was so hoping to get out of this damn outfit." She touched his face the way he'd done to her several times now. It made her feel precious, and she hoped it had the same effect on him.

"And I was so hoping to be the one to take you out of it." He led her to the dining area for the elders. "But I still have plans for us this evening. Once everyone is gone, we shall lock ourselves in our room and not come out until we land. I've got almost two days to make up for."

"Sorry about that. I had no idea your mom would interfere the way she did." She smiled up at him. "But at least it's over. There isn't anything else is there?"

"A few formal dinners, you'll meet the rest of the council. But no more surprise ceremonies."

"Good. I'm over all the surprises." They stepped into the room and found it crowded with dignitaries from all over the world. "I'm surprised they allowed anyone on this ship."

"There is always a reason for what they do." The moment they entered, they found themselves surrounded by people. Most wishing them well.

Heather had a few who wanted to speak to her about the treaty so she would know what they expected. And all she would do was smile and ask them to submit it in writing. There was no way she would be able to remember anything after all she had been through.

They took their seats at the head of the table. Toasts were made. Dinner was placed in front of them. People talked around them. Heather took a bite of her food but didn't taste a thing.

"I know how to clear this room." Storm leaned toward her, speaking softly so no one would overhear him but her. Heather fought the grin trying to spread across her face when she noticed his mother had pinched the inside of his arm.

"You will do no such thing, young man. You will show respect to all of our guests." Her movement was discrete. No one but Heather saw it.

"Mother, you are walking on a thin line if you plan on embarrassing me in front of all these people." He turned an angry glare on his mother.

"Storm." Heather placed a hand on his. "Relax. I'm the only one who knows your mom can control you that way. Although I'll have to ask her how she is able to do that so I can get my way every once in a while."

"You don't like the way I monopolize every aspect of your life." He feigned a pained look as he picked up her hand and kissed her palm.

"Have you ever thought about what I could come up with if given the chance?" She moved her hand and ran it up the inside of his leg. She smiled when he perked right up.

"Maybe I should be a gentleman from time to time." He leaned over and nibbled on her ear for a moment.

"You might enjoy it." She gave him a smile that had him hard in seconds.

"The sooner we're done here the happier I'll be." He touched her face tenderly. "I need you badly."

Heather wanted him just as bad, but knew they were stuck for a while.

She picked at her food. As hectic as the last two days had been, you would think she would be starving, but food didn't appeal to her. The headache was back and this time it hurt more than it had in the past. Something wasn't quite right, but she didn't want to worry anyone.

The doctor stood nearby, and she tried to be discrete in catching his attention.

"Problem?" Storm caught her movement.

"Just a little headache." She smiled at him. "Nothing for you to worry about."

"Anything plaguing you is something for me to worry about. I can escort you to the medlab if you need me to."

"All I need is a quick shot."

The doctor came over and pressed the hypo against the back of her neck. Normally she would feel instant relief, but this time it just took the edge off. She still nodded and smiled, pretending everything was fine. Hoping the dose was just slow acting.

The meal finally finished, and they were able to leave their seats. Heather snuck over to the doctor. "That dose didn't do a thing for me."

"I can give you another one, but you need to come to the lab so we can see why the dose isn't enough anymore." The doctor looked concerned.

She nodded as he gave her another shot. "I'm sure it's just the stress of the last few days." That one she felt relief from. She smiled as the headache abated this time. "Thank you."

"Are you okay?" asked Storm's mother.

"I'm fine." She gave her a bright smile. "It's just been a hectic couple of days."

Storm came up to her side. He wrapped his arm around her waist. "What is going on?"

"She is complaining of a headache." His mother looked concern.

"I know, the doctor gave her a shot at the table."

"And she got another one just a few seconds ago."

They looked at Heather.

Goodness, she had to calm both of them down now. "I promised the doctor I would stop by the lab as soon as I could. It's no big deal. I have these headaches from time to time. It's okay, there is nothing wrong with me."

"How about we go to the medlab right now?" He started to steer her toward the door.

"How about not embarrassing me like that?" She got out of his hold. "Isn't that what upset you with your mother not too long ago? This can wait until our guests leave. It's only a headache."

"Can't help but worry." He looked into her eyes. She knew he was trying to see how bad the pain was. "I have plans you know."

She had to laugh at him. "And heaven forbid if I mess those plans up. No need to worry. I'm fine. I promise."

The evening finally wound down and they were free to head to their room.

"But first you must go by the lab." Storm escorted her down one corridor, then another.

"Anyway, I can change out of this suit first?"

"Sorry. It would make us backtrack and once we're in our room, I'm not letting you out for a while." He brought her to the doctor on call. "She's still having headaches."

"Yes, sir. I have been told what tests to run." He held a small device in his hand. It took him seconds to use it. "The doctor will call you once he has had a chance to go over the information."

Storm scooped her up and strode down the hallway to their room. He didn't let her feet touch the ground until the doors closed.

"Please help me out of this thing." She tugged at the collar as she kicked off her shoes.

He took the small device the fitter had given him earlier and waved it over the seals on the jacket. Then he helped her pull it off. The skirt was easier to release and soon she stood in just her shirt. The seams separated on that quickly and after removing the cufflinks she was able to slip out of it as well.

"What is that?" His fingers rubbed against the delicate straps of her bra before he noticed the same lace on her panties.

"Something I thought you'd enjoy taking off me." The sparkle in his eyes let her know she had made the right choice. They weren't the most comfortable things and not needed with the way clothing now did all the supporting a woman would need, but if he liked her wearing his shirt, she knew the undergarments would meet his approval.

"And how do I do that?" Like a kid with a gift, he wanted to tear into his present but didn't want to tear the wrapper. He liked it too much.

"There is a snap upfront." She undid it so he would know how it worked before redoing it.

A bell sounded, but Storm decided to ignore it.

"Door," she reminded him.

"It can wait." He released the little piece of plastic and palmed her breasts.

"It's probably the doctor." The heat of his hand on her breasts made her close her eyes, but she knew they couldn't ignore the door. "He said he would get back to us."

Storm sighed. He had taken off his jacket, but that was as far as he got before she caught his attention.

Heather snapped it back and pulled a shift out of a drawer. How she was always the one underdressed made her wonder, but it didn't take long for her to slip the shift on. Once she was covered, she opened the door. A nurse stood there. She gave Heather a sympathetic look before turning on her heels and heading back to the medlab without saying a word.

"Let's find out what the doctor has to say." She walked out of the room and followed the nurse down the hall. Storm came out of the room a few seconds later. He wasn't happy to be interrupted.

The doctor, his mom, and a few other people were waiting for them. Heather didn't like all the extra people. It probably meant there was a problem.

"So this isn't just a simple headache, is it?"

"What do you know about that device in your back?"

"Only what I've been told. It's been there all my life." She took the seat Storm offered her. "The doctors couldn't figure out what it was for other than some sort of inhibitor and it doesn't like being too far away from me."

"So what would happen if it were removed?"

"The headaches, mainly. The first time they removed it and moved it too far away I did pass out. But that was the only time that happened." She looked up at Storm who placed his hand on her shoulder. She looked back at the doctor. "I'm not quite sure what you want to know. Anything the doctors along the way learned should be in my records."

"That's just it," said the doctor. "There is nothing in your medical records about it."

"What?" She stood up. "There should be. I saw the doctor looking at it not too long ago."

"What doctor?"

"I'm not sure. I've seen so many over the years. That little device is a bit of an oddity." She went to the computer. Her file held several folders, and she worked her way through them before finding what she was looking for. There, on the bottom of her last physical, was another file. She pulled it up and entered her password. The file about her device opened up. "Sorry. I figured you people had already figured out where it was and how to open it."

"Thank you." The doctor looked over the file for a moment. "There are two things I have learned about the device. One, it's beyond our technology because it is ancient in design. The other is that it is disintegrating now."

"Is that why the headache didn't go away?"

"Is it still bothering you?" The doctor ran the scanner over her once again.

"It's tolerable."

"The device is being absorbed by your blood, so the metal and all will always be with you. It kept you reading as human, but I'm not sure you are."

"Excuse me?"

"Your blood work says human. Anyone who doesn't know what to look for will believe you're human. But you have several markers that humans don't have. I've never seen these markers before. I need to do more research before I can really pinpoint your race. But I think you were put on Earth to keep you safe as a child."

"So, why is it disintegrating now?" asked Storm.

"I have no real answer."

"How long will it take to disappear?" Heather rubbed her back absentmindedly.

"I'm not sure when it started. Based off of the readings I have, I'd say within the month it will be gone."

"And whatever it is hiding will show itself, then."

"I can only assume at this point. I need to read the file you unlocked and run a few more tests of my own before I feel safe answering that question." He looked at Storm apologetically. "I know you wished for some time to yourselves, but the sooner I run the tests the faster I'll have answers."

"How long will these tests take?"

"A couple of hours."

Heather had fallen asleep during the tests. He knew the day had taken its toll on her and she had dozed off about fifteen minutes ago. She was curled up on her side, looking so peaceful.

"So how long have you suspected this?" He knew his mother stood beside him. She had remained to keep him company.

"Believe it or not we didn't have a clue." His mother watched her sleep as well. "This whole thing was because of your uncle. He's the one you need to talk to."

"And you will keep an eye on her?"

"I will guard her as my own."

He kissed his mother on the cheek. "She is one of your own now."

"Just seeing if you were paying attention."

He headed to his uncle's room. He had conversed with him so rarely he wasn't sure what to say to the man. He had no real power yet was the most revered man of their race.

His door opened. "Ah. Wondered when you would show up. Where is your mate?"

"Sleeping on a gurney in the medical area. Mother recommended I come speak to you."

"Come. Sit." He stepped aside so Storm could enter the room. The door closed behind them. "You wish to know why her? You have already asked me that question."

"Well, yes. But what do you know about her no one else seems to?"

"I don't." He sat in a chair opposite Storm. "When I was young, long before you and your sister were born I had a vision of you and this woman. I had no idea who either of you was until you grew into a man. I'm not sure how to explain it but I knew she would be important to you."

"That's why you came along on this trip. You knew I would run into her."

"What can I say? Are you upset you met her?"

"No. I have enjoyed my time with her." He wasn't about to go into detail about his sex life with their religious leader. "But I don't understand how my presence has started a series of events that has made her life hard. There have been attempts on her life and now she has a strange device that is disintegrating in her system."

"I have heard." He gave him a grin. "I wish I could give you more, but I have learned in the past that when I reveal the future I change the future and it has always ended badly. Keep her safe and everything will work out in your favor. I promise."

NINE

Heather stretched. Opening her eyes, she realized she was in their room and their bed. Storm held her close, his deep breathing like music in her ears. He looked so peaceful sound asleep like that. She brushed a lock of hair out of his face. He probably had stayed up all night listening to the doctors drone on about what they didn't know.

She didn't want to wake him so inched herself over so she could slip her feet onto the floor. A cup of coffee would be great right now.

"And where are you going?" He hadn't opened his eyes, but his grip around her waist tightened, pulling her back against him.

"Was going to look for some coffee."

He released his hold on her and opened his eyes. "Get two. You know how to use the replicator?"

"Learned that yesterday." She stepped over to the replicator. "I thought you were in a deep sleep."

"Learned how to sleep with one eye open while in the military. Comes in handy when your mate tries to sneak out of bed on you."

"Blame the coffee. It told me to sneak out." She programmed it to give her two cups and she carried them back to the bed. "So glad your computers can synthesize coffee. It would be the one thing I would miss the most."

He leaned on one side and took the cup from her.

Heather sat on the mattress next to Storm and cradled her coffee in her hands. "So now that the device is starting to dissolve, you starting to question your decision to be with me?" She tried to be nonchalant about it.

He sat up, took the cup out of her hand, placed both on the floor, then pinned her beneath him. "I regret nothing other than the time we're losing because of that stupid thing. The doctors asked me to bring you back the moment you woke up, and they would know if I hadn't followed their explicit orders. I'll probably get into trouble over the coffee, but they didn't say you couldn't eat or drink anything and I know how cranky you get without your coffee." He reached down and grabbed the two cups. "So drink up before they send security after us."

She laughed and hugged her cup to her. Taking a sip, she realized she had a few articles of clothing missing. Her night gown lay in a heap next to her on the floor, but she wasn't sure what happened to everything else. "Where's the underwear? You know those little pieces of lace that had you drooling last night?"

"Under my pillow, waiting patiently for you."

"Bet that gave the doctors something new to talk about." She had planned that only for him, not half the medical staff.

"They never saw them." He winked at her.

"And how did you remove them without anyone knowing?"

"Those doctors don't pay attention to everything." He pushed up to a sitting position before setting down his empty cup. "You ready?"

"Guess, but didn't it show up in their scans?"

"You are worrying about something you don't need to." He pulled on a pair of trousers before pulling on a shirt. "Now, you going like that or getting dressed?"

She knew he would love to keep her naked, but she didn't have the confidence to walk around with nothing on, so she quickly pulled out another shift.

With other visits, the doctors always made her change to something that wasn't formfitting and she hoped this gown would be perfect. Lifting her arms above her head, she let the gown slide down her body. Once the gown fell to her feet, she turned to face him.

His face was priceless. He wanted her so bad he couldn't move. "God, woman, do that again and we won't be going anywhere but to that bed."

"All in good time. Let's find out what is going on with me. I'd like to get to the bottom of this." She walked past him and through the door into the corridor. Their room wasn't far from the lab. "Good morning, Doctor."

He smiled at her as he picked up his scanner. "Good morning. Any headaches?"

"Same one." She looked around the place. Last night she was so tired she really didn't pay attention to her surroundings. The center wasn't very big, but to her a medlab was a medlab and she hated them all. "What have you learned?"

"Not as much as I would have liked." He pulled up her DNA strand up.

Parts were still blank, but she watched as newer data filled in. No one had gotten this far before. Maybe there was hope.

"Most of what the device is inhibiting hasn't come to life in you yet, so I still don't know a whole lot." He isolated one particular strand of her DNA and brought it to the forefront. "I have learned you have ancient blood in you."

"And what is ancient blood?" That was new too. The odd markers in her blood had stumped the other doctors.

116

"The bloodline of the elders. We all have it." Storm stepped up to the screen. He tapped a section that broke down the DNA to show what race she was from. That still hadn't been filled in yet. "Yet you can't prove she's Vespian. You want to explain that?"

"It is possible that they were involved with more than our race." The doctor shrugged. "We just have never run across anyone else with that blood in them who wasn't Vespian until now. We know so little about the ancients I'm not sure what to tell you. It just means more tests."

Storm took a step toward the doctor.

"I'm sorry, sir. I have no other explanation. I'm hoping I'll have more as we go along. Once her DNA sequence fills in completely, I will have all the answers." He pointed to the arch she had been through before. "If I can get you to enter that once again?"

Heather nodded. She entered the machine and felt a strange wave of heat as several tests started at once. They were over in seconds, but the after-effect lasted longer. She wanted to see the research the doctor had. She knew her file better than anyone and might be able to help. "Can I have a copy of everything you've learned?"

"Well…"

"Of course you can," Storm finished for him. "We'll go over it in our room." He stood at the doctor's shoulder, watching as he made copies, making sure he gave them everything she requested.

One of the elite guard stepped into the room. "Your mother wishes to speak to you."

"Tell my mother I'll speak to her later. I have something I want to do."

Heather watched the man's face at the thought of telling the head elder he had refused her. "We can give your mother a few moments."

"Which will turn into a few hours and then we'll have to

do something. My mother can be very manipulative when she wants to be."

"Then humor me. She has accepted me without question. The least I can do is see what she wants from us." She touched his arm. "If she does as you say, I will learn from this lesson and follow your lead from this point on."

"How is it you have this way to make me do things I don't want?"

"Because I am the only one who puts up with your voracious appetite, remember?" She stepped up to him so he could look down the gown she wore. He saw his favorite playground only inches away, yet he couldn't touch it.

"Now who's not fighting fair?" He growled but allowed her to have her way. He walked her to his mother's room. "You wish to speak to us?"

"Yes." She walked to her view screen. "There has been an incident at one of our remote bases, and your expertise is needed."

"What happened?" He walked up to the screen and pulled up the file so he could have as much information as possible.

"We're not sure." She offered Heather a seat. "There was an explosion, and then a riot ensued."

"Riot?" Heather looked from Storm to his mother. "What exactly do you make there?"

"Most of our satellite locations are for those who can't quite fit into our society. Every person is important to us, so we work hard to find a way to utilize their particular talents." Storm's mother sat down across from her. "It's harder there, but they have their own society and lifestyles. Every once in a while things will get a little out of hand and we have to step in, but other than that we leave them to themselves."

"And what if one of them wants to come back here?"

"We have a tribunal that oversees that. You and I will have time to go through a lot of this while he is away."

"Yes, Ma'am." Her fear of being left alone on a strange planet must have been evident in her face, because Storm walked over and pulled her into his arms.

"Mother will look out for you."

"I know." She felt a little silly. "I have been on my share of missions where I didn't know the people or what to expect, but for some reason this is different."

"Part of it is because you can't just come in, do what you need to do and leave. You need to fit in." He touched her face with his fingertips. "And you will do fine."

But she knew people would be staring at her. Wondering if she had what it took to blend into their society. The thought made her nervous.

"When do I leave?"

"You have a few hours before we're within the raptor's distance." She gave them a shooing gesture. "I have kept you long enough."

Storm grabbed Heather's hand and practically dragged her out of the room. "If you don't pick up your pace, I will throw you over my shoulder and carry you."

"A bit impatient?" She found herself almost running to keep up with his long stride.

"Aren't you?" He stopped to look at her. "It has been too long."

"What, a day and a half? Is that a new record?"

"It is where you are concerned." He pulled her close. "I seem to become desperate when I'm kept from you too long."

His gold eyes darkened, warning her he wouldn't wait much longer. She was grateful their room was only a few feet away or he might take her in the hallway. The doors opened and she found herself half carried into the room. The doors closed and Storm made sure it was locked before thrusting her against it.

"I am sorry, but I can't wait anymore." He lifted the skirt of her gown and freed himself just enough to enter her. A sigh escaped him as he slid home. "I promise to make this up to you, but I must have you now."

It gave her power to know she could reduce him to this. He could have used any of the people here and no one would have thought a thing yet he knew it would upset her so abstained. His desire was for her and not just the act.

Even in his desperation, he was gentle with her. His body pushed for release, but not at her expense. She felt cherished. She could feel his wants and needs deep inside, and she did her best to give it to him. Nothing seemed to matter except for his need. Her body reacted to the constant pounding, tightening and squeezing him, heightening his desire, causing little quakes to shake his control. She could feel him getting close.

He drove into her harder, his breath quick, his release imminent. She felt it, reveled in it, knew it would send her over just as quickly as any other time with him. Her muscles gripped him in a vise, one that had him straining for control. She clenched and he lost it.

She felt her release start slowly, deep inside. Storm's started first, he drove into her deep and hard, his breathing erratic. Then her orgasm wrapped itself around her, causing everything to freeze in time. Muscles jerked and tightened. Like a spiral, it circled around her, pulling her in. All of her shook as the powerful orgasm took control. Every time he touched her like this, the planet moved. She prayed it would never change.

"You are the most amazing woman." He buried his face into her neck. Nibbling in his favorite place.

"You have a lot to do with it." She finally found her feet

on the floor again. "I'm amazed you made it back to the room. You did have me worried for a few moments."

"I was worried too." He pulled her into his embrace. "Thank you."

"I could say the same thing."

He pulled back to look at her. "Why?"

"I've learned enough about your society to know others wouldn't have waited. They would have found relief so their mate wouldn't be molested like that." She loved it, though.

"It wouldn't have been the same." She could tell he wasn't sure how to answer her.

"Admit it, you only wanted me."

"Ah, fishing for compliments." He hooked his hands in the hem of her gown and pulled it over her head. "Not about to give you any more control over me than you already have."

"Oh too late, honey." She worked on the seals of his shirt and pulled it off him before she worked on his trousers. "It's nice to know that all I have to do is look at you and I can make you hard. Plus, I'm the only one who can make that hardness go away." She ran a finger along his length and found him growing hard again. "Considering all you have to do is touch me the right way and I turn into a boneless mass at your feet, I feel a little more even."

"You do have your feminine weapons. What was the name of that outfit I have under my pillow?" His eyes brightened at the thought. "I believe you called them underwear."

"Aroused you?"

"More than you know." He walked to the bed and pulled them out for her.

"And I'm assuming you wish to see me in them again?" She took the little bits of cloth from him.

"It will keep me warm while I'm away."

She laughed. "You make it sound like you'll be gone for

months." She held out her hand when he went to help her. "You can't touch me until I say."

"Why?"

"I won't put it on."

He didn't look happy but agreed. Sitting on the bed, he watched as she slipped into the panties and bra. She would watch him out of the side of her eye and swear he was salivating at the thought of taking them back off of her.

Her hands dropped at her sides and he stood.

"No pouncing."

"I don't pounce."

"Really?" She put her hands on her hips. "Then what do you call it?"

"Showing my desire for you."

She had to give him that. "Okay, promise me you won't rip it off me, so we can't use it again."

"I can promise I won't rip it but can't promise it won't get hurt. It looks too delicate to be reused." He stepped up to her, sliding his fingers around the contour of the cup that supported her.

"It's made of pretty sturdy material." She allowed a strap to slide down her arm.

His fingers followed it down. He was gentle, almost afraid he'd break something. The snap came apart quickly, letting her spill out into his hands. "Oh yes. I do like this."

She felt the heat of his mouth on her. He knew what she wanted and needed to make her desire spiral out of control.

His hands didn't remain idle, sliding down her hips to the bit of lace framing it. His fingers traced the edges, reveling in the sensation between her skin and the material. He maneuvered her to the bed and eased her down. Lifting one of her legs, he slid the skimpy material to the side and entered her once again.

"You know those can come off."

"Didn't see a need with only that strap in the back." He

closed his eyes as she flexed her muscles against him. "I like the sensation of the lace rubbing against me as I move in and out of you."

A tremor raced through her when he pushed in a little deeper in response.

"I had wished to spend this trip exploring every part of your body. Figure out how many different ways I can bring you to arousal." He murmured in her ear as he built up the friction between them once again. "Instead, I have to steal my moments with you."

His body shuddered and he started to move faster.

She hitched her leg a little higher. "We will have our time together."

"It had better be soon or I will have to kidnap my own mate so I can live out my fantasies."

"Fantasies?" She arched against him as everything tightened once again. Her body sent the signals that she was close. "Perhaps I can have a special incentive for you to return to me quickly."

"Like what?"

"It's a surprise," her voice sultry. She could feel her world start to splinter around her.

"That isn't fair." He ground himself against her.

Her nails dug into his back. "Like you ever play fair."

"True." He nipped the soft skin on her throat. "But you'd never complain."

"Of course, oh God, not." She could no longer focus on their conversation, only the feelings racing through her. She felt like she was flying. It was a glorious feeling, dipping and soaring through space and time. It took her a while to come back to her body. "Sorry. I seem to leave you every time."

"I love watching you when you're caught up like that, no inhibitions, no faking, just a beautiful, powerful release." He pressed a soft kiss to her forehead. "And the grip you have on me takes me right along with you."

He pulled her into his arms and closed his eyes. "Let's just enjoy these few moments before I have to go."

She snuggled against him with a sigh.

Somewhere along the way, she must have dozed off and Storm had taken those moments to leave on his mission. Heather sat up and looked around. Now she had time on her hands with nothing to do. Slipping on the gown he had tossed aside earlier, she got up and wandered around the small room for a moment, wondering how she was going to keep herself busy.

The first thing she decided to do was go through Storm's file. See if he had any enemies who might want to cause them harm. She found his file amazing. Everything was in there including how many partners he had throughout his life.

"Wow. He did put someone in the hospital." She sat back. He felt so bad after that he stopped any contact with non-Vespian women. He even tried to find a mate. There was a picture in his file and Heather recognized the woman as Miss half-a-dress. The one her sister-in-law dragged her away from. Toki had said their relationship hadn't lasted long and it was right there in the file. The relationship ended quickly due to lack of interest on either side. There was no animosity between them and they just both moved on to other partners.

She wondered what he thought when he went through her file, and there was nothing about her sexual history. Did he think she was a virgin because of that? Then she remembered the man she gave a black eye to. Laughter escaped her. Poor man, he went to kiss her and she took it as an attack. She put him in the hospital and that was in her file.

It didn't take her long before she realized that he had touched lots of lives and for the most part he was well liked and respected. No one had any grief with him. If they did, they hid it well.

The door sounded.

"Come."

One of the nurses stood in the hall. "The doctor would like to see you."

She stood and followed him to the medical area. Her mother-in-law was also in attendance. "Have you learned anything new, Doctor?"

Heather already knew the answer. She had been through it all before.

"Your device has already dissolved into your body. Although I thought it would take a lot longer. The metals it was made of will take longer to leave your system, if they leave at all." He pulled up her DNA strand. "As the compounds break down, most are being re-assimilated into your DNA."

"And what race has those compounds in their blood?" asked Storm's mother.

"There are a few races, Anseri, including ours, but Heather has a few extra sequences that still baffle me. They're common and in most species, but there is no real pattern to them."

"Unless they were to combine a certain way." Heather said it so matter-of-fact. Although not something she heard from every doctor, those who made it this far had tried to figure out why she didn't quite fit into any particular race. A lot never got as far as these simple elements, but there had been a few brilliant doctors who had. This was where most stopped.

"You don't seem to be upset about it," commented Storm's mother.

"Because I have heard it before." She walked up to the screen. "May I?"

When the doctor nodded, she touched several things at

once, bringing them to the forefront. "Understand that very few doctors have made it this far, but I studied science and have a knack for it. I took the research those doctors had and went a step further." She pulled the chemicals up so everyone could see them. "These two are the ones that make us humanoid. And why some races can mix with others and produce children. But then there are these five compounds that no one understands. If they were combined, there would be no problem. I'd be human. If these two combined…" She pulled the two compounds she spoke of forward. "Then I'd fit these races." The screen brought up a series of races that had that combination. "If these two were to combine, then it would be another set of races. There are a lot of variables. But when someone tries to get them to combine nothing happens. The five compounds just sit there, floating along, totally ignoring each other. That's where I hit a wall. I kept hoping for a breakthrough." She sat down. "Been waiting a long time."

"Doctor?" Storm's mother looked at him for confirmation.

"She's right. They're not combining. But I'm wondering if it is still some type of safety mechanism. That device was put in her to make her read as a race she didn't belong to. Perhaps the catalyst to activate everything hasn't happened yet."

"What sort of catalyst?"

"That's what I'm working on now. I don't want to do any damage to what is happening to her." He turned the screen off and faced them. "There is one thing. The last time we put her through our scanner Heather drained all the power out of it and it took several hours for us to get it up and running again."

"You talking about the arch?" Heather pointed to the contraption. "I felt a little funny after walking through it, but it passed in seconds."

He nodded. "It's possible you just needed an energy boost then and took it from a strong source. It could have been a safety mechanism again. Since I don't know what caused it I would like to try something a little different." He held out a necklace. "This has a monitoring device. And will transmit your readings to me. It has its own power source. One you shouldn't be able to drain."

She took it from him and turned it over in her hands.

"Have you ever worn anything like this and not have it work?" asked the doctor.

"Have to say this is a first." She looked up at him. "You sure this will work?"

"No. Since we're not sure what is happening. Your body might be shutting down anything that is trying to figure out what is going on to protect itself. I'm hoping this will bypass any safety feature your system has and will allow us to monitor you."

Heather wrapped it around her neck. "Okay. Guess you'll know pretty quickly, won't you."

He nodded.

Storm's mom touched her on the arm. "Toki has been sent on an assignment as well, so I thought it would be good training for you to work with me when we get to Vespia."

"Keep me out of trouble?"

"Teach you your duties as Storm's mate."

Heather sat in the grand hall, listening to the two farmers arguing about how one guy's livestock was eating the crops of the other farmer. She tried to act interested, but after realizing they were totally ignoring her, she decided to find something else to occupy her mind. Her mind continued with the conversation while she studied the architecture.

The walls and pillars in the place were beautifully carved

with images and words. Some spoke of old times and how the race first struggled to survive, but then it went into stories of great heroes. She found it fascinating.

A hand touched her arm, bringing her back to the arguing farmers. And she found everyone staring at her. Great. What did she miss?

"They wish for you to make the decision."

And if she made a mistake the whole planet would hear about it. If she backed away, they wouldn't believe she had the spine to be part of this society. Military training kept her features calm and serene. Inside she wanted to scream. She needed to think.

What was the real problem? The animal wandering onto the neighbor's land and eating the crops or was it more of a jealous jab because one was considered better than the other? She touched her mother-in-law's arm. "Anseri, may I ask a few questions first?"

"Of course." She smiled at Heather.

She looked at the two men, not missing how she had everyone's attention now. She spoke to the crop farmer first. "Can I assume you have access to technology that will keep animals away from your crops?"

"Yes, but it will also keep the bugs needed for pollination away, so I can't use them."

"And you?" She looked at the second farmer. "You have access to technology that would keep your animals from wandering?"

He nodded. "But it can harm the meat and bring down the price."

"Brothers?" She had noticed they had a family resemblance.

The two men looked at each other.

"I'll take that as a yes." She looked at one of the pillars and smiled. The answer was right there in front of her. "I find it interesting that we're here in the great hall covered with the rich history of the Vespian race. Your most basic laws are etched here for all to see."

That had her mother-in-law turn in her seat.

That couldn't be good. What did she do wrong now? Heather feared she was burying herself, but it was too late to stop. The brothers had dropped their gaze from her.

"You know what I'm about to say." She adjusted herself in her seat.

They nodded.

That caught her off guard. "Then why would you come here? The problem isn't your animals eating his crops or his animals wandering onto your farm. You two are jealous of the other. One thinks the other has it easy. You think your brother doesn't have to work as hard as you do because of what he raises. I know each of you works as hard as the other. But who am I?" she paused for a moment. "Sometimes it takes an outside source to see the real problem. Personally, I think you two should switch places for a season. See what the other does. Learn from firsthand experience what each other must do day to day and you'll learn to appreciate the work each of you do."

They seemed to be happy with what she said and were soon ushered out of the hall.

"That was very good." With the nod of her head, Storm's mom had the hall cleared. "We have a little time before the next session starts."

"Huh uh. You looked at me when I said something about the writing on these pillars. And now you want to question me to death about what I see."

"I was a little curious about your comment." She stood and gestured for Heather to walk with her. "Did Storm teach you how to read some of our language?"

That was Vespian language on the pillars? No wonder she got such a weird look. It looked like English to her. "When we were together he had other things on his mind, but when I had time I studied a little. Wanted to at least be able to read a menu."

"And what does this particular section say?" she brought them in front of one of the arches.

Heather looked at the area she pointed to. "This one is part of a storyline about the planet explorers. Here they are, showing a landing on one of the shores where they meet indigenous natives."

"Interesting." She remained quiet for a moment. "I'd like for you to try something for me."

Once again, she was under the microscope. Why did she do this to herself? What was her next challenge?

"The university is in session and we have a class I'd like you to see." She ushered her out the door into the warm afternoon.

"Okay. It has something to do with this language here, doesn't it? Is it a secret? Something you don't share with all your people?"

"Oh, no. We don't keep things like that from them." She walked her across a park to a tall spirally building. "It's just not everyone can read it. It is an older language and cannot be taught to everyone."

"Oh." She found that a bit odd. "So you taking me to some expert who will prove once and for all that I'm either faking it or telling the truth?"

"Yes."

"Okay, then I can save us a trip and just say it was a fluke, and I promise to never do that again?"

The doors were opened for them and they passed into a much cooler interior. "Sorry. It's a little too late. I just want to see to what extent you can read it."

"Fine." She followed her to a large room filled with students. The teacher stood up front, speaking in a very boring tone, all the while showing a section of a wall filled with writing. Not one she had seen but she recognized the language and could read it easily.

"To translate, you look to the third picture for your subject."

Heather crossed her arms. If you did that, half the sentences would be translated wrong.

"Like here. How would you translate this?" He looked up and noticed the elder leader standing at the back. "Anseri."

He gave her a formal bow, which caused the students to turn. They all stood and repeated his gesture.

"You cause quite a stir." Heather said it softly.

"So do you, my dear."

Heather had nothing to say to that. When people realized she was the Earther she got strange looks and heard the whispers. She knew Storm's mother heard it as well.

"What brings you to our class today?" The teacher puffed up his chest with the knowledge of having the supreme ruler in his classroom.

"I have a guest here who wants to try her hand at translating some of the text." She gestured to Heather.

"Of course." He looked at Heather.

She could see his questioning look. He didn't know who she was, but that wouldn't last very long. Everyone else did.

"Go ahead and translate, then." He pointed to the image.

"Why don't you go ahead and do this one since you have already been working with your students on this and let her read the next one?"

"Of course, Anseri." He turned back to the image on the screen and started to translate. "So what we have here is the subject." He pointed to the third figure, "Which is we or us."

"Our." Heather said it under her breath. She couldn't understand how he didn't see how the translation really worked.

"This," he pointed to another image. "Means land."

She rubbed her hand across her forehead. That was wrong too. "But in this text it means planet."

"You believe you can translate this better than I can?" He had been watching her muttering to herself and his body language showed his disgust with her behavior.

Obviously, he had never had anyone question his translations before.

She didn't mean to be overheard or be so rude, but when it came to things like this, she had trouble keeping her opinions to herself. "Sorry. Please continue."

"Please. I would like to hear your interpretation."

Heather looked at her mother-in-law who nodded. Everyone wanted to see what she could do. "Okay, but you're asking for it."

"Where are you from?"

"Earth." She watched as his face went from confusion to that look she had seen so many times. Disgust that the Earther thought she knew more than the man trained in the language.

"Please translate."

"Our planet is precious. Treat it with respect."

"And how about this?" He brought up another phrase. This time no images were involved, so she had to translate the words themselves.

"Life is ever changing. Fill yours with love and laughter."

He gave her an unbelieving look. "And this?"

"Your name." She was getting annoyed. If she was by herself, this man would be on the ground right now with her foot at his throat.

"Come." Storm's mom ushered her out of the room. "We need to be getting back to the hall."

"Happy, Anseri?"

"I see you have learned the people's name for me. Do you know what it means?"

"Yes." Heather walked beside her as they headed back to the hall. "It means great one, leader, mother of all."

"Very good. Did your translator give that information to you?"

"No. I just knew it." Heather watched as people stopped to bow to Storm's mother. There was something about the question. "Anseri is an ancient word, isn't it?"

"Very good." She strode into the building and led Heather to a set of doors to their left.

Heather knew this wasn't over yet. "So who's next?"

"What makes you think I want you to see someone else?" two guards opened the door for them to enter.

"Oh, my goodness, it seems to be your thing." She knew better than to believe her innocent comment for a moment. "Heather, I have a doctor I need you to speak to. Heather, I have a teacher I'd like you to meet. Heather, I have a linguist expert I think you could learn from."

Storm's mom laughed. "Okay so I am that way. We still have the afternoon session, but I would like you to have dinner with some people."

"Experts?"

"Yes."

"Of course."

The rest of the day was pretty quiet. She kept her mouth shut and worked hard on keeping her attention on what was going on around her. No one else asked for her opinion, which made her happy.

They made it back to the house without any incident.

"I am sorry I keep getting myself into these situations."

"Heather, please understand you are doing nothing wrong. You did surprise me, but there is no crime for anyone being able to speak ancient."

"Ancient? Really?" She had suspected as much as she started to pace. "Couldn't have been the normal Vespian language? I have to make it worse by speaking a dead language? How many people can speak it?"

"Three."

"And once I'm confirmed I'll make four."

"Yes. Drink?" Anseri gestured to a small table where a servant stood.

"As strong as you got."

"It will be fine."

"Sure it will. Can't even prove I belong to one particular race, but I can speak the language. Of course, I'm sure this will thin the list down a little. How many races have even heard of ancient?" She took the glass from the servant and looked at the doors that had opened. "Holy cow."

Two people she didn't recognize were ushered into the room along with the one she called the strange little man.

"Heather, this is Streya and his mate."

She bowed to them and was a little surprised when they bowed back.

"My son's mate can read ancient and I need your help confirming it." She greeted her friends. "First though we will get to know each other."

Heather was thrilled. Lots of small talk with these people staring at her when she wasn't looking.

Storm's uncle walked up to her and handed her a soft leather book. "Read for me."

At least he was honest with her. She took the book and looked at the page he had it opened to. Within seconds, she closed the book. "That is the mating ceremony."

It went into graphic detail of what the mates needed to do. More than Storm ever told her. She felt the heat in her cheeks.

He patted her on the shoulder and smiled. "She can read it easily."

"We were going to wait until after dinner, Hynna."

"Why? Everyone wants to know." He picked up a glass

near him and drained it. "Waiting will only make her worry."

Streya spoke next. "So there must be a few things you miss from Earth?"

"Some things, but not as much as I thought I would." She was greeted with a bunch of grins. "You asked me that in ancient, didn't you?"

"And you answered it in the same language."

"Great." She felt her head start to hurt just a little more. "How many people can read it, understand the spoken version, and speak it?"

"One."

"Me."

TEN

Heather sat there, looking at the people who confirmed that she was more of an oddity than she realized. She had always had a knack for languages but nothing like this. She had never been normal and she sure wished it would happen for at least one day.

"I'd like to try something." They nodded. She turned her translator off to see if it was the equipment or just her. "Okay. Please speak to me. Let me see if I can understand you."

Storm's mother spoke first and although she could catch a few words here and there she didn't really understand her. But when Streya spoke she understood every single word. "At least the translator isn't the reason I understand the language."

Heather just wished she wasn't the one who could do something no one else could do. Her life had been filled with too many of those crazy little moments.

She spoke to the couple as nicely as she could even though her head was going in circles. Why her? Why did she have to have this special ability?

They had dinner and then excused themselves. They

knew she needed time to absorb what was going on with her.

Storm's uncle came up to her and touched her chin so she would look at him. His lack of height allowed him to look her in the eye. She wondered why he didn't hit the seven-foot height the rest of the men reached. "Your time to be strong is coming soon."

"Okay." What did he mean by that?

He then walked to his sister and kissed her on the cheek before letting himself out.

"So what did my brother say?"

"He was being his cryptic self." She sat down and dropped her head back. "Wish Storm was here."

"He will be. Tomorrow."

Her head snapped up. "And how am I allowed to greet him?"

"Any way you wish."

"Okay, what is proper protocol?" She could tell Anseri didn't understand the question, so she tried again. "On Earth, when a loved one came home from a mission the families would be at the space dock waiting. They wanted to show their support and most didn't want to wait until their loved one got home."

"I see. As his mate, you may greet him at the site. As the mate of the next leader of the elders you must be protected."

"How discrete." Heather wasn't happy, but at least he'd be back. Her plans to greet him like a normal person had been trashed by her new station in life.

"You wish for discrete? I can arrange that."

"Please?" Heather stood. If it didn't look like she had half the Vespian army around her, she would feel one hundred percent better. "If you don't mind, I need to get ready for him. I promised him a surprise and haven't had a chance to get it ready."

"Do you need any help?"

"Um, I've got it, but thank you." She went to the room his mother had offered to her when they arrived. It had been Storm's when he used to live in the palace.

Being alone on the strange planet hadn't been as hard as she expected because she was surrounded by his things. The clothing was older and probably didn't fit him but when she felt a little lonely, she had taken out a shirt or two and put them on. She could feel him near when she did that. It brought her a little comfort.

She had brought several data links with her so she could access some of Earth's files without having to ask permission every time. The links had all been cleared when she first set foot on the Vespian ship. Now she had to find the lingerie she had in mind.

The rays of the two Vespian suns lit up the landscape. She stood off to the side of all the other women and men, waiting for their mates to arrive. Storm's mother didn't seem to understand the meaning of discrete with the giant blue and white tent she had erected on the site. All the guards standing between them and the other well-wishers didn't help either.

"His ship has landed." She offered Heather a drink.

"I'm sure he'll be able to find me now." Heather shook her head. All she wanted to do was meet him at the ship. Not make a spectacle of herself.

"You had hoped your reunion would be a private one." Storm's mother stood and walked to the opening of the tent and lifted the flap. "I do understand that, but someone is after you and my son would never forgive me if something happened while you were in my care. This will work out just as well. You'll see."

She left Heather inside as the soldiers aboard ship started to debark and head to their homes.

"Why is your mother here?" asked Fridon.

Storm looked at his friend. "What are you talking about?"

"The big blue and white pavilion up there?" He pointed in the direction of the tent.

"I'm not sure, but I'll go find out." Storm grinned. He had an idea and wondered what his mate had said to get his mother to make such a spectacle. It wasn't her style at all.

He stopped in front of his mother and gave her the proper bow before he gave her a bright smile. "My soldiers and I are honored by your presence."

"I wanted to thank them for their hard work and sacrifice." She looked out at the sea of faces staring back at her. "I wish to honor all by opening the palace to you and your families. I know you just got back and wish to spend time with them before coming to some formal function." She shooed her son into the tent behind her.

He found his mate standing there, waiting for him. In two strides, he had her in his arms and his mouth on hers. "I have missed you."

"I have missed you too." She looked around the tent at the different servants. She had been working on her courage all day to do what she knew would surprise him. With them in the area, she was losing her nerve. "I had hoped to greet you alone. Your mom didn't think it would be proper without a little spectacle thrown in."

"So she did all this for you?"

She nodded.

Storm noticed she was a little skittish. Something was up. Her quick glances to the help and a slight nibble on her bottom lip made him wonder what she would do if he got rid of them. So he did. "Out."

In seconds, the room cleared. "Now, what has you acting like you did something wrong?"

She looked at him. "How do you know me so well so fast?"

"I'm a good study."

Her bright eyes held a promise in them. What was she up to?

"Well, I promised you something when you left."

"I remember." He watched as she reached for the tie that held her gown together. The garment was pretty simple, wrapping around her waist and keeping it snug. She had his undivided attention as she slowly pulled the belt free and held the gown open.

He became instantly hard. Her body was encased in another bit of lace. Red in color and it fit her perfectly, but what had his total focus were little straps going from her waist to the tops of her thighs. They attached to more material covering her legs. "Woman, you can greet me like that every time we're separated."

He traced the edges of the lace that surrounded her breasts. Her nipples hardened when he brushed his fingers against the tips. His hands slid down her stomach to the straps holding the material wrapped around her legs. It was soft and sensuous. He felt his body shake, knowing he couldn't touch her until they made it home. "Why would you do this to me?"

She rubbed him along his length. "Because I remember the last time when you saw a bit of lace and you couldn't touch me. You lost control for just a moment. Knowing I can do that to you the way you do it to me was too much to pass up."

The flap started to move and he pulled her against him. That was his gift, and he didn't want to share it with anyone.

"Secure your dress. We're about to have company."

One more flash of red filled his vision before she covered herself.

Her whole demeanor changed then. Knowing she was able to affect him the way she did gave her power she didn't know she had. She swished her hips at him and held herself proudly.

He took her hand and led her out of the tent. This was the first time the people, especially those who worked with him regularly, saw her. Many were curious, straining to see what she looked like. As a unit, they all saluted him and bowed to her. He was very proud when she gave them the proper bow, her modesty keeping her behind him and allowing him to still show dominance.

"So what did you end up deciding to do about this celebration you want to have?" he asked his mother.

"It will be in two days time." She stepped back so her son would have the limelight for a moment. "That way, you and your mate can have some time to yourselves."

"Thank you."

It didn't take long for her people to take the tent down and move it toward the main buildings of the elders. Storm followed his mother, keeping an arm around Heather. He couldn't keep his gaze off her, wishing he could just find a secluded spot and show her how much he missed her. His heart beat faster every time he caught a hint of red. Or heard the soft swish of her legs rubbing together.

"What is that?" he said it softly in her ear.

"Silk."

He squeezed her hand. "You are in trouble when we get alone."

"I hope so." She said it softly and it was music to his ears.

"So, what happened while I was gone?" He expected an answer, but both women were quiet. Never a good sign. "That bad?"

They still remained silent. He saw the look that passed between them. Then Heather finally sighed.

"You know how I didn't want to cause any trouble?" She gave him a bright smile, but he could hear the sarcasm in her voice. "Well, I was minding my own business and learned I have a new talent. I kinda blew that staying out of trouble right out of the water."

"What are you talking about?"

"I can speak ancient. Wait, that's not quite right. I can speak it, understand when it's spoken to me and read it in any form and the best part? I'm the only one on your planet with that particular talent." Her voice took a sad edge. "Turned the translator off and everything."

He looked at his mother, who nodded.

"I decided I wasn't enough of an outcast on this planet I had to add something to the list." She released his hand and wrapped her arms around herself.

"You are not an outcast." He pulled her body against his so her feet couldn't hit the ground. He touched her face with his free hand. "You are my mate and I will show you how much you belong here when we get home."

She pressed her face into his neck and wrapped her arms around him.

"This has been bothering you."

"How would you feel if you were on my planet and suddenly you could speak some language that had been dead for so long no one was sure what it sounded like anymore?" She pulled her face back so she could look at him. "And you weren't from the planet."

"Knowing I had you to come home to every night would make it all right." She remained silent. He stopped walking and put her back down. Touching her cheek, he wanted to remove the painful look on her face. "You don't agree."

"Then your mom needed to verify my talent." She took his hand and urged him to start walking again, her grip tight. They caught up with his mother quickly after she spoke.

"You took her to the university?" He wanted to throttle his mother. She could have waited for him to get back before subjecting his mate to all of this.

"Is she not the mate of our next leader? Should she be given special treatment because of who she is mated to?" His mother kept her back straight and her eyes in front of her. Her tone let him know she didn't like his questioning of her decisions.

She was right. Heather had to stand on her own. "And how did she do?"

"Magnificent."

He hugged her tight. "I knew she would. Um, why are we walking past my apartment?"

"Because it was easier for me to stay with your mother." He was sure there was more to it than that but had to agree she was probably better with his mom than by herself in his apartment.

"Is that where you wish to go now?"

She gave him a confused look. "I'll go wherever you want me to."

"Then tomorrow we shall move into my apartment, for tonight we can stay at my mother's." He looked at his mother, wondering if staying with her was a good idea. "You don't have some weird agenda to keep us apart do you?"

"Storm, that is your mother." Heather slapped him on the shoulder. No matter what his mother had done Heather still wanted him to show respect to her. He couldn't help but grin.

"Yes, and you've been at the receiving end of her agendas too." He watched his mate stand there looking all proper. She didn't argue with him but gave him a look that begged he show his mother respect. The dress got caught in the wind, giving him another glance at the slip of red underneath. He knew better. Storm looked at his mother. "If you interrupt us once this evening I will carry my mate out, naked if I have to, to my apartment where you can't reach us as easily."

"I promise to leave you two alone this evening."

"Good." He scooped Heather back up into his arms and took off. He made it to his old room in record time. "Now, take that dress off."

"And if I say no?"

"I just might tear it off you."

She stepped away from him. Now they were alone her bravery seemed to be coming back to her.

What was she up to? "You trying to make me chase you?"

"No." She smiled. "But I do have another surprise." She turned her back to him and started walking into the bedroom, dropping the dress along the way. The lace gently cupped her, those straps keeping the silk high on her legs. The red heels she wore accented the whole effect.

His erection was turning painful. He shed his clothes as he followed her.

She had converted his room too. Candles covered the dressers and just about any flat surface, setting a wonderfully cozy mood that would help suspend the rest of the world once he closed the door. The bed was covered in a shiny material that he recognized as satin sheets. He had tried them out while on Earth one time. She had chosen a dark color to wrap his bed in.

"Hmm, I'm thinking you want something from me."

She laughed as she turned back to face him. "I do believe it is the other way around. I remember the last time we were separated for more than a few hours. You barely made it in the door."

"Be glad when I'm on a mission my mind is too busy on what needs to be done to think about your luscious body or you wouldn't have made it out of that tent." He walked up to her and, pushing her hair away from her throat, he started to nibble. "But in case you can't tell, I'm in pain because of my need for you."

She tilted her head so he could nibble to his heart's content. "Which is why I picked this outfit for you."

"Really?" His fingers slid along the soft lace across her stomach. Storm found her backing him up and pushing him down on the bed. He sat, wondering what she would do next. Her eyes sparkled with a touch of fear as she bent in front of him. His gaze fixed on her beauty.

She took a hold of his length, giving him a little massage before she seemed to be happy. The silk of her hose slid up against his legs as she straddled him, her body inches away. She wrapped her arms around him as she eased herself down. Her heat made him harder, if that was possible. Then her muscles tightened against him, setting him off almost immediately.

She wasn't going to send him alone. Tilting her backward, he found the hard pebble of one breast and started to suckle her. The material of the bra added a dimension to the sensation. Through the lace, he felt her nipple thicken. She felt it too. He turned his attention to the other and continued to focus from one to the other until she lost control.

Everything exploded when she hit her climax. He was amazed at the intensity. Her body clenched around him, squeezing him so tight he found his breath taken away. She shook a little as she lifted her face to the ceiling. That was all it took for him to go over the edge with her.

They clung to each other, little tremors setting off smaller waves of release in her. Stretching on the bed, he pulled her with him, keeping himself buried deep inside, marveling over how she had done all this just for him. His fingers played with the lacey material that covered her hips. "How did you do that? We didn't have to move anything aside."

"Crotchless." She fell against him, her body happy and

spent. "It doesn't cover your favorite spot, so you don't have to do anything to access it."

"I think this is my favorite one so far."

"You have only seen two."

"Doesn't matter. Of course, if you were to stand before me naked I would still get hard, fall to my knees and worship your body the way I always do. It's you, not the little outfits you create for me." He wrapped his arms around her, thanking whatever brought her into his life. "But the outfits do add something wonderful. I keep wondering what you will do next."

Storm opened his eyes, enjoying the feel of her next to him. The suns were rising, and he decided to bring her coffee in bed before having his way with her once again. As he eased himself out of the bed, he grabbed the quilt and pulled it over her, covering the little red outfit, minus the garter, as well as her body. That garment had seen a lot of action last night but was sturdier than he expected. Good thing. It was something he hoped she would wear for him often.

He covered her because he shouldn't be gone long and didn't want her to wake because she drew cold.

Last night had been a first for them. They had found some time to explore each other. No mad desire spiraling out of control. Just joy. She was amazing, just as curious of him as he was of her. She wasn't afraid to touch or caress to see what he liked best. And she made sure what she liked more than others was obvious to him.

He moved quietly into the main room of his suite only to find his mother sitting there waiting for him. Three cups of coffee ready.

"Mother." He looked back at their bedroom and sighed,

knowing his thoughts of rejoining his mate had just been squashed.

"I promised to give you last night, which I did. It's time to talk." She was oblivious to his nakedness. "Sit."

"Why do you plague me like this? I have always been the good son and as the future leader have done everything you have asked but when I wish time for myself and my mate you seem to be in the way. Why?"

"No matter what the circumstances are, you have obligations to this planet and these people." She smiled as Heather came out of the room as well. She held up a cup for her to take.

Heather stepped up and graciously took the cup offered. She kissed him on the cheek before she slipped into one of the chairs.

He turned to find her covered by one of his old shirts. It didn't quite hide her red garment, but it covered her enough so his mother shouldn't ask any questions. He grinned as she held up a pair of his old workout pants.

Silently, he took them and slipped them on.

"You do your people and your mate a disservice by keeping her isolated like this." His mother looked at Heather, then him, and smiled.

He frowned at his mother. He wasn't quite ready to share the joy he found in her arms.

"If you wish the people to see her as she really is and care for her the way you do, you have to let her mingle with the people. Let them get to know her. She has proven her worth to me and the council, but no one else knows anything about her. Except she was there to greet you yesterday, and that caused quite a stir." She turned on a monitor to show the news feed. Heather's face was everywhere, with reporters wanting to know more about her.

"You know I don't mind being a kept woman." He knew Heather hated being the center of attention, which was why she joked. She stroked the rim of her cup as she continued. He wanted to be that rim so bad. "I don't know how to behave around your people. Our ideals are very different. Perhaps keeping me away a little longer is a good thing."

"You will find they're not so different after all. Being afraid isn't the Vespian way. You need to face it and charge on through." His mother stood and turned to face him. "Tomorrow night you have to let her be herself. Let everyone see why she is your perfect match."

Heather stood in front of the mirror, adjusting her dress for the fifth time. Storm had argued that he wanted her to wear the red under her dress. She tried to make him understand it wasn't a good idea. She was even willing to create another garment like the red one but in a neutral color so most people wouldn't spot it easily, but he didn't want to hear it. He wanted red.

So red he got. She chose a long black gown instead of the white Anseri had her wearing all the time. Her red underwear would show through the white too easily. The dress was a soft jersey type material she had never seen on Earth. It hugged in all the right places and fell softly where it needed to. The neckline had a high collar just touching the bottom of her ears. Heather assumed it was to hide her mark, but the neckline plunged deep and made her worry about things popping out again. The red lace would hold her in place, but how many times would she have to check her bosom to make sure no one would get little flashes of red because the neckline allowed something to expose itself? If Storm had never seen anything like her little lace outfits she was sure the rest of Vespia hadn't either and she didn't want to give them an education on it.

Storm had already been called to stand with the elders.

As next leader, he had to be there when everyone arrived. They had other plans for her. Ones she wasn't too happy about. She walked down several corridors by herself. Her black heels gave her a little more height, but she still found them to be small torture chambers for her feet.

Several servants greeted her near the reception line, ready to help her as she worked her way through it. They escorted her to the beginning of the line and followed her as she moved down it and greet each of the elders. It was to show she was one of the people. But it just made her feel more isolated.

Using all her training, she worked her way through the elders, bowing at the proper time, smiling and nodding when spoken to. She reached Storm and his mother. After she gave the leader of Vespia a proper bow, Storm grabbed her and gave her a resounding kiss. One that could have melted the clothes off her body and definitely letting everyone know she was his. All the work she went through to show proper decorum and grace gone in one kiss.

"That was evil." She felt a little breathless. Her body hummed.

"How?" He smiled at her as he kissed her again.

"I can't think when you kiss me like that." She knew her body vibrated with desire and wondered how he was dealing with his reaction.

"And things like that have a tendency to backfire." She palmed his length to see how hard he was, the fullness of her skirt hiding her movements. A smile spread across her face when he sucked in his breath at her touch. His stiff member jumped at the contact. "That is something you're going to have to deal with."

"So, is that how we're going to play tonight?" He looked at her, his eyes glowing with need, accepting the challenge she had thrown down.

She hadn't planned on challenging him and knew she

would lose, but in the end they would both win, so she gave him a smile, then a wink as she took her place beside him. "If that is what you wish for."

He gave her a bone-melting smile that she knew meant trouble.

"You two are going to behave, right?" His mother's voice was very soft, but in that tone mothers across the universe seem to know how to use.

"Yes, Ma'am," Heather answered. She looked at Storm. At least she hoped they would try. It really depended on how much they planned on teasing each other all night. She could be discrete, but she wasn't sure about him or how quickly it could get out of hand.

Heather had been the first one to walk down the receiving line, so they stood there, greeting the soldiers and their families as they passed through. Most showed their curiosity about her but maintained their best behavior. There were a few who didn't hide how they felt about her, drawing a few growls from Storm.

She was used to it and chose to ignore the lewd glares and sexual comments. It didn't matter what they thought, she was there to stay and sooner or later they would have to get used to her. Just like every person who ever worked with her. She had a lot of rocky starts, but in the end, all of them learned she was a valuable ally.

Once the line ended, they took their seats for the meal. Instead of sitting up on the dais which the elders used all the time, the council sat at tables scattered amongst their guests. It surprised her to know they didn't keep themselves separate all the time. Heather found herself sitting opposite Storm. A nice safe distance away. She knew his mother had something to do with that.

She held up her glass to him. He winked at her and held his glass up as well.

Small talk started at the table and it didn't take too long

before Storm was answering a lot of questions about her. They were thinly veiled ones about Earth and how interesting he found the planet, but she knew they wanted to know about her. The little oddity he mated with. Too afraid to ask her directly, they went through him.

She let him answer. Wanting to laugh as he tried to keep his temper under the barrage of questions. He finally hit his limit when he looked at the woman who wanted to know more about the Earth wedding and said, "I'm not the one from Earth, she is. Why don't you ask her?" Then stuffed whatever he had speared with his fork into his mouth so he wouldn't have another outburst.

"I meant no disrespect." The poor woman looked stricken.

"And none was taken." Heather leaned over to pat the woman on the hand, giving Storm and several other people at the table a little flash of red in the process. "If we were on my planet right now, the situation would be reversed. People would be asking me all the questions because they would be a little hesitant to speak to Storm."

"Thank you." The woman adjusted herself in her seat and asked. "So, how does your ceremony work?"

She spent the next hour explaining the whole process from engagement to the reception. Including having to explain the rings.

"So that tells your world you belong to someone?"

"Yes." She flexed her fingers, making the light in the hall bounce off the diamond.

"And you can't have multiple partners?"

"Depends on the culture and the couple. My planet has a very diverse group of people. What one might find taboo wouldn't offend another." She touched the engagement ring. "This ring shows that I have someone specific in my life and have promised to spend the rest of my life with that person, but it doesn't mean I am his. There is a second ring that is given during the ceremony that shows I have chosen to be with the one person for the rest of my life, excluding anyone else."

"I'm not sure I understand."

"It's her mark," Storm spoke up. "Humans use it to warn people that the man or woman is taken and they don't want any other partners."

"Must be awfully boring," the woman commented.

"Not so far." His comment might have been seen as a quip, but she knew he was being honest and she felt his sincerity deep inside.

Heather watched Storm. He looked at her and gave her one of his smiles.

The dinner was cleared, and they were allowed to mingle with the other guests. Storm was at her side in seconds.

"I see you wore it." He slipped a finger under the collar of her dress to expose a red strap.

"Yes." She slipped it back into place. "Now you will know and still have to wait."

"Not really." He looked around to see who was paying attention to them. "No one would think twice if I were to take you right here, right now."

"And you'd have an audience to see what your sexual prowess is like." She ran a finger around the edge of his shirt, smiling when she saw a row of goosebumps pop up with her touch. "You sure you want to know what your friends think of your technique?"

"You'd go along with whatever I decide?" His finger dipped a little deeper into her neckline, playing with the lace as well as her skin.

"I trust you." The words were so simple, but the effect they had on him was immense. He bent his head toward hers just as someone stepped between them.

"Mom said for you two to break it up." Storm's sister looked up at him and grinned. She enjoyed being the bearer of bad news. "She wants you to mingle, not steam up one corner. So I have come to steal your mate for a little while. Introduce her to some of the people here."

Heather waved bye as she was ushered off. She felt she needed to defend herself. "We had only been talking for a few moments."

"Please, you two were all over each other. No one would dare interrupt, and whatever you just said to him thrilled him to the bone. I sensed it. If I hadn't stopped you, I do believe everyone would have gotten quite a little show." She brought her over to a small group of women. "Besides, my brother needs to learn to wait."

"You trying to teach him patience?" Heather nodded to the ladies. Let the awkwardness begin. No one spoke for a few moments.

"Mother is."

The women around them just stared at Heather. As usual, she was some strange oddity, no one knew how to deal with.

Storm's sister rolled her eyes. "Heather, do you bite?"

"Well, I guess it depends on the circumstances." What was she getting at?

"Like now. Would you bite any of these women? Growl at them? Take their heads off?" She pointed to the silent mob staring at her.

"That is more your brother's job. He's the one who growls and bites heads off." She looked up and found him watching. He stood amongst several young men who vied for his attention. As they spoke to him, he would look away from her to answer a question, but only for a moment. He only had eyes for her. Heather had to ask her sister-in-law. "Is he going to do that all night?"

"What?" Storm's sister looked over before looking back at Heather and grinning. "I'm afraid so. He's been like that since he met you. Be flattered. A lot of the men here don't pay any attention to their mates."

"Aren't you warm in that?"

Who said that? The comment came out of nowhere. Heather glanced to her left and there stood the woman she had met before. The woman Storm had dated for a short while. She ran her fingers through the soft material of her dress as she thought of an answer.

"You look like you've been dressed by the elders." She looked at Storm's sister. "You should have dressed her so she could at least fit in."

So many thoughts ran through Heather's mind. The first was, look who she's been living with. Of course, it would look like she was dressed by elders. Another was why did it bother her? It wasn't her body that it covered, and to Heather she was exposing a lot of flesh, but instead Heather elected to be nice. "The median temperature of your planet is about nine degrees lower than mine, so I find it to be a little cool and cover for comfort. I'm sure as I adjust, it will change."

And then the woman moved on.

Heather didn't know what to say.

"Forgive her. She talks that way to everyone."

"And she dated your brother?" Heather's gaze followed her until she got lost in the crowd.

"Yeah. He tried. She's a beautiful woman and the daughter of one of the elders, but the moment she opens her mouth. Well." She grinned at Heather. "You can see why it didn't work out."

"So, why did you rush me away from her the last time?" Heather shook her head. "I wondered if there was anything between them because of that."

"You have to be kidding." Toki gave her an odd look. "Who is my brother still watching?"

Heather looked up and found his gaze hadn't wavered. "Okay. Point taken."

"She is a beautiful woman, Storm."

"I know." He looked at the young man who made the comment. "Remember that she is mine."

"You know we would never approach her without your permission." He took a sip of his drink. "Besides, I have heard that humans are a bit prudish."

"They are sexual beings, too. They just feel that it is a private thing and what she does when the doors are closed makes me want to keep them closed all the time."

"Really?" The young man set his drink down. "Perhaps I should ask for that permission now."

"Only if you wish a pounding." He glared at the young man's audacity. "My mate is not to be approached by anyone or I will cause bodily harm."

"You never cared before." One of the other young men commented. "What makes her so different?"

"I say he just hasn't grown tired of her yet," said another.

Storm growled. He didn't like the comment at all. Grabbing the man by the collar, he lifted him up into the air. "Keep up your thread in this conversation and I will take you outside and teach you how to show respect to me and mine."

The man swallowed hard. "I am sorry, sir."

He felt the gentle pressure of her hand. It didn't matter that she couldn't have heard what anyone said, she knew enough to stop him before he made a mistake. Heather's soft voice washed over him. "Everything okay?"

He dropped the man and took her into his arms. "Of course. Why?"

"I don't know." She looked at the man holding his throat. He knew she had sensed his anger. Just like he could sense her awkwardness of being around all these people without knowing how to talk to them.

"Everything is fine now." He bent his head to hers. No sister to stop him now. She tasted a little like the wine she had been drinking. He tightened his hold on her for a second more but released her before someone from his family ran interference. "Go on back to my sister."

She nodded and started back to Toki. Unfortunately, she didn't watch where she was going and ran into one of the servers. Glassware and drinks went everywhere. Heather crouched down to help the young girl. She leaned forward to pick up fallen glassware, allowing her dress to gape open and give him a beautiful view of the red lace underneath.

He was hard again in seconds. The lace hugged her, moving as she reached for the fallen glass.

"What is that?" someone asked.

He wanted to enjoy the view as long as it lasted, but something told him to turn around and find out what intrigued the men behind him so. He found every man nearby staring down the front of her dress as well.

ELEVEN

He moved fast. As much as he liked what he saw, he didn't want everyone else gawking at his mate. Grabbing her by her hands, he eased her to a standing position. "Don't do that again."

"What?" She looked confused.

As discreetly as he could, he rubbed a finger against the collar of her dress, his finger slipping inside where she would feel the heat of his hand.

She looked down and then back at him, her eyes widening as she realized what she had done. "And everyone saw?"

"It was a beautiful sight." His eyes sparkled with his desire.

She buried her face in his shirt in mortification. "Well, I just became the subject everyone will be wondering about for the next week." She peeked up at him. "A very good look?"

He rubbed himself against her so she would know what it did to him. "My men are speechless at the moment, and that is hard to do."

"Well, great." She thought about it for a minute, then cocked her head to the right. "Then I guess I'm winning for the moment. I not only got you, but half the ballroom. Can you top that?"

He grinned, need still blazing in his eyes. "Let me think about it."

***

She smiled and gave her skirt a little swish as she headed back to Storm's sister. All the women stared at her in awe.

"They want to know what that was," said Toki.

"It's known as lingerie. Undergarments. Years ago, women on earth wore them to keep things in place. Now it's used for arousal." Heather picked up the drink she had been nursing and downed it. She needed three more, fast. "Unfortunately, I was only trying to arouse one person, not everyone here."

"Can we see it?"

She wasn't about to parade around for these people, so they could see her little outfit. "There is more than one piece and I don't think my husband, sorry, my mate wants me to make this public knowledge. He's asked me not to bend over like that again."

"He's got it bad," said one of the women.

Heather grinned. She did feel empowered after it was all said and done. She made men speechless and didn't have to do anything more than bend over. And Storm now had that gleam in his eye. The 'you're about to have a wild night' look that she had come to enjoy.

The waitress she had run into brought her another drink, which she downed just as fast. "Three more."

The young waitress nodded and went to the bar.

"Have you drunk our alcohol before?" Her mate's sister looked concerned.

"I've done a little research and the content isn't too far off that of Earth's. I have been able to out drink anyone who

challenged me there. Just need something to help relax me."
A shadow fell across her path and she became alert. Someone
was about to do something stupid. All she saw was a hand
reaching for the top of her dress. Before it could come too
close, she had grabbed the hand, and using a simple joint
lock manipulation, had the owner on his knees. "Don't move
or I will break it."

"I only wanted to see." He tried to turn around, but she
applied more pressure.

"I said don't turn around." She bent it a little more,
pushing it to the breaking point. "I can snap your hand that
fast."

"I'm sorry, mistress."

"I'm not really the one you need to apologize to. Do you
see the angry thundercloud coming at us?" Using the hold,
she turned him so he couldn't miss Storm, or the anger
etched on his face. "I'm his, and he doesn't like to share. He's
the one you're going to have to apologize to, and I'd make it
good because he looks like he wants to kill you."

Storm noted the hold she had on him and the fact that the
man started blubbering the moment he got within earshot. It
didn't matter. No one was going to get a chance to do that
again.

"She's going to stay at my side from this point on. Warn
Mother, I won't tolerate her interference anymore." He
wrapped a possessive arm around Heather as he stared
down at his sister, daring her to argue with him.

Heather found herself being carried over to where he had
been standing. "Can I at least walk?"

"Nope."

"You mad at me?"

"No." He looked at her. "I'm mad at the way everyone
has avoided you like you were some strange disease, but the
moment you spiked their curiosity they feel they can do
whatever they want to you. They show you no respect."

"It was only a little peep show." She tried to make light of the situation. "And I think I have stopped anyone from trying to get another look without my permission."

"Peep show?" He put her feet on the ground when they reached the now growing crowd of men. It seemed like his translator took its time finding the proper way for him to interpret it because it was a long time before he smiled. "A tease? You saw what you did to all these men with that bit of lace as a little tease?"

"Let's pretend it was only for you." She sure hadn't planned on flashing the entire group.

"You know how I get when you tease me like that." He stepped up to her, not touching her but so close she could feel his heat.

"I do." She looked up at him, a soft smile on her face. "It's those moments I live for."

The men made a small circle around them. Knowing how Storm had reacted to the view and the man who wanted a second look, they made sure they kept their distance.

"What was that?"

Heather wasn't sure who was brave enough to interrupt the banter between her and her mate, and the question made her leery. If they were still questioning her undergarments, she was going to scream. She slapped on a smile and turned to look at the circle of men. "What?"

"That hand thing you did?" One of the men wiggled his wrist, trying to show the move. "It didn't look like much, but he didn't move after you had him in it."

"A little Earth trick." Finally, a subject she felt comfortable talking about.

"Do all your women know how to do that?"

What an odd question. She looked up at Storm before answering them. "You gentlemen do realize I had a life before I came here, right? That I was a security officer in my government's military?"

"Sir, you have to let her work with us," one of the young men said. "See if there are things we can learn from her and her training."

He didn't respond right away, and she knew he didn't want to say yes. He still didn't see her security training equal to what he put his soldiers through.

"Oh, I have learned I can't work with Storm." His silence angered her. If he didn't think she could do it, neither would they. She remembered when she tried to work out with him before. It was a lot of fun, but she never got to accomplish her real goal, which was prove she was good at what she did. "He doesn't fight fair."

"Of course not. He's our trainer." It was said so matter-of-factly she wanted to laugh. So they did know how he worked.

"You do to them what you did to me?" She batted her eyelashes at him. How was he going to answer her question?

"No." He crossed his arms over his chest. "But they are smart enough not to challenge me when it comes to training. They know to do what I say when I say it."

So was he saying she wouldn't listen to him? He was asking for it if that was the case. "So are you saying that when you challenge me, I don't respond properly?" She tried to word it so he wouldn't be seen as anything less in the men's eyes. He watched her with his predatory gaze and she didn't think he was going to rise to the bait until a sly smile spread across his face.

"I had to use a different strategy with you and making you lose one piece of clothing every time I pinned you seemed like a good idea. It did work out in my favor."

"Ultimately." She smiled back. "But if you feel I didn't learn my lesson properly perhaps we need to redo my training."

"We can continue that lesson anytime." He looked at the

men before looking back at her. "When we don't have such an audience."

"I look forward to it." The spark in his eyes grew to a distinct flame.

"What about her training with us, sir?" They weren't going to give up on their request.

She could see he didn't want to give in, but how could he say no? She'd think he thought her unworthy of working out with them, and his men would probably think the same thing. Heather crossed her arms and waited.

"Fine. We will start training again in a few days. I will make sure her schedule is clear so she can join us."

In other words, he was going to run her through the paces so he could be sure his fragile little woman could keep up. She was looking forward to showing him what she was capable of doing.

One of the suns was starting to peek up over the horizon when they finally made it back to their suite. Storm had planned on moving them to his apartment yesterday, but things got in the way. He thought about taking Heather to his apartment when they headed back, but knew he hadn't been there since he went to Earth and had no clue what condition it was in. He needed to get a crew in there to get it ready for them. Then he looked over at his mate.

Heather had sunk into one of the overstuffed chairs in the main room and curled into a ball in slumber. She wanted to wait for him, but sleep wasn't letting her.

"Come on, my heart, get to bed." He helped her up and pointed her in the direction of their room. He wanted to set up the cleaning before joining her. It only took seconds for him to send the message.

Trying to be quiet, he followed the trail of clothing she

had left on her way to the bed. He picked up her dress, the bra, panties and garter. The hose she had removed before they headed back. He placed them on a chair near her side of the bed.

He was tired too, but watching her slumber there filled him with a peace he hadn't felt before. Most arranged marriages ended in disaster, but he didn't think he could have picked a better person to be his mate if he tried. A yawn reminded him he hadn't gotten much sleep since arriving home. A few hours of rest would do him a lot of good. If he could keep his hands off his mate.

The smell of coffee brought him around the next morning. He found Heather fully dressed and sitting on the edge of the bed with a cup for him. Normally, he was the one waking her in a very pleasurable way. Had he slept that late?

"We have company." The worry on her face told him to dress and come out as quickly as he could.

He leaped out of bed and out into the room in seconds. There stood three of his security men. What were they doing there? "Problem?"

"Yes, sir." That was all they needed to say. He stalked back into the bedroom and dressed in his uniform. Heather stood to one side as he walked past and out the door. Whatever happened to make them come to the palace had to be bad. They filled him in on their way.

"You hired a crew to clean your apartment this morning?" asked one of the men. He held a small handheld and started entering data in it as Storm answered his question.

"Yes. Why?"

"They walked in on someone ransacking your apartment. When they were late in reporting to their superiors, the crew's leader sent out someone to check on them. They found your apartment broken into. One of the cleaners is dead and the other has been taken to the med area. No one has been able to give a description of the assailant or what they were after."

Storm walked into the apartment. It was a mess. He couldn't believe the devastation done. "What about the security cameras?"

"They were turned off."

He stepped over items that had been strewn about the room. This was aimed at him. It got worse as he headed back to his bedroom. He found his bed slashed, furniture smashed and in tatters about the room. Across his bedroom wall in black letters was the question. 'Where is she?'

Whoever was after Heather was now on his planet.

Heather could feel his distress. Whatever he was dealing with he was taking personally. Several guards took up residence outside their suite, making her nervous. Not knowing what was going on made her trepidation worse.

Storm walked in the door and went into their room, ignoring her and closing her out for a moment. When he came back out, he had a uniform in his hand. He dropped it on the table. "Put it on."

She was surprised to find a Vespian uniform in her size. Once she had it on, she asked. "You going to explain what happened?"

"They're here."

"Who is here?" She wasn't sure what he was talking about.

"Whoever has been after you. I had hoped it was someone from Earth, but they were at my apartment today. Looking for you." He pulled up the image of the words scrawled on his bedroom wall onto the main screen in the room. The words explained what she felt from him. "This is now very serious. You have training. I know that, but you're going to learn to fight as a Vespian, think the way we do. You need to understand what you are up against."

She wanted to argue that she knew what she was up against, but knew he was in no mood. The anger etched on his face showed his worry over her safety. What she had to do now was prove how good she was at her job. Earth picked her to protect him for a reason and he needed to see that to help him understand she wasn't defenseless. "So when does my training start?"

"Now." And he came after her. His first lunge came up empty-handed. She had been quick enough to jump over the couch, but he wasn't stopping.

She didn't want to hurt him, but she had to prove that she could protect herself against someone much bigger than her. Everyone who saw her only saw her size. That included her mate. It didn't matter how many times she had stopped someone from harming her, until she could stop him, it didn't matter.

His sole intention was to protect her, and she knew that, but the whole thing reminded her of her training when she was pitted against some big lumbering ox who didn't think a skinny girl could get the best of him. He used his weight and strength to try to subdue her. The first time he did triumph, but only because she allowed him to. She made a misstep to see what he would do. To learn from it.

Her security instructor made them do the technique again, and she outsmarted him. Ten times in a row, she knocked that big guy down and secured him before he could move.

Storm was a lot smarter than her opponent years ago, but then again, she had a lot more training. She studied him, trying to figure out what she needed to do to triumph.

His height could be what she needed to use against him.

Get him off balance enough and he would fall. Once she got him down, she would have to move quickly to secure him. So what was she going to use? She needed a rope or cord to bind him. Glancing around, she did find something that would work, and she slipped it into her suit.

No matter what, though, she needed to be sure she was out of the way of his long reach. He reached for her again and she dropped back far enough that he ended up with air a second time. He was determined to get her, and she was determined to prove he couldn't. She watched his movements as he stalked her. She needed to plant a sidekick right between his shoulder blades to knock him down. Now she had to figure out how to get him to move past her long enough to hit him.

They seemed to know what the other was thinking most of the time, anticipating needs and wants, and she knew he would use it to best her here. She had to do the same thing.

He watched her. So far, so good. He was trying to read her. She gave him a smile, making him frown and make the first move. His first mistake. He moved to the right, and she started left. The moment he compensated and headed in the same direction, she stopped, back-stepped and spun around him. Jumping, she landed the kick square between the blades and knocked him to the ground. She grabbed and pulled one of his arms back and as quickly as she could she wrapped the cord around his hand. She had thought about wrapping it about his neck, which was what she would have done if it wasn't Storm but found she couldn't. She didn't want to hurt him, only stop him for a few seconds. Then she pulled his foot behind him toward his back and wrapped the other end of the cord there.

She stepped back because she knew it wouldn't hold him long. "That should take you about thirty seconds to get out of. But you need to know I can protect myself, even against the head instructor of your planet."

"What makes you think I am the head instructor?" He pulled his hand free then rolled over.

"I have a brain in here, too." She tapped her head. "It's the little things like the comment one of your men made. Something about that was the way you trained them. They didn't refer to anyone else."

"So I could just teach the men who were there with me."

"The next leader of the planet? Please." She offered him a hand up. "Know I can put up a fight and I'll do my damndest to win."

"And I will worry every second until we end this." He took her hand and got to his feet. "But I do have to say that wasn't bad. There aren't too many people who can get the drop on me."

"Your focus was off. I'm sure if you had been on your game it wouldn't have happened."

"Really? And what do you think interfered?" He took a step toward her.

She gestured to her body as she stepped back. "And don't think I'm going to relax enough to let you take advantage of the situation."

"Glad you're paying attention, and as much as I'd like to take advantage of you once again, I need to be sure you know what to do with someone who knows our ways. I'd never forgive myself if you weren't trained properly."

"Because you're the best?"

"Yes."

She worked hard. Harder than any of his other trainees. He had never seen anyone like her. If he knocked her down, she got right back up and tried again. Once she mastered it, she never lost at that particular maneuver. No matter how many times he might throw it at her.

He could push and push and she never complained and always gave more than one hundred percent. If she was any other trainee, he would probably force her to go home, knowing she was working too hard. But part of him knew she had little time to learn as much as he could teach her, so he kept pushing.

Their lessons were private. What he taught her never went past the two of them. Her training was more intense and sometimes more advanced than anyone he had ever worked with. He wanted her up to speed with the seven men and two women he had been training. They were the best of Vespia, and she needed to be able to keep up.

When she worked out with his team, she learned what everyone else did. She never received special treatment, was normally the first one to volunteer to try a new maneuver, and always asked the right questions.

His men and women grew to respect her quickly. He would give them challenges and her ingenuity always helped whatever team she was involved with, to win. She excelled in a group that already had the best. He had never been so proud of a student before.

She was now as good, if not better, than the elite team she was working with. There was one more test he wanted to give her, but no one could know what he was about to do.

"Tomorrow we get to play." People nodded and smiled. Heather just watched, arms behind her, legs slightly apart. Some sort of military stance from Earth. "Go home, get some sleep, be back here first thing in the morning."

Everyone filed out one by one until they were the only two left.

"You've been so serious lately." He picked a few weights that were accidentally left out and put them back on the racks.

"Yeah." She picked up her gear and wiped her face with a towel she had sticking out of the bag. "My mate would expect nothing less. My teacher would tell me I've learned faster than any of his students, but my mate would argue that I don't have as much time as the rest might and I need to push, and to be honest I want to keep my mate happy."

"Well, you've earned a well-deserved rest." He grabbed his towel and swung it around his neck, then picked up his bag.

"Is that my mate or my teacher speaking?"

"Both." He gestured for her to go out the doors first so he could power down the exercise building.

She nodded.

"Unless you feel we need to train." He gave her one of his heart-stopping smiles. "Like we did on your planet. I do have a lesson I never finished."

"With all the cameras running in this place?" She stepped out the doors, shaking her head. "Really don't want to see that on any of your newsfeeds. We were at the embassy the last time, and I know you took care of the recordings."

"You do?" After closing the doors, he wrapped an arm around her waist and ushered her back to the palace.

"Yes, because I went to have them erased and was told the cameras weren't even on."

"How about that." He stopped moving when he noticed the large screen in the middle of the park. "How did they get that information?"

Heather looked up and saw her picture flashing across the screen. They were talking about the intensive training she had been going through since his apartment had been vandalized. Somehow they knew, as she did, that the exercise tomorrow was to test her. "Oh, boy, that is going to make my mate very angry."

He looked at her, wondering why she kept speaking of him as two different people. "And what do you think your instructor will do?"

"I'd like to think he would take this opportunity to show

how good he is at training and what an apt student the mate of the future leader of this planet is. That she can prove that she is up to the challenge despite the publicity."

He didn't say anything, just started moving again. His arm still around her urged her to walk with him.

Who would dare leak this information? None of the team would, because they knew he would extract a hard payment for betraying the team. They learned that a long time ago. Besides, he had only informed them of the exercise just before he released them. This information looked a few hours old. Heather had been by his side the whole time, so she couldn't have, and she hated that kind of attention anyway. Who else did he tell?

His legs started moving faster when he realized who the culprit was. He released his hold on Heather when she couldn't keep up with his quick, angry stride. He charged through the main door, yelling at the first person he saw. "Where is she?"

"I'm right here, dear." His mother must have anticipated him.

"How could you?"

"What?" She walked deeper into the main hall of the palace, smiling at Heather when she ran in, trying to keep up with Storm.

"Besides having to set aside the land for the exercise and the equipment they would use I kept this information from everyone. The council were the only other people I told my plans to."

"I didn't say anything to the news people."

"But someone from the council did." He couldn't believe they would put his mate in jeopardy like this.

"You know I don't speak for them, nor they for me." She shrugged. "Do you want me to call an emergency meeting?"

"No." Heather spoke up. "The damage is done. Let's not

make it worse by getting angry." She then took him by the hand and practically dragged him into their rooms.

"You don't speak for me." He pounded on their bedroom door.

"Even when I know you're going to make a mistake and I'm trying to save you from it?" She jammed her hands on her hips. "If you want to make a fool of yourself, go right ahead. All you will do is tell these people that you have no faith in me and they shouldn't either. Is that what you want?"

"I want you to be safe." He stepped close to her.

Storm found her anger breathtaking. Her eyes snapped fire. The intensity there mesmerized him. He went to touch her.

"Oh, hell, no." She darted behind the couch. "None of that I must dominate you to prove my manhood stuff."

"But I'm so good at it." He wanted to laugh at her words. She knew him so well. That was what he was thinking. Her body language said her pride was speaking and if he could overcome her pride, he'd get his way. Of course, he would have to set his pride aside too and that was what was wounded here. He knew she could do the job. He wouldn't allow her to participate tomorrow if he didn't think she could do it, but she shouldn't even have to face this situation. She was his mate and he should be able to protect her properly.

And there it was, the slight smile. She agreed with him. She did keep dodging him, though. He went one way, she went another. Even when he tried a few different tactics to catch her off guard she was ready for him.

He needed to distract her. What was the one thing that always worked? He smiled as his fingers opened the seam of his uniform and he peeled it off.

"You have to fight fair." Her gaze went from his face to his naked body and back again.

"It was cumbersome." He took a step toward her.

She didn't lose focus and kept moving away from him. "I could do the same thing, except it seems to have the opposite effect. You become hyper-focused on whatever I expose."

"Really? Try it and let's see." His anger had vanished the moment he saw the smile brighten. He found an opening and made a grab for her. She almost got away, but he had a hold of the back of her uniform and slowly pulled her back to him. "So, what should I expose first?"

"My feet?" She turned to face him. "The shoes do need to come off."

"True, but not a part of you I'm interested in right now." He slid his hands up her arms to her neckline. His fingers rested against her collarbone. "I'm pretty methodical in my ways. I like starting at the top and working my way down."

He parted her top in one swift movement. "I helped design these uniforms so I know how they go together." His fingers relished the feel of her soft skin. "Helps in moments like this."

"Do this a lot?" She watched his hands for a moment before she looked up at him.

"What?" He looked into her violet eyes. She was serious.

"Remove clothing from your female warriors."

"The uniform is a unisex garment." His fingers continued to caress her skin, but he didn't move on to anything else. He didn't want to make light of her question. "It was created with the doctors in mind. The easy in and out is for treating wounds. I just figured out this extra little perk because of you."

She didn't say anything, but he knew something bothered her. "What is it?"

"I want to do well tomorrow." She let out a shaky breath.

"You'll be fine." He started to follow the seam of the uniform all the way down but found her hands on top of his. "Why does this bother you so much?"

"Because I don't want to disappoint you."

"What makes you think you would disappoint me?" He didn't realize she was so worried about this. "You have been an exemplary student. You've far exceeded any expectations I had for you."

"And if I make one misstep, I will never hear the end of it." She sighed as she stepped away from him. "I have done thousands of missions and have had things go wrong and handled the problem easily, but knowing you are going to be there to judge me has me second guessing everything."

"Heather, I never meant to undermine your belief in yourself." He stepped close again and took her face in his hands. He wanted to be sure she continued to look at him. She needed to know he was serious. "I've read your file. You have more commendations than any of my people. You have been in twice as many situations as any of my most seasoned soldiers. I want you at my back anytime, anywhere."

A single tear ran down her cheek. He brushed it aside with his thumb. "You're beautiful, strong, and the most precious thing I have. I push you because I can't control and stop the things that could hurt you. I don't want anything to happen to you."

Another tear trickled down her cheek before she closed the distance between them. In one quick move, she captured him in a deep kiss as she shrugged her way out of the top of the uniform. She became the aggressor this time. Wanting him to possess her, show her how much he cared for her.

He was happy to oblige. He eased the seals of her uniform open in silence. The only sound in the room was their breathing. Storm felt her nimble fingers wrap around his staff and he sucked in his breath. He brushed a nail across the tips of her breasts, causing the same reaction.

The bed was too far so he lowered them to the carpet. Heather's hand pressed against his chest. He laid down, his hand touching her softly, a brush against the underside of her breast, across her stomach and around her hip.

She straddled him and slid him home, her head back and body arched. She was exposed to him. Vulnerable to his will. His hand went to her hips first, helping her set a rhythm that worked for them both, then he slid his fingers into her folds, looking and finding the button that set her off every time. His other hand played where it landed. Tickling her navel, caressing her breasts. Whatever she needed to heighten the experience.

She was getting close. He could feel it. Storm pulled her down toward him and rolled them over. Her silent communication begged him to take over, make this mindless for her. She was his and needed to feel him possess her.

Storm changed the tempo of the strokes. He slowed them down, much to her frustration, and made them deeper, much to her delight. He could feel her body welcome him every time he surged in, those wonderful muscles of hers tightening against him. Her hips tried to urge him to move faster, but he would have none of that. He took his time, pleasuring her in a way she would never forget.

He brought her back to the edge again. The little tremors had started with each stroke. Her hands were at his backside, urging him, begging him to give her what she wanted. He reveled the feel of them on his body.

He was ready this time. Three strokes would be all that it would take to send them both to their orgasms. He took her face in his hands and placed a soft kiss on each side of her mouth.

"You are the air I breathe, the light in my life. My world." He entered her one last time and felt his world crack. Joy raced through him when he felt her body stiffen around him. They were caught in a vortex as sensations overwhelmed him. He had never experienced sex like this before. It was like he was in her body and she was in his.

More tears slid from her eyes.

"Why are you crying?"

"That was profound." She laughed as she wiped the tears from her eyes. "I have never felt that before. It was as if we were sharing each other's orgasm."

"I felt that too." He cradled her in his arms, not ready to move or break the spell they were wrapped in. "But I have noticed we seem to have a silent communication going on between us. We seem to know what the other wants or needs before they have to say anything."

She shifted a leg and found him growing inside her again. "I see what you mean. I was wondering if we could try that again to see if we'll have the same experience."

"You do realize if your experiment works, I'll never leave you alone." He closed his eyes when she slid a leg up around his hip. How did she arouse him so easily?

"You don't leave me alone now. How would this be different?" She closed her eyes and licked her lips when he pulled out and surged back in again.

"I'd never pull out."

Heather stood next to her air cycle, listening to the last-minute instructions for their exercise. She knew that no matter what they were told, she was going to be the one truly tested. How it would be done was her big question. Storm hadn't hinted it to anyone.

They were given permission to take off.

She pulled her helmet on and locked the suit together. The uniform was very versatile. Adding the helmet and gloves allowed them to seal the suit so it could be used in any hostile environment, underwater, non-breathable air, even in space. The person inside would be totally protected. She could also dial up the strength of the armor built into the suit to its highest protection. The moment she sealed the suit, her holographic readout popped up inside her helmet. It took a few seconds for her to adjust, but then it became just another extension of her suit. She could hear commands coming through the earpiece. The chatter became background noise as she ran through her checkpoints.

She climbed onto the bike and took off. The bike was fun. Easy to maneuver. A slight turn to the right or left and the bike took off in that direction. She had only ridden one in simulation before this and she liked the freedom she felt with it. She would have continued to play with it except they were watching their every move and it didn't take Storm very long before he reminded her of that.

She headed in the direction of the challenge, weaving her way through the wooded area. She heard another reprimand when she darted between a few trees, when she should have gone straight through. Once she passed a certain point, she had to dodge drones designed to bring down their cycles. They weren't a surprise to her and were easy to outrun in the beginning, but suddenly they were coming from in front of her. Finding them hard to dodge, she tried to use the weapons on the bike to find they hadn't been loaded.

Great. How was she supposed to fight these stupid things?

"Who's smart idea was it to have the drone come at you and not give you any way to defend yourself?" she shouted into her mike. She used evasive maneuvers to try to keep out of the range of fire, but she found it a bit hard to talk and fly at the same time.

"What are you talking about? Each bike has blanks designed to stop the drones from attacking." She heard Storm's voice in her ear.

"Well, they skipped one. I have no weapons and…" She shifted her bike to the right to avoid another tree and spotted the drone coming at her that she hadn't seen before. "Oh, crap."

This one was going to hit the bike dead on. There was no way for her to avoid it. She had seconds to get herself safely out of the way. She launched herself off the bike and turned the suit up to its highest settings. The suit should protect her from a one-hundred-and-twenty-foot drop and since she was only up about eighty feet, she should be okay. Her descent would be sharp and she would have no control over her trajectory but the area was pretty clear.

The bike exploded, pushing her back a little, then she suddenly had to avoid the flying shrapnel. Something she hadn't thought about when she first pushed off the bike. Pieces whizzed by her head, making her shift her body and changing the direction she had been falling. Pain exploded in her shoulder when one piece found her. It knocked her a little further off course and leaves on branches slapped her helmet.

Heather wanted to check to see if the suit had been breached, but at the highest setting she couldn't move her arm behind her head until she was stationary and could move the setting down again. Any command she could try to give it now would be overridden by the safety protocol built into the suit. The ground was coming up at her pretty fast and she felt like a rocket heading straight into it. She crashed through a few more branches before she hit a clear area where she could see the ground once again. She hoped that was all she had to deal with.

Voices sounded in her head, demanding a response. Along with the weird alarm she kept hearing inside the suit. The effort to speak through the pain took its toll. She answered best she could. "Bike is gone. Will have to make it to the checkpoint on foot."

She could still hear them wanting to know what was going on, Storm's voice urgent in its demand. That blow must have knocked out her mike so they couldn't hear anything she had said. She spotted another problem. There was a large limb coming at her very fast and she couldn't move out of the way.

"This is going to hurt." She closed her eyes and hoped she would survive the blow.

TWELVE

"Somebody talk to me." Storm watched the data stream onto the screen. It didn't explain what caused the bike to explode or the silence from Heather they were now dealing with. Her life signs were still on the screen, but nothing else. "What's happening out there?"

Silence filled the command center when the data stream suddenly stopped. No life signs from her, no data at all.

"I want answers. Now!"

"Sir, we're still trying to get the information for you. All we know is that her bike exploded, and she turned her suit up to maximum."

"I saw that part." He growled at the man who spoke. "I want to know why. Her bike was supposed to break down, not explode in mid-air. Who loaded her bike? Why didn't she have weapons? And why don't I see any medical information coming up on the screen?"

"Seconds before everything went out, she took a blow somewhere in the midsection." The doctor moved data from one screen to the main one Storm was looking at. "It took out the medical reader. That's why we have no readings."

"What about the backup? That damn helmet should be giving us something."

"Your family doctor hasn't been able to use a backup on her, sir. She keeps killing conventional power sources," the doctor said. "But the blow she took wasn't life-threatening."

"And the helmet?"

"Also took a blow. We stopped getting that data about a minute before. It's why we aren't getting any communication from her."

"Send the team back to where we got the last set of readings. Find her and bring her home."

Heather opened her eyes and found her body filled with pain. "That hurt." She moved her fingers slowly to touch the armor settings in her wrist and brought it down so she could move. Her ribs hurt like hell. Probably broke at least two of them from the pain she felt. She found her right arm hard to move as well from the first blow.

She reached behind her and found the suit intact. That was good. Everything else seemed to be in working order. Standing, she found simple movements excruciating and set the medical setting on her suit to help take the pressure off her body. It tightened around her ribs, which made her lose her breath for a moment before she was able to adjust. It also immobilized her shoulder so she wouldn't do any extra damage to it until she could be examined.

Storm had to be going crazy. All of her readings had stopped flashing inside her helmet when she hit the branch, so she knew they had no idea what happened to her. Her medical reader was gone too. She had no idea what happened to it.

Time to get to work. She checked the perimeter for traps and parts of her bike. Somewhere on it should be a beacon and a med kit. If she could find the right part. Then she'd be able to assess the damage she did, maybe repair enough to take some of the pain away.

A sound to her left stopped her in her tracks. Since she hadn't taken her helmet off yet, she put the uniform in camouflage mode and moved into some low-hanging foliage. Not knowing who she could trust in this exercise had her trusting no one.

One of the other soldiers stepped into the perimeter. Part of her wondered if this was also part of the mission. She not only had to make it to the safe house, but not get caught along the way. It would make perfect sense. So she remained hidden and allowed her stalker to get in front of her.

Whoever this was wasn't very good. He wasn't using any kind of stealth mode. What did he think would happen? She'd blithely go along with him capturing her?

Ten other cycles flew over her head, heading toward where the explosion happened. Everyone was looking for her. This just got a lot more complicated. Should she go back and let them know she was living proof the suit worked or finish the mission as expected? It took her seconds to make the decision.

Storm waited for their initial report. It seemed to take forever.

"Sir, whatever hit her bike totaled it. There are fragments everywhere." The images they were recording filled the screen.

"Any sign of Heather?" Shrapnel covered the ground. There was nothing left. How the hell did she survive that?

"Nothing. We have found prints that fit her height and mass. Oh, that medical device that she wore? Mangled like the bike. Must have gotten caught in something during the fall. Found it under a large branch that shows new damage. She probably hit it on the way down."

That went along with what the doctor said. She had taken a blow to the mid-section. Now she was out there and wounded and knowing her, she was going to finish the mission.

"Sir? Did you set up a tracker as well?" one of the men asked as they showed another set of footprints in the area.

"Yes."

"He's been here."

"He shouldn't have been." The soldier he assigned was one of Storm's closest friends and never went against orders. "He was told to wait near the site where the bike was to become disabled. This is too far back."

"Could he have seen the accident and gone to help her? Because there is definitely another set of footprints here."

Storm turned to one of the communication officers. "Did the tracker alert us to the explosion?'

"No, sir. He's been silent, as you requested."

"Contact him."

The communications officer did as commanded. "Any sign of the lieutenant?"

"No, sir, but I was told to give her up to an hour to pass by here in case the bike broke down a little early. As per your orders."

Fridon was right, that was what he had told him. "Any unusual activity?"

"Only the cycles going overhead twice. Wasn't aware they were to double back during the mission."

And they weren't supposed to either, but that meant he didn't know about the explosion.

"Wait. I have movement." Silence filled the room for a moment. The next few words he heard sent a chill down Storm's spine. "Sir? Did you assign a second tracker? There is another guard, in uniform, and the height and mass is all wrong for your mate."

"No one else was assigned. Take out that target." He wanted to climb through the mike to stop the danger he now knew Heather was in. Danger she wasn't aware of.

He heard the release of a blaster.

"Sir." The voice came from the doctor. "He's been hit. I'm losing vital signs."

Everything was spiraling out of control, and he had no clue where she was.

She knew the safe house was to her right a little. The same direction the soldier was heading in. As long as he stayed in front, she should be okay.

Something caught her eye, and she spotted another soldier. He just seemed to be standing there as the first one took aim and fired. She watched in horror as the man's face shield shattered before she saw a spurt of blood shoot out from his face.

Heather inched her way over to the guard, keeping her eye on the shooter who had begun to move on. Everything just got a whole lot more dangerous. This guy was playing for keeps, and she had to be careful or a few damaged ribs could be the least of her worries.

The soldier just turned and continued on the path he had been on. That was strange.

Keeping a low profile caused the pain in her ribs to intensify, but she didn't want to be detected. She made it to the side of the young man hit and pressed her hand to his neck. There was a slight pulse. He was critical, but still alive. First, she activated the med seal on the uniform so he would go into a suspended animation until he could be worked on by a doctor.

The next thing she looked for was a working weapon. Since this guy wasn't acting normal, she wasn't sure what to think. If she didn't know better, she'd swear he was artificial intelligence.

She recognized the young man. He hadn't spoken to her but once or twice, but Storm said he was one of the hardest working men he knew. The weapon she found on him worked and would give her a little extra protection. She sure hoped the doctor would be able to help him.

Keeping the other soldier in her line of sight, she continued to the safe house. After following him for a while, she was sure it was an AI. It didn't move like a human. Kept in a straight line and when it made changes to its direction it was done like a computer. Hopefully, she would be able to over-take him before the safe house was compromised. She bided her time, watching and waiting for just the right moment.

The small house didn't look like much and she sure hoped the people inside knew about this little wrinkle. The soldier walked to the front door and smashed its way in. She could hear shouts and blasters going off, but the soldier hadn't stopped.

Heather closed her eyes for a second. She didn't know what type of weapon she had or if it would do any damage to the AI, but she had to do something. Hoping she would do more than just alert the thing to her presence, she got as close as she could before aiming her weapon and shooting. This had better work.

"Fridon should be fine." The doctor stood as the paramedics took the young man into the transport. "I'm not sure who turned on the suit, but they saved his life."

Storm nodded. This shouldn't have happened.

"Sir?" One of the communication officers stepped out of the ship for a moment. "She has made it to the safe house."

Relief washed over him.

"Let's go." Personally, he didn't care if everyone made it back onto the ship. He needed to make sure his mate was okay, but he had to give his people time. This was the first time he found his personal life taking over when he needed to keep it under control. The ship seemed to crawl to the house where she was. He knew it was moving fast and they would be there quickly, but he hated the waiting.

He was the first one off the ship. Trying to keep himself together, he walked into the farmhouse. All he wanted to do was to see with his own eyes that she was all right.

Heather stood near one of the walls as Storm and the doctor moved to her side. She held her right arm against her body and he could tell her shoulder wasn't sitting right, but everything else looked fine. As much as he wanted to touch her to be sure he wasn't dreaming, he had to remain professional. "Doctor."

The doctor nodded and pulled out his equipment as he crossed in front of Storm to run a diagnostic on Heather. "Three bruised ribs and two broken ones. You have also dislocated your shoulder." He opened her uniform and placed one piece of equipment on her ribs, then the second one on her collarbone. "Give this one about half an hour." He tapped a few places on the small piece on her shoulder. "That one will need about five hours." He programmed the one he set at her ribs.

"Just snap my shoulder back into place and I'll be fine." She tried to move her arm and grimaced at the pain.

The doctor placed a hand on her arm when she tried to lift it above her head. "Give it a moment and you should feel relief."

The device made a strange whir before there was a loud

snap. Heather found she could use her shoulder without as much pain. "Thank you."

"Both devices will heal all the tissue so you won't have any tenderness once we remove them." He checked the information his system picked up. "Once the one on your shoulder is done you will be able to have full movement, but until then, please don't push it. I'm also giving you a sedative to help with the healing."

She nodded. Heather hadn't really acknowledged Storm standing in the room. She knew if she did, a part of her would want to run into his arms and cry her relief. She had a point to prove to all these people, and there was no way she was going to ruin it by following her instinct right now.

Next, she spoke to two of the officers that came in with him. "I have a present for you." She pointed to the beheaded AI. "I don't know where it came from, but I sure would like to know if you people are responsible for him."

"Not ours," one of the officers responded. "But we will check it out."

She nodded again. Once she was sure she had done her duty, she walked right at Storm. She kept her body ramrod straight, wrapping her professionalism around her like a blanket. "Why did you make the bike explode?"

"We didn't." As unprofessional as it was, he couldn't stop his hand from touching her cheek. He needed to be sure it was really her. "It was sabotaged."

"And the creepy AI?" She stepped back from him. Her eyes begged him to treat her like a professional right now, not his mate.

"Like they said, not ours." He held himself in check. As much as he wanted to pull her into his embrace, he had to be mindful of her injuries and the injury he could cause to her ego if he followed his instincts. "I did plan on making your bike go down, but I would never put a soldier's life in danger like that. It was supposed to just stop working and coast to the ground."

"And Fridon? The young man I found?" She found the world around her started to spin. Her knees grew weak, and she knew they were about to buckle. The sedative started to work.

"He's going to be fine, thanks to you."

"Glad to hear it," she said it softly. Everything went fuzzy and her body went limp.

He moved fast, grabbing her before she fell to the floor. He nodded to the doctor, who got two of his staff to help get her to the ship. He still had a few questions to ask. He had noticed the splintered door. "Did the system not stop that thing before it could enter?"

"No sir. Must have had a jamming device. Your student had it all in hand, though. She somehow had gotten a blaster and tried to use it. The stun setting neutralized it long enough for her to kick the head off to stop it from doing any more damage." He handed him a small stick. "As a precaution, she pulled the memory out of it so if it had a failsafe it wouldn't remember its program."

Storm took the stick. Once he was sure everything was secure, he headed to the ship and had it head back to base. He checked on Heather and found her resting comfortably. He started barking orders to get everything secured before they landed.

He watched as each of the team went to check on Fridon and Heather.

The doctor approached him just before landing. "I'd like to keep her for observation."

"No."

"Sir."

"Doctor, someone is trying to kill her and your medical area isn't secure enough. I'm going to do my best to keep her safe while she heals. Download all your data to my family doctor and he will care for her."

"Yes, sir." The doctor didn't seem happy, but he didn't argue with Storm anymore.

Storm had the men secure the transport while he went to help his mate. He knelt down by the bed. "Ready to go?"

Her eyes opened as she gave him a lopsided smile. "Yes."

He wanted to pick her up in his arms but knew she would stop him. She would want to walk on her own. He'd be the same way. He offered her his hand.

"You understand." She took his hand and got to her feet. She was a bit unsteady, but grateful he wasn't going to humiliate her in front of everyone.

"I have been in your shoes before and know how hard you worked to gain the respect of these people. Something as simple as my carrying you would destroy all that work in seconds. I know they would never question me, but they would question and wonder if you got special treatment because of who you are. You are a soldier and still in uniform." He made sure she could move on her own before backing off. "However, one wobble and your feet are off the ground. I don't take anyone's health lightly."

"Agreed." She took a few steps away from the bed. "What was in that sedative? I feel a little rubbery."

"You want the whole list?" He offered her his hand, which she shook off.

"I need to prove I can do this on my own. I don't want people questioning my ability on another mission."

"What makes you think there will be another mission for you?" He helped her down the gangplank when she needed it and onto the tarmac. "I have never been so scared."

"You? Imagine how I felt." She stopped moving when she saw the rest of the team standing there waiting for the transport. The doctor accompanied Fridon out of the ship. The team stood at attention on either side of the walkway, giving him a salute as the doctor moved his bed through. She waited until they had passed through and expected them to break up, but they didn't.

"Your turn, Lieutenant."

"Me? Why?"

"You saved his life today. That earns you a place of honor."

"I did nothing out of the ordinary."

"It could have been any one of them and you would have done the same thing." He urged her forward. "Go."

She didn't want all this attention. She had been fighting back the tears threatening to spill since she knew she was safe. This would just force the waterworks to start. Holding her head high, she walked between them, trying her damndest to not make eye contact with anyone. That would be all it would take.

There, at the end of the lineup, was Fridon. She felt the first tear fall.

Storm called everyone to attention as he dismissed them.

Once she saluted Storm for being relieved of duty, she walked up to the bed Fridon lay in and took his hand. "I am so sorry."

"This isn't your fault." He squeezed her hand. "If you hadn't been there, I wouldn't be here."

"That damn thing was after me." She wiped one eye. After a few more tears slipped down her cheek, she was able to regain control of her emotions. "But saw you as a threat. None of this would have happened if I hadn't gone on that mission."

"You got the intruder, didn't you?"

"He wasn't going to hurt anyone else." The satisfaction she felt in ripping off the head was something she had never felt before.

"And more than likely, it would have come after you sooner or later."

"Probably, and I see where you're going with this. Better to have it happen on a mission instead of in the middle of the city. Doesn't make me feel any better."

"Imagine how I feel." Storm's voice came from behind her. "This shouldn't have happened at all."

"Who is after your mate, sir?"

"We don't know." Storm didn't say anything else. He looked at her, concern etched on his face.

"Anyone heard anything?" She knew he didn't want to get anyone involved until he knew who he could trust, but she did trust these people. They were her team and had put their life on the line to save hers.

"Heather." That was all he said.

"Eyes and ears, sir. We don't have that. These people walk amongst the rest of the students and soldiers. They would hear something a lot faster than you or I would." She hoped he wouldn't get upset by her cornering him like this. "Let them in. We need their help."

She got the glare she had only seen aimed at other people, and she waited for the anger to follow.

"You do realize the more people involved the more can get hurt." His voice was flat.

"Sir, they don't have to be involved to get hurt. Today's mission proved that." She made sure she kept this as professional as possible. If she made it personal and he was made to look weak, he might never forgive her.

"If we involve your team, you will follow my rules, not some hair-brained scheme someone might come up with." He looked at every one of them. "We will do this by the book."

"Of course." She might regret that later, but she knew he only had her best interests at heart. "All I ask is you don't pull me from the team to protect me."

He watched her, silent. As the silence stretched she

wasn't sure if she could stand the wait. "Agreed." The single word sent joy through her heart.

"Thank you, sir."

"We will meet in the morning. I'll send coordinates to each of you later." He grabbed Heather by the hand and started walking.

He didn't say a word, but she could feel his anger. She was surprised he didn't pick her up and throw her over his shoulder when she stood up to him like that. Then again, he was probably trying to be mindful of her ribs as they still had a few hours to go before they would be completely healed.

"Storm. Please." She found it hard to breathe as she tried to keep up with his long gate.

He stopped and turned his angry glare on her before he scooped her up and carried her the rest of the way. She knew better than to fight him. What she worried about now was what would happen once they were alone.

The moment they passed through the main doors of the palace, he deposited her on the ground, wrapped his arms around her and pressed his lips to hers. She felt his hunger in the gentle sweep of his tongue through her mouth. The way it searched her mouth for hers, begging it to dance with his. Her blood started to move faster. Her heart beat at a quicker tempo. Time seemed to stop as they kissed. Storm continued the kiss for a long time, and she found herself breathing hard when it ended. She wanted more.

"My heart."

She was waiting for the anger and frustration to come out, but it was all he said before he realized other people were standing around, including the family doctor and his mother. As she went off with the doctor she heard Storm shout at his mother. "I hope the council is happy about that little leak. They could have gotten her killed."

That wasn't a conversation she wanted to hear more of, so she was glad to be heading into another area.

"I heard you broke the medical scanner."

"Not on purpose, Doctor." She sat on the table he pointed to. "I just had a little mishap."

"So I see. A dislocated shoulder, two broken ribs and three bruised ones isn't little to me." He eased her uniform to one side so he could check the device on her ribs. "What happened?"

"Got the raw end of a fall." She tried to make light of it.

"You and your mate will be the end of me yet. The scrapes he used to get into." The doctor shook his head. "Your shoulder is repaired, but the ribs are going to take a little longer. I'd like you to stay here tonight. Make sure nothing goes wrong."

"What can go wrong with a few broken ribs? I've done worse and never had to spend the night in the medcenter."

"You fell how many feet?" He resealed her suit. "There is no evidence of a concussion, but I have had stranger things happen over the years. I have learned to not always trust my equipment."

"Storm won't be happy."

"He normally isn't too happy with me, so I'm not going to be too upset about it." He gestured to a small room toward the back of the area. "You'll be comfortable back there and your mate can join you. As long as he behaves."

"Who behaves?" asked Storm.

She didn't hear him come into the room. Lately, she had been sensing his presence long before she actually saw him, but not this time. Must have been the medication.

"You. She is to stay here to rest. Let her body heal."

"And what makes you think I won't let that happen?" He tried to put on an innocent act, but she saw right through it.

"I am your doctor."

"As long as she is one hundred percent healed. I have plans for her." At least his humor was back. Yelling at his mother must have done some good for him.

"Good. Then you'll behave yourself." He looked at Heather. "You know where to go. Bring him with you or he'll be in my hair all night long."

She grinned as she took Storm's hand. "I do believe your wonderful charm doesn't work on the doctor."

"He's known me too long. He brought me into this world."

"That explains so much." She climbed into the bed. "It also explains why he gave us such a small bed. There is no room for you."

"There is if I want to be your mattress." He winked at her. "But the bed would then pick up both our readings and drive him crazy."

"Something I think you'd enjoy doing." She shifted and sucked in her breath, then she felt a slight pain in her side. Storm just about jumped on her with worry. She had to touch his arm to stop him. "Shouldn't have done that."

He touched her face. "You okay?"

"Fine." She pressed her check into his hand. "It doesn't hurt that bad. Just need to move the right way."

The doctor popped his head into the room. "Rest or I'll separate you two."

"Yes, Doctor." She lay down on the bed and closed her eyes. "So, did you have a good talk with your mom?"

"Yes, why?"

"Your whole attitude changed since we got home." She yawned and snuggled against the pillows. "I thought you were angry at me earlier."

"Why would you think that?"

"You...gave me...that look." And she nodded off.

Storm moved the moment she drifted off. "There is no reason for you to keep her."

"Her readings are changing again." He pulled up the image of her DNA strand. "And I'm not quite sure how to read it anymore."

"What do you mean?" Storm stared at the screen.

"The information is no longer loading for me. The program might be deciphering the information, but I'm not getting any new data. It's like it doesn't want me to know what she is. Something is blocking me from being able to finish the strand." He turned the screen off. "Have you noticed anything out of the ordinary between the two of you?"

"Like what?"

"I don't know." The doctor scratched his head. "Something you don't have with anyone else. I know you've been trained to keep everything to yourselves for her protection, but I have been here with you all your life. I need you to trust I have both of your best interests at heart."

Storm remained silent. What could he tell the doctor? Then Storm suddenly looked at the room she slept in. He felt her distress. Ignoring the doctor, he hurried into the room.

Heather was caught in a dream. He watched as she moved in the bed, like she had her hands tied. She screamed his name and shot up into a sitting position. He was beside her, pulling her into his arms in seconds.

He held her shaking form, trying to calm her down. "Heather, it's okay. You're safe."

"Storm?" Her hands touched his face. "Oh, thank God. It was horrible. It was a trap. He used me to lure you in and, and he killed you."

"It was only a dream."

She was panicky as she continued. "It seemed so real. The whole place was dark, like I was in a cave or something. He had me secured to a big metal bed. He wanted something from me, but he never told me what it was. His first goal was to make sure you wouldn't be able to stop him. He didn't want any interference and he knew you would be coming to save me."

"Who?"

"I don't know." She looked up at him with a tear-streaked face. "I never saw his face. But he knew things about us." She grabbed his arms to make him look at her. "About me."

She wasn't acting like it was a dream. She was too lucid. Her fear real. "Tell me what you saw and heard."

"I was strapped to a table. My hands tied above my head." She paused as she tried to maintain control. More tears streamed down her face.

Storm placed his hand on her heart. He could feel the fast, erratic pace. "Relax. I'm here with you now."

She nodded, gulping for air. "I have never been so frightened. I was in an old building. There were cobwebs and skittering sounds like it housed animals that had suddenly been disturbed. Lights hung over the bed so I couldn't see as well as I wished. There was someone else, but I couldn't see who it was."

"He hated you so much, Storm, you can't go after him." She grabbed his shirt. "Promise me you won't let him get the upper hand."

"You are my heart and I will never do anything that would put you in danger." That seemed to mollify her. She leaned into him, wanting to hear his heart beat steadily as she shook off the last of the dream.

The doctor signaled to him and Storm tried to leave Heather's side for a moment, but she wouldn't have anything to do with it. He had to wait for her to relax enough to doze off again so he could find out what the doctor wanted.

"She was a bit frantic after that dream."

"The dream seemed real to her." Storm wasn't sure what he was getting at.

"Are you sure it was a dream?" The doctor held up his hand before Storm could argue with him. "Let me tell you what I noticed this evening. You were aware that she was caught in something that frightened her long before she made a sound. You were there at her side before she woke up. Then she described something that was a lot more detailed than most dreams. I only wish to ask you to try something. I don't care if you tell me or not, but if you two are noticing clairvoyance developing between you, develop it as much as you can. Test it, see what grows from it. It could help you later."

The doctor turned around and walked away then. His words made Storm wonder what he knew.

THIRTEEN

Heather sat up quickly when she realized she wasn't in her room with Storm. Then it came back. She touched her ribs to find them completely healed. Her shoulder moved with ease. Looking to her left, she found Storm with his eyes closed. He looked so uncomfortable in the chair.

Her heart skipped a beat at how he reacted to her dream last night. Even though he didn't believe she had seen the future he knew whatever she had experienced affected her and wanted to help her calm down. Right now, he guarded her against whatever he could stop.

Too bad it wasn't the dreams.

He didn't know she had dreams like last night before. That they were warnings to protect her. Each one she had saved her life somehow, although she couldn't say that for everyone involved. Many times, when the dream started to unveil in real time someone ended up dying in her place, but that was at the beginning when she didn't really know how to interpret them. Now she did. But that was the first time she had ever feared for someone else's life like that. Normally, it was only about her.

She needed to get back to their room and meditate, as more of the dream would come to her when she relaxed and opened her mind.

"I see you're awake." Storm stretched in the chair and sat up.

"Yes." She swung her legs off the bed and stood. "Did you sleep well?"

"No, but I'm not the one to worry about." He stood. "Are you okay?"

"Yes." She smiled up at him as his hand touched her face. "But we do need to talk about the dream."

She saw a fleeting look of concern cross his face.

"I agree, but we have an appointment." He gave the doctor a smile as he ushered her out the door.

"If you don't mind, Storm, I'd like to make sure everything is healed before you take off with her." He ran a quick scan and nodded. He unsealed her suit and removed the small metal device from her ribs. "You are fine now but let me know if you have any trouble."

Heather nodded. Storm took her arm again and practically dragged her out the door.

"You don't trust anyone, do you?"

"They knew too much about the mission, Heather." He kept his voice slow so only she could hear him. "They knew which bike you'd be riding when we were taking off, our course and destination. Information I didn't give one person. Was it out there to be learned if you knew who to go to, probably, but they had to work to get that information and that worries me."

"Because they did?'

"Exactly." He contacted everyone to meet back at the transport. "You're going to be stuck in that uniform a little longer."

"I know." She brushed her hands against the material. "Very durable outfit."

"They've been known to stand up against a lot of fire-power, but I don't want you to test it."

"Promise." She followed him as fast as she could, but found his long legs kept widening the distance between them. He would notice from time to time and stop to give her a chance to catch up.

"Want me to carry you?"

"No." She tried to look indignant but knew the smile on her face belied any frown she might have tried to muster. "Look, I might not be as tall as you people are, but I can keep up. Right now, you are just pushing too hard."

He took her elbow and slowed his pace enough so she could keep up without doing a mad dash.

"You're afraid." She said it so matter-of-factly.

"What?" He looked around to make sure no one heard her. "I fear for your life, my heart. They've tried to kill you now."

"But what if that wasn't the goal?"

"Your dream?" He looked down at her.

"Yes. I have impressions of emotions, bits and pieces of conversations that are running together. I need to sit down and analyze it better. See if I can make some sense of it all." The transport loomed in front of them. "Didn't realize that thing was so big."

"Holds a full battalion for our missions, plus the backup crews running communications and weapons." He banged on the hull. "This is my home away from home."

The floor lowered so they could walk up the gangplank into the belly of the ship. He led her to a large oblong table. "I don't know how much time you need, but I'll try to leave you alone so you can meditate."

She nodded and sat in the first chair to her right. Clearing her mind, she brought up the strongest emotion she felt when she woke from it. Her fear for Storm's life. She wasn't sure why the man in the dream hated Storm so much.

Had he hinted to it? Said something she needed to isolate to find?

The voice was distorted so she couldn't recognize it, but she was sure it was male. It was in the way he talked to her about her and her relationship with Storm. He was jealous of their relationship. But why? She never had a real relationship before this. Never had anyone tell her that someone was interested in her for anything other than sex. So she didn't understand what he would be so jealous of. He had her at that time, and Storm didn't. It didn't make sense.

She could see a woman wanting to do this, but a woman wouldn't keep her alive. Get rid of the competition.

Voices came from the background, letting her know some of the team had started to arrive. Too bad. She felt she was getting somewhere.

She smiled as they came and joined her at the table. They were concerned for her, hoping she was feeling better.

Once everyone had arrived, Storm sat next to her. The fact that one chair next to her had remained empty hadn't gone unnoticed.

"We're going back to the site." Storm brought up a three-dimensional image of the forest area. "The data collected yesterday has been analyzed and loaded into the handhelds in front of each of you."

"You think we missed something?"

"I'm hoping." Storm crossed his arms. "You were very thorough in your search, but we didn't have Heather's eyewitness report to help us pinpoint more details that could have been overlooked."

She wasn't sure what she could add to their findings. Everything happened so fast.

The ship landed in the same clearing and the bikes, minus Heather's, were brought out. "Now, did anyone pay attention to the lineup?"

"Not really."

"Who went to what bike? And in what order?"

They all walked to the bike they used. Storm made notes on his handheld before walking to the new bike where Heather's would have sat. "We ride together."

He climbed on first, then slid back so she could climb in front.

"You know, it would have been easier if you let me get on first." She had to swing her legs over the front of the machine to get seated properly. Once she nestled against him, Storm fired it up. They put on their helmets and set the seals.

"I know, but this way I can get a little extra contact since I haven't been able to touch you in almost twenty-four hours."

"Is this going to be another up against the door because you couldn't wait times?" She said it like it was a common occurrence.

"I have only done that to you once." He wrapped his arm around her as the bike took off. "And if you keep rubbing that derriere against me like that it might."

"You're the one who had me move up front so you get to suffer."

"Um, sir. Your mike is open."

He laughed as Heather's head dropped. It figured everyone heard that.

"Take us to where the drones started." The laughter still laced his voice.

She took control of the bike and headed in the direction she had gone before. Looking at the readings, she got the bike to follow the exact flight she programmed into it the day before. "The drones started here." She pressed the popup screen to start a clock.

"That goes with the ones we had set up." He touched the screen a few times as well, and new information joined the clock she had started. It showed how many drones were released, the intervals of each release, and the location they came from. "The goal was to outrun them."

"Right. There were three behind me." She waited until she passed a certain spot. A lot of it was all visual for her. The information had been streaming in her helmet, but she hadn't really focused on the data. She touched the screen again, starting a second clock and showing the location of where the other drones had come from. "Then I started noticing them coming from in front of me to the left."

"That's about the time your bike started to show signs of acting up. Did you follow your coordinates all the way?"

"Yes. I had to adjust altitude a little to avoid the second set of drones, which might have shown up as erratic behavior, but I stuck to the path."

Storm steered the bike to where the trajectory put the weapons at. He turned off the bike and walked around. "Did you see or hear anything out of the ordinary?"

"Besides missiles coming at me?" She couldn't keep the sarcasm out of her voice. "No. Everyone had already moved beyond my line of sight and I was trying to catch up."

"How did that happen?" He gave her a serious look that showed his displeasure at that bit of information.

"No one knew. I didn't even notice the bike wasn't working at its full capacity until the missiles started coming at me and I couldn't dodge them the way I should have. Until now, I thought it had something to do with your plan to down the bike later." She pulled her helmet off. "Oh, and I had never flown one, so was checking everything out before I took off. That put me a little behind everyone."

"When you checked the bike, did you notice anything out of the ordinary?"

"No." But did she? She needed a few moments to think.

Everyone else landed in the same area.

"You know what to look for." Storm pulled his helmet off as well and walked around the perimeter. She wasn't sure what he was looking for.

Heather worked back through when she approached the

bike. There was no one around the bike which should have caught her attention. Normally, there was a technician standing by. She went through the checkpoints she had been given and everything was in the proper perimeter but if she had paid attention, she would have noticed all the items she was to check were on the low end of the spectrum. Heather let Storm know what she remembered.

Storm made notes in his handheld. "So the shooter waited until you were by yourself. He could have set it up so you were the last bike to come through here." He called three of the men forward. "I want the three of you to go back to the landing site. One of you is to set your bike to these parameters, and I want you to come this way. Push the bikes just like you did during the mission. I'll signal you when I want you to land."

They nodded and took off. Within minutes, they were flying overhead, not much of a difference in their speed.

"Come on back," he said in his mike. Storm put more info into his system before looking at her. "The bike with your settings was the bike in the middle, so those readings have nothing to do with the speed of your bike. How would he know you would be last?"

"Isn't that the way you had it set up?" asked Heather.

"It wouldn't have mattered." Storm shook his head. "The bikes were identical, the suits with the helmet on makes everyone look the same. How would he know who was who? Unless someone in camp alerted the shooter to your location."

"Then why didn't they finish the job? They could have sent another one of those drones while I was falling, and that would have been it." The look on his face was something she had never seen before. Her words caused a strong emotion she could feel emanating from him. Having everyone around stopped him from grabbing her and showing her how happy he was to know she was alive. She wanted to tell him it was okay. She was here and his and nothing was going to change that.

He stood there for a moment before he ignored everyone and reached for her. His lips found hers, drinking in the soft feel of her mouth. His tongue delved into the recesses of her mouth, caressing hers. He held her so close. Afraid if he let go she'd fade from sight.

No one said a thing. Work was being done around them. Both oblivious to anything else.

He finally broke the kiss. With a gentle caress of her face, he regained his composure and took control of the mission once again.

"There isn't much here, sir. Footprints, pad marks from the mechanism that housed the weapons. That's about all."

Storm nodded. Heather found he kept her in his sight the whole time. Her one comment knocked him for a loop. He stepped up to her. "What happened next?"

"I went around a tree." She used the three-dimensional display on her hand set to show which one she was talking about. "I saw the missile coming at me and knew it was going to make my life miserable. I turned my suit up to max and launched myself off the back of the bike."

"And you landed where?"

She headed back to where she thought the bike blew up. It didn't take long before she found the branch she hit on her way down. She gave it a little kick. "That thing hurt."

"What probably hurt the most was that medical remote. You must have landed on that when you hit the branch. Shattered it to pieces." Storm held up the remnants of the device.

"You're kidding me. I didn't realize it had been damaged. I thought the chain had been broken and I just lost it." She rubbed her newly healed side. "That would explain the broken ribs, though."

"So what happened next?"

"I wanted to look for the medpack in the bike, but then I

heard a noise. I figured you would send someone after me to try to keep me from reaching the safe house, so I put the suit in camo and hid. The guy walked right past me. I thought he was a horrible soldier since he didn't try to disguise himself. He just kept walking." She looked in the direction he had headed in. "I followed him, figuring if he was in front of me, then he wouldn't be able to capture me."

"That made sense."

"I moved in this direction. Once I cleared the wooded area I slowed down but still kept the soldier in view." She swallowed as she chose her next words. "I saw Fridon off to the left of me. He just stood there. I'm not sure what set that AI off so he knew Fridon was there, but I was too far away. I watched his face shield shatter." She walked to the spot where she found him. "I got to him as quick as I could without being detected and turned on his medic seal. I wasn't sure how well it would work with his helmet destroyed, but I had to try."

She paused for a moment.

Storm put a hand on her shoulder. "You okay?"

"There was so much blood. It frightened me. It made me realize that whoever was willing to shoot a secondary person was no one to play with." She shook her head. "Anyway, the hostile turned and started walking again."

"You saved his life, that's what you need to remember."

"I know, but at this stage I knew I wasn't dealing with a simple exercise. This was for real. I took Fridon's weapon, hoping it would do more than just anger the hostile once I caught up to him." She smoothed her hands against her suit. "I also knew this thing wasn't human at this point."

"Why?"

"Because a trained assassin would have made sure Fridon was dead. Once the target was out of the way, the AI continued to move to his destination. He removed the threat according to his program and continued to move to his objective." She kept her eyes on the ground because she knew her next words would upset him just like the last time. "And if their goal was to kidnap me, the AI only had one set of commands. A real person would have tried to capture me right after the bike blew up when I could have been most vulnerable, or at this moment. Instead of shooting Fridon the way he did, he could have captured him and lured me in."

"But he didn't."

"Exactly." She took his hand in hers and started down the path she followed. She pointed as she talked. "It walked in a straight line instead of sticking to this path. Lots of little things that made me realize what I was dealing with."

"Let's get back to the bike." He kept a hold of her hand, this time letting her climb onto the bike before he slid in behind her. Once they secured their helmets, they flew to the safe house, followed by everyone else.

The door had been repaired. In fact, there was no sign of what happened there the day before. Heather opened her visor to look around.

"I watched it smash through the door and knew whoever might be in here could be in danger, and considering it was close quarters I felt this was my best chance to take it out." She climbed the stairs and opened the door. The scene replayed in her head. Several had been wounded, but they had reacted pretty quickly when the AI had smashed through the door. "It had gotten to here before I was able to put the blaster against its head. I put that on the highest setting it had and hoped for the best. It short-circuited the AI long enough for me to take its head off and remove the memory chip."

"That must have been glorious to see," said one of the other men.

"Yeah, you're going to have to teach us that technique."

"All right. Head back to the transport." Storm held her back for a few moments, waiting for the rest of them to take off. He touched her face with tenderness. "The moment things went wrong I feared for your life. You are my heart."

"And you are mine, but it doesn't matter where I am. Whoever is doing this is determined to get their hands on me. That first night at the embassy, your apartment, this exercise." She placed her hand on his heart, the same gesture he had been doing lately. "You can try to protect me but keeping me in a bubble isn't going to fix the problem and you know I won't allow you to lock me away like that."

"Even if I promise to keep you so busy with so much inti-macy you won't have time to complain?" He placed his hand over her heart as well.

"Um, sir? The mike is still on."

This time Heather laughed.

Heather sat on the bed in their darkened room. Storm had been called to his mother's chambers, which gave her some time to meditate. She could have jumped into the shower the moment they returned, but she needed to focus on the dream while it was still fresh in her mind.

This time, she had the handheld so she could try to recreate what she saw. The ceiling was the first thing she remembered. The way the shadows kept everything dark and hard to see. One big lamp hung over her head. It reminded her of the old films from the twentieth century, an old seedy warehouse where no one should be. The image she created reflected that too.

Next, she looked to her right. There were a row of old cabinets or maybe lockers. They were dark, a metal grey or dark brown? They were a little harder to see because of the lighting. To her left was a blank wall. It had been white at one time, but over the years it had faded to a dull grey. Had anyone been in the room with her? She didn't remember anyone.

The bed she was strapped to was made of metal. A leather band went across her stomach and her hands were secured above her head. Her feet had to have been secured too, but she didn't remember that. She had tried to sit up in the dream, which was how she knew her movements had been restricted.

The voice she heard was distorted. Strange. If she didn't know who the man was, why did he distort his voice? Was it someone she knew? But she knew so few people here on Vespia, how could it be one of them? Maybe someone from Earth? The only people she knew were through her work. Why would they be after her?

The conversation with the strange voice floated in and out. She had said something about Storm coming to rescue her and he laughed, letting her know of the trap he had set. So what was the trap? She couldn't remember. All she knew was it frightened her and it was palpable. It had to have been one that would work on him. Some sort of ambush.

Deep in thought, she didn't focus on who walked into the room, she was just aware someone was there. A hand touched her shoulder, which she grabbed, twisted and forced away from her. When she focused back on her surrounding, she found she had Storm down on one knee in another one of her joint locks. She released him immediately with a sheepish grin. "Oh, sorry. Guess I should have warned you not to do that when I'm meditating. I've caused a few injuries in the past."

"You are full of surprises, aren't you?" He rubbed his hand. "You want to try that one again now that you're focused?"

"Why? You don't think I could do it again?" Was he crazy enough to challenge her? She knew her capabilities. They had been tested time and time again.

"I have a few tricks I have learned over the years." He gave her that if *I win I get to have my way with you* smile. The one that always melted her to the core.

"If you're going to cheat." She stood up and found herself wrapped in a hold that kept her immobile. He had moved so fast she didn't have time to react. With her front pressed to his, she couldn't see a reason to complain.

"I never cheat." He nibbled on her ear. She could feel his smile as he spoke against her throat. "Manipulate things, maybe, but never cheat."

"Storm." She pulled back to get him to look at her. Instead, he pressed his lips against hers, his tongue swept into her mouth, swirling with hers, touching her deep inside. Once he broke the kiss, he continued to plant soft little kisses along her jaw and neck.

Part of her wanted to melt into the sensations he was drawing from her, but she knew everything he was doing was a calculated move. He wanted to throw her focus off.

That wasn't going to happen.

Her feet didn't touch the ground or she would have tried stomping on his. Going boneless wouldn't work. She was pretty much there, anyway.

"Thought you were going to try to get out of this." He said it so nonchalantly, his lips still working on her neck. He knew she hadn't figured out how yet. In three strides, he had her at their bed.

The bed she could use. Gaining purchase on the mattress, she pulled her weight backward, throwing him a little off balance. That was all she needed. He had to adjust his hold on her to keep them from falling onto the bed, and she used that to slide through his arms and drop to the floor. She didn't get very far as his hand closed on a leg before she could pull it out of the way. Heather wasn't sure if she really wanted to, but she did prove she could get away from him if she wanted to.

He pulled her toward him until he could wrap his arms around her and pull her back against him. "You can be quite slippery, can't you?"

"And you can be devious, so I think we're even." This time, she relaxed in his arms.

"So I guess the question I should ask is what should I do to make you understand that you'll never get away from me." He started to work on her uniform, releasing the seams slowly. "Make you beg for it?"

"You can't go that long without needing me. I think I'd win that one." His fingers skimmed across her skin, sending little frissons of desire spiraling through her. "And what makes you think I want to get away from you?"

"Good answer."

"I do have a request, though."

"And what is that?" Her uniform opened and gave him complete access to her.

"Shower? Please? I need to feel clean after all of that." A soft sigh escaped her as his hands slid across her body.

"The suit did that for you. You're probably cleaner now than when you put it on."

"True, but there is something about water falling on the naked body." She felt his fingers slide into her folds. She leaned her head against his shoulder as sensations washed over her. "Remember the last time we were in water?"

That was all she needed to say. He moved them to the bathroom. A large stone area stood in one corner. It looked more like a waterfall garden than a shower. "You asking for a real running water shower had my mother baffled."

He put her down so he could release the last few seals on her uniform.

"If she knew it was just another place for you to mark your territory, she might have said no." She worked on his, being just as quick as he had been with her uniform.

Heather set the temperature and climbed in. Tilting her

face up, she reveled in the feel of the water washing away the emotions of the day. The fear and the anger ran down with the water and washed out through the drain. She wished she could do the same with the dream, but ignoring it didn't work, that was another tactic she had tried that failed miserably.

After soaping and rinsing her hair, she looked up at Storm, who watched but hadn't climbed into the small space.

"Are you okay?"

"I could have lost you." He had a tight grip on the shower frame.

"But you didn't." She stepped up to where he stood and placed her hand on his heart. "I know you don't believe me, but every time I have been in any mortal danger, I've had those dreams to warn me. I was perfectly safe."

"And so you trust them?" He placed his hand on her heart. "Aren't you afraid that the dream could be wrong?"

"It never has been in the past. Questioning it would just make me fear everything. Believe me, if I have one before a mission, I will tell you. As you saw, they're kind of hard to hide." She took his hand and gave it a tug. "Come in with me. Let's forget about everything but each other."

He allowed her to pull him into the water, but she could still see his worry over her safety. She took some soap and lathered her hands, then slowly she spread the soap across his chest, fingers teasing his nipples, making them hard with a simple brush of her nails. She loved the feel of his hard muscles under her palms. A little more soap and she worked on his waist and his hips before she wrapped her lathered hand around his length, gaining a little shudder out of him.

Storm came alive then. His hands caressed her as he lifted her, centered her, and entered her in one movement. It took her breath away. His desire to keep her safe turned into a hunger she had never felt from him.

Swept up in the tumult of fear, anger and desire, he swept

her away with him. He pumped into her. In and out he moved, building her desire with his. She felt desire lick at her insides as he started to move faster. Her slick sheath hugged him as he slid in and out. Everything in her squeezed him, increasing the sensations they loved so much. Each time he drove into her, she could feel her orgasm getting closer. Her body begged for release and she could feel he was close, too. She tilted her hips, and that was all it took to send them plunging into their orgasms.

Everything exploded around her. She felt like she was freefalling through space. Then she felt his release, just as powerful, racing through his body, sending him soaring along with her. They flew together, their releases inter-twining and blending to a point where they couldn't tell which orgasm belong to them.

The only sound they could hear over the hiss of the hot water was their heavy breathing. Heather felt her heart beating hard in her chest.

Storm kissed the edge of her jawline. "What was that? I have never felt anything so powerful."

"You felt it too? I felt like I had two orgasms. Mine and yours, just like the last time." She closed her eyes and tilted her head as his lips continued to work their way down to her collarbone.

"I think we need to do that again just to compare."

"I may never want to get out of the shower if it happens again." She felt him pulse inside her, felt herself grip him tight, her body fitting him like a glove. The muscles surrounding him caused a delicious friction.

He pulled out and surged back in, and both of them groaned. She felt everything. His tension filling her, her muscles hugging him, how he stretched her, the way her body surrounded him each time he filled her. It took very little to send her off again.

Once she took off, she felt him tense before she was hit with another wave of pleasure. "Oh my."

"You thought I was demanding before, but you haven't seen anything if it's going to be like that every time." He pressed another kiss against her throat.

"How is that possible?"

"You questioning something so phenomenal? I want it again and again." He still stayed inside her, holding her against him.

"You think you could do that again?" She wasn't sure if her muscles could take another round. Feeling his as well as hers made the whole experience so much more intense.

"Sure would like to try." He held her close, the intimacy between them profound. "Oh my heart, you have changed my world."

"You've used that phrase before."

He eased her off him and allowed her feet to touch the tile in the shower. "You know how on Earth they like to use the phrase 'I love you'?"

"Sure. Heard it a lot between couples." She turned the water off and stepped out into the area where the dryers were.

"It doesn't translate into our language. We use phrases to show our appreciation to the person who is our mate, not an expression of an emotion. My heart is about as close as we get to I love you."

She opened a cabinet and pulled out a big, fluffy towel. "My heart is very close to my love."

He took the towel from her and started to dry her off. She reached for a second one and dried him off. Such a simple act had such a profound effect on them. Their feelings went way beyond the physical. They were one.

"I supposed it is. But I want you to know you are my heart. How you got there so fast I don't know, but I'm not complaining." He wrapped the soft towel around her, pulling her into his embrace at the same time.

She snuggled against him, happy and content. He needed to know about her recording the things she had seen in her dream, but she didn't want to break the moment they were sharing. She just hoped there were many more just like it.

FOURTEEN

Storm stared at the readouts to see if he could figure out anything new about the AI. Heather stretched beside him. Their limbs entwined. The feel of her soft skin against his brought him joy.

"That is going to drive you crazy, isn't it?" she said it softly, her voice still laced with sleep.

"Not as much as you and your luscious body will." He rolled over on top of her.

"I do believe I have created a monster." She smiled up at him.

The door sounded.

Storm dropped his head against hers. "That is the drawback of staying with my mother. They know we're here, so I can't just ignore them."

"You were the one who felt it was safer here." She stretched a second time. "Go answer it before they call the guards."

He placed a soft kiss on her forehead and got up. "Don't go anywhere."

She laughed. "Like you'd let me."

He slipped on a pair of pants and padded to the door.

Why he started doing that, he wasn't sure. Heather must have rubbed off on him. He opened the door to find Streya and his mate.

"We're sorry to disturb you, but we wish to speak to your mate."

"Of course." He opened the door wider to allow them entrance. Just as he turned to alert Heather, she came out of their room fully dressed. Somehow, she must have sensed they were coming. "For you."

She smiled at him and gave his face a brief touch as she passed him. She then focused that smile on their two visitors. "How may I help you?"

"We wish to speak to you about the treaty," said Streya. "Perhaps we could walk in the gardens?"

She nodded as she looked at Storm. As much has he wanted to keep her for his own plans, he knew she had been getting communiqués from Earth asking why the treaty hadn't been finished yet. She was doing a great job balancing both world's wants and needs, but it was taking its toll on her. This was something she needed to make her old world happy.

He gave her a quick kiss. "Hurry back."

"My planet will be very grateful for an update." She followed them out the door and outside. Heather hadn't seen the gardens before this and found them beautiful. The flowers were exotic to her, but she wasn't as familiar with the plant life of Vespia as she'd like to be.

"You have been very patient with us, unlike other citizens from your planet."

"They are very anxious to see this treaty done." She knew they hadn't understood why it was taking so long.

"And you aren't?"

"Please don't misunderstand. This will help our planet immensely, but I have learned that you move at your own pace. Pushing doesn't really help. I knew you would come to me when you were ready." She walked beside them. "My leaders haven't understood my silence, but they will be very happy once it is done."

"You seem to understand the Vespian way."

"I've had a good teacher." She smiled at them.

"Your mate." They looked to her left.

She nodded and looked as well. Storm stood nearby, watching as they walked.

"He seems very attentive," said Streya's mate.

"He is." She knew he feared someone would snatch her from him, so didn't want to let her out of his sight for a moment.

"You're happy with your mate, then."

"I am." He had been there for her from the beginning. Not many others would have done that. But she wasn't there to talk about her love life. "What can I tell my planet?"

"We will sign your treaty and give in to the concessions they have asked for, but there is something delicate we need to ask of your people."

"And what is that?" One more thing she would have to ask her planet to give into. They were tired of these requests.

"If you haven't noticed, we have very few children born to our new generations. We need an influx of fresh DNA to help build our progeny."

"But you want to be able to pick the donors." She stopped and crouched down so she could enjoy the aroma of one of the flowers. "Can I also assume you wish to only have tissue to implant?"

"Yes."

"I will make my people aware of your request, but I'm not sure how they will take it. Just like the Vespians, humans are very proud. Children are the future and very precious.

This will be a decision the individual person will have to make, not our government." She wasn't sure if anyone would want to go along with their request. Their desire to remain isolated from other planets wouldn't make it easy for anyone to want to help them.

"Do you miss your home?"

"Earth?" She hadn't really thought about it. "At times, but I spent most of my life away from the planet, so it's hard to say I'm homesick."

"Do you feel at home here on Vespia?"

She wasn't sure how to answer that. Storm was her anchor. Wherever he went, she would follow. "It is a beautiful planet. What little I have seen of it."

Streya's mate laughed. "Our males can be a little overbearing at times."

All she did was smile. Storm did a great job of dominating her, but she loved it. It made her feel safe, loved, cherished, and very satisfied.

"We wish to invite you and your mate to have a meal with us," said Streya. "We wish to get to know our future leader's mate."

"We would be honored." She hoped Storm would agree. He didn't like sharing her very much.

"Then we shall let you go to your mate. He seems to be losing his patience with us."

"Thank you for your time." Heather bowed before heading back to her mate. "I hope to have an answer for you quickly."

"Done?" He wrapped an arm around her, watching Streya and his mate leaving the gardens.

"Yes. No thanks to you." She wrapped her arm around his waist as well.

"What do you mean?" He tried to look innocent but didn't do a very good job at it. He urged her to move so they could walk along one of the garden paths.

"They knew you were about ready to pounce." She walked slowly, enjoying their leisure time together. They had so little of it.

"Sorry, but they did interrupt." He squeezed her waist. "Did they say anything worthwhile?"

"Gave me one more stipulation to offer Earth, which I think is a deal breaker if Earth doesn't go along with it. They are tired of the delays. I'm not sure what they will think of this last demand."

"I'm sure you will handle it with your normal grace and wit. I've been amazed at how you have put up with them in the first place."

"And I could say the same thing about how you put up with the council." She leaned her head on his chest. "Oh, and they invited us to have a meal with them. I'm not sure why or when. They also didn't mention a date or a time."

"Their family has been part of the elders for as long as my family has. They do have a say in who takes over when the time comes."

"Thought you were the next leader."

"I still have to pass their test. Most of them have not been too happy with my overactive libido or the fact that I couldn't seem to find a mate. Mother has probably told them you have centered me and helped me mature and they just want to see so for themselves." He smiled at her. "A meal means we can choose which meal to have with them."

"And which one would show the most respect?"

"Good question. Let me speak with their servants and I'll find out which one they wish us to pick."

The meal was three days later in the evening. Storm found out it was their daughter's birthday, and for some crazy reason that was the day they picked.

"What happened to the daughter?" Heather sat in a chair, waiting for Storm to finish getting ready.

"Mother never really talked about her. She was younger than me and died when I was a child." Storm stood in front of a mirror and brushed his hair. "They were heartbroken when she passed and have celebrated her birth every year."

"Then why would they want us there today of all days?" She didn't like the idea of invading on such a personal day. It was a little bit creepy to her.

"Their daughter was to be my mate." He turned to face her. "We were promised when we were children. This is their way of accepting you into the family, so to speak."

"Storm, how can I live up to that?" It made her feel a little sick to her stomach. Such an emotional day for them and she had to make sure she didn't say something stupid inadvertently.

"Ready?"

"No. Can I feign an illness?"

"Come on."

They headed through the large plaza to the home of Streya and his mate. Heather wished she knew the woman's name, but since Vespians didn't use proper names that much when speaking to each other, she hadn't heard anyone use it. Asking had crossed her mind, but only when she was in the woman's presence and it just didn't seem right. She was about to ask Storm when she felt butterflies in her stomach take flight. Something didn't feel right.

The door to their home stood ajar. She grabbed Storm's arm.

"This can't be right." Storm entered first. The whole place was a wreck. Storm and Heather had carried weapons on them since the last attack and they pulled them out as they worked their way through the house. They found Streya crumpled on the floor near a bedroom door, his mate prone on the floor inside the room.

Heather stepped into the room, knelt beside the woman, and pressed her hand against her neck. "She has a pulse."

"So does he."

"What is her name? No one has said it yet and I think I should know it if she wakes before a medical team arrives."

"Helia." Storm called the medics as they continued through the house, securing one room at a time. Once again, they were too late. Streya's mate started to stir, making Heather reenter the room and beg her to stay where she was until she could be checked out.

"What happened?" A point to the walls made Heather look and swallow hard. Whoever attacked them had been looking for her. Angry words covered the wall.

You thought to hide Heather from me, but I have found her, anyway. She will be mine.

Heather remained quiet as the medics came and checked out the elders. They weren't required to go to the center, but the medics didn't leave until they were sure they were okay.

Storm spoke to the security men who had come to take statements.

She found herself wandering around the place, looking at nothing in particular. On one wall was a screen that flashed images. Watching the images, there was one that caught her eye. She stepped up to it, waited for the picture to flash again and felt the blood drain from her face. She turned and asked Streya about the picture. "Can you explain that?"

"What?" Storm dismissed the security men and turned his focus onto the picture.

"That's me."

FIFTEEN

"Um, my heart, why would they have a picture of you?" Storm wasn't sure what to make of her comment.

"That is a very good question and one I would love to hear the answer to." She turned to them and waited. When no one said a word, she wanted to scream but knew there was only one way to get their attention. "Can we access my files from here?"

Storm nodded and held up a small device. "Have it with me all the time." He popped it into a terminal and stepped back.

She had one of the very first images after she had been found on the screen in seconds. Once the picture was visible once again, Heather touched it to freeze it. There was the same little girl with violet eyes and long blonde hair. The outfit was identical. "What did you do? Take this, then send me away seconds after?"

"It's not like that," Streya said, his voice quiet.

"Then explain this to me."

"It's complicated." He looked at his mate.

Storm's brows creased together. That thunderous look

was appearing on his face. "I think you need to start explaining why you would send a child away."

"It was to protect Heather." Streya rubbed his face. "There is so much to explain."

"How was this to protect me?" Heather could feel Storm's anger growing. He didn't like this any more than she did.

"I can't believe my mother allowed any of this to happen," he said, his voice flat.

"She had nothing to do with this," said Streya.

"I don't believe you." Storm shook his head. "No one could do this without her permission."

"They could if your uncle was involved. He was the one who put all this in motion."

Heather rubbed her head, trying to comprehend what was going on. She was suddenly sitting in her parents' house? Parents who abandoned her years ago on another planet? What could have been so bad they would do that to her? And what did Storm's uncle have to do with any of this? "Can we start at the beginning and focus on one thing at a time?"

Streya nodded. He gestured for Heather and Storm to take a seat. "When we learned we were having a child, we were ecstatic. As you know Vespian children are rare. Children born to the elders are rarer. We have more of the ancient blood in us. It takes more than the physical act to bring a child into the world."

Heather wanted to ask them what they meant by that, but they continued before she could say a word.

"It didn't take long before everyone knew of the pregnancy and that I would have twins," said Helia. She had joined them but kept quiet until this point. "Storm and his sister were young then."

She looked at her mate before continuing. "Long ago, the three families had decided that if we were to have children, there should be a rotation to how we would mate for progeny. It was to keep the bloodlines even so no one family could say they were the strongest because they were the ones who had the leadership bloodlines. Most of the time it never came into play because when there were offspring, only one of the three families had them so mates were chosen from the general population. Once we had two families with children."

Heather looked at Storm. "Only one time? Then how did you and Storm's parents end up with twins? Plus, the third family had a child as well. Considering there is normally only one child born, your council has five?"

"Twins are rare, but not unheard of. There are quite a few sets of twins running through the ancient bloodline," said Helia. "The fact that all three families had children was more of a surprise. That's never happened before."

"What you might not know, Storm," said Streya. "Is that there were five ruling families originally. How they became the ruling families has been lost to us, but we have to assume it has something to do with the ancient blood we all carry. The families constantly fought amongst themselves to see who would dominate. When one family was destroyed by another, it was decided to set up the council to protect the planet from constant warring. Four families ruled when the council was first created."

"But there are only three now," said Storm.

"The fourth family decided to try to take control of the planet, so our three families worked together and defeated them. Most of the rules for the council you now know, Storm, came into being then. Once the war ended, the fourth family was banned from the planet."

"So what happened to the fourth family?" asked Heather. She reached for his hand as all the information they gave them sank in.

"No one knows what happened to them after they were

forced to leave Vespia. We figured they had mixed with another race and diluted that line, but now we're not so sure."

"So you think they are the source of the attacks?" Storm took her hand in his.

"It's highly possible but we can't be sure. They didn't attack when the other children born from two parents mated. We don't know why they seem to be focused on Heather," said Streya. "We only have your uncle's vision to make decisions on."

"I'm not sure I understand." Heather rubbed her head.

"I wish I could tell you more, but we can't. Hynna came to us and said we had to send you away or you would die. We feared for your life."

"Why didn't you ever bring her home?" asked Storm.

"Every time we tried, Hynna had another vision forcing us to leave Heather where she was. He said the only person who should find her was her mate, so we had to wait for you." He looked at Storm. "It was the only way to keep her safe."

"That message on the wall says they knew you hid me, but they found me, anyway. How do they know so much about us?" asked Heather, moving the conversation back to where the attacks could have come from. "If they've been gone for that long, why would they suddenly have an interest in me?"

"We don't know."

Not the answer she was looking for. "Can you give us more details on the vision Hynna gave you?"

"I'm sure he will be ready to give you the information you need now you know this much of the story, but we only know what we told you."

"Do you think the third family could be after her since their daughter should have been my mate?" Storm asked.

"We did suspect them in the beginning, but you two tried

and it didn't work out. Why would they try to force something they know won't work?"

Storm nodded. He didn't seem convinced, but he let it go.

"You mentioned something of a twin brother?"

"I will explain it all," said Streya. "I know all this hurts, Heather. You're trying to figure out why we sent you away. I want you to know it was out of affection for you and fear for your safety. We were forced to do this. When you were about two, Storm's uncle, who was still new to his position, started to have visions. Some very violent and always centered around you two." Streya pointed to Storm and Heather. "He came to us and made us aware of two separate visions. One was your funeral at the age of eight. The other was you as a grown woman giving birth."

"I can't have children."

"And we'll get to that as well," said her mother.

"We had to make a decision. Either keep you here and run the risk of you being killed at a young age. Or send you away and hope we'd be able to bring you home one day."

"What does that have to do with the threats now?"

"The visions showed someone after you. Wanting you, but we never knew the reason." Streya took his wife's hand. "A few months ago, Hynna came to us and said it was time to bring you back. That you were in danger where you were and you needed the protection of your mate."

"Which is why you sent me as an ambassador. I couldn't figure out why my mother was so adamant for me to do this." Storm wrapped an arm around her. A protective gesture she had learned to love. "I'm not happy with how you went about doing this, but I am happy with the result."

"We're sorry for the subterfuge, but it was the only way. You couldn't go charging to Earth and demand your mate, which is your normal tactic. We don't know who is after Heather, so followed Hynna's visions. He told us if they were watching us, then they would find her when we found her." He grew quiet for a moment. "We sent you, hoping we would find her quietly. That's why you went to Earth several times. It took us that long to locate her and get her government to send her to you."

"You took a chance in hoping we would be attracted to each other," Heather said.

"To you, it might have seemed like a chance, but we knew it would work out. Hynna guided us the whole way and his visions have never been wrong."

"That's why he wanted to go on that mission, wasn't it? He knew Heather would be present. He needed to be sure everything would work out the way his visions showed." Storm was able to understand what was going on while Heather couldn't.

"I'm sorry, but you sure are taking this well." She turned to look at him, anger snapping in her eyes. "As much as you like to be in control, how could you go along with this so easily?"

"I have tried to explain the power my uncle has, but until you experience it personally, you won't understand what he is capable of." Storm gave her hand a squeeze. "He is an amazing seer."

"Don't really care how wonderful he is. I don't like my life manipulated this way."

"My heart, how would you have reacted if you knew none of this? Do you feel we don't belong together?" He pulled on her hand to get her to look at him.

"Of all of this, you are the one thing that keeps me centered. But it is hard for me to believe any of this. There are so many questions no one can or will answer."

"We will get to the bottom of all of this, trust me on that, but you need to believe in my uncle's power. You need to feel it for yourself."

"I agree." Hynna stepped into the room. "You don't know what you are, do you, Heather? That is your real question and I wish I could answer that for you. It will be revealed as time allows. But you do need to know why things have happened the way they have."

He gave a slight slap to Storm's hand so he would let go of Heather. "You have visions of your own, right?" He touched her hands.

"How did you know that?" Having his focus on her made her realize she didn't want his attention. He scared her a little.

"I have my ways." He sat on a small table in front of the couch she sat at. "Tell me about the vision you have had."

She didn't want to go there. Looking around, she found everyone staring at her, waiting for her to do as Hynna asked. "Fine. What do you need me to do first?"

"Clear your mind. Take me with you." He held her hands at the wrist. "What do you remember about it?"

"I haven't been able to go through everything."

"In other words, you want to work your way through this information alone, like you have all of your life." He smiled. "You are afraid to go through what you saw with help, aren't you? Afraid to see everything clearly."

"Okay. This is crazy." She pulled her hands free. He was right. If she didn't look too hard it might not come true. The other times when she examined the dream, too many terrible things had happened. "There is no way you could see what I saw in my dreams."

"There is only one way to find out, isn't there?" He took her hands once again, closed his eyes and settled his mind.

Heather found herself back in the room where the metal bed was. She stood in front of it. None of her other visions were so clear. "What is going on?"

"Is this what you saw?"

She looked around. It was. The low-hanging lamps hung just above their heads. "How did you do this? I was on that bed. The lights are right where I remember them. These dark items are lockers aren't they? How did you see them so clearly when I couldn't?"

"It is easier for me to see things without the emotional ties you felt when you dreamt this. So this is the room you remember?"

"Yes. The wall there was the only one I saw. The dull grey stuck in my memory. Being on the bed kept me from being able to see much else."

"What did he say to you?"

She didn't want to think about what she had heard. "I don't know."

"Yes, you do, you just don't want to face it."

He had that right.

She sighed. "Then why are you forcing the issue?"

"I'm only hoping to help you, Heather. This is coming, we both know that. The more information we have, the quicker we will be able to solve it."

Her heart picked up a little at the thought. Storm could walk into a trap if she were to resist. Maybe this time she could actually beat her dream. "This is all I saw. I remember a voice. I'm positive it is male, but I couldn't get much out of it, except Storm's life is forfeit if he tries to rescue me. He must not fall into the trap set for him."

"Show me."

Heather wasn't sure what she could show him, but she did her best. She had never shared a dream before. The energy drained her. By the time she was done, she could barely lift her head.

"Do we need to go?" Storm was worried about her and ready to whisk her away at a moment's notice.

"I'm fine." She rubbed her head. "I just need a moment to refocus myself."

Storm's uncle pushed him aside and helped Heather stretch out. "This will take a toll on her. The doctor can take the edge off if you wish."

Storm sat on the edge of the couch and touched her face. "Call him."

Heather found her mind hurt. It hadn't done this before. "Why does it hurt like this?"

"You're pushing your mind beyond its normal capabilities. The device was designed to stop that from happening. It's still doing its best to protect you and will do that until it is completely absorbed."

The doctor walked in then. He saw Heather on the couch and went to her side. "You okay?"

"Just another one of my headaches."

"Another one? I don't remember you having headaches before." He ran a quick scan. "I can give you a sedative to take the edge off, but I'd like to do a little more research before I give you anything else."

Heather looked at him. He had given her several shots but now acted like he didn't remember.

"The sedative will be fine, Doctor," said Hynna. "I'm sure it's nothing and she'll be fine in the morning."

"Of course." He put down his medical pack and pulled out a small hypo. Heather heard the slight hiss of the release as the drug entered her blood. In seconds, she felt a difference.

"Thank you." She was able to sit up and gave him a smile.

Storm sat beside her again. "You okay?"

"Yes." She smiled at him and took his hand. "I feel much better."

The doctor nodded, gathered his things, and headed out the door. Once he was gone, Hynna sat the scanner on the table near the couch. "The doctor remembers nothing now. When the device started to disintegrate, he was the one who could understand what was happening to you, but now it is too dangerous for him to know anything. This is for you to use instead of going to him every time. As far as the headaches go, I'm not sure if the sedatives are a good idea from this point on. Even though they help with the pain, it will keep your reaction time down. You're going to need a clear head in the days to come."

"Days? That soon?" Heather now wished she hadn't taken the shot.

"I'm afraid so."

"You two want to let the rest of us in on the conversation?" Storm didn't look pleased.

Heather touched his heart. "My device should be fully absorbed by that point."

"But I thought the device had already disintegrated." Storm frowned, worried about her.

"It has, but we're now talking about the minerals and residue from it." She looked up at Storm.

"That means your special ability will manifest," said Streya.

"Now, what are you talking about?" asked Storm.

"Each child born to an elder has a special ability because of the ancient blood. Storm's uncle is a perfect example. His visions have made a difference in our world."

"So what's so special about speaking ancient?" Heather wasn't sure being able to understand a dead language was something someone would covet.

"That's not your gift. You inherited that ability from our side of the family. It just proved that you were our daughter. The marker put in your body to disguise you has kept that suppressed, too. Once it fully disintegrates, then you'll see your gift manifest."

"We think it is your gift they are after."

"But you're not sure." She stood and started to pace. "It seems to me that everyone is grasping for an answer right now. What sort of gift would I have?"

"We don't know. Each child is different."

"Okay, what gift would be something someone would

want so badly they'd be willing to come after me for?" They had no answer for her.

"What gift are you talking about?" asked Storm. "My sister and I don't have any special ability that I'm aware of."

"For most of us, it didn't show up until we went through the mating ceremony. For others, it didn't show until their first child was born." Hynna grinned. "I was special. Mine started when I was a child, but mine was because of the role I would play. Your sister has ignored hers because she doesn't want the role she is destined for."

"Yours hasn't shown up because we've had to inject you with the same compound that is in Heather's device," Streya said it quietly, knowing Storm would be angry when he learned the truth.

"You feel no qualms about manipulating anyone's life?" Storm's voice held a note of anger.

"Let me ask you something, Storm. With Heather's life in jeopardy, have you allowed her to mingle with society?"

"You know the answer to that." He glared at them.

"And have you forced her to work with your latest training team so you can be sure she can protect herself?"

He didn't answer.

"And you complain about manipulation? You wish to protect her as much as you can. We were no different." He sat next to his mate. "What upsets me is no matter what we do she will still be taken and her life will be in jeopardy."

Storm stood and took two steps toward him before Heather touched him and stopped him. "Hear him out before you tear him apart."

Storm just stared at him, waiting.

Streya swallowed hard. "When we sent Heather away, you two had already gone through a ritual. One designed to allow you two to find each other if you were separated. We knew we'd have to send our daughter away and wanted to give you two a fighting chance in case we weren't there to guide you two back together. What we didn't know was what would happen to Storm when we had to send Heather away."

"Get to it." He had sat back down, and she followed suit, but Heather could feel his anger rolling off him in waves.

"Your blood started to call out for Heather's. The mating call was so powerful you would enter a room and cause grown men to fight amongst themselves. We had to do something, so we used a version of the serum in the device to mute that call. That's why you didn't affect the humans as much. The natural ability every Vespian has to call their mate to them was suppressed."

"I have my mate now."

"The moment you and Heather were together that injection stopped. I'm sorry, but we did what was necessary to protect our child. You will do the same thing when the time comes."

"I'm sterile." Heather said it so matter-of-factly.

Storm took her hand. "We both are."

"Right now you might be, but that was a side effect of the drug."

"What?" Heather stood, not believing a word. "I have seen my medical records. My body doesn't produce eggs."

"Or could the device have been able to disguise that to make it look like you couldn't?" Streya asked.

"No." she shook her head. There was no way that could be possible. She was sterile.

Hynna picked up the scanner and ran it over her. "Check the readings then. See for yourself." He dropped it into her hand.

Heather looked at Storm. "I don't think I can."

"Then we'll look when you're ready." He stood, pulled her to her feet, and wrapped her in his embrace. "I think we're done for the night, but we will continue this conversation another time."

He led Heather out of their home. The night breeze warm on their skin. "Speak to me."

"Storm, it's all too crazy. I don't know what to think. If it wasn't for that device in my back, I'd think they were out of their minds." She had her arms around him. "I'm part of a crazy plot? I am something so special my parents sent me away for protection? Everything that has been real for me all my life is totally destroyed in one night by strangers who claim to be my parents. How would you feel?"

"I would be very glad I had a mate who understands. We need to take this one thing at a time. First, we'll use the scanner to see what it says."

"Do you think it's possible?"

"Children? I have accepted the fact that I would never have any. I'm not sure what to think about that."

They entered their rooms. Storm went to the security panel and turned all the cameras and sensors off so whatever they found out wouldn't be recorded. "Ready?"

"No, but we need to know."

Storm sat beside her and put the scanner on the table between them. She stared at it. "Do you believe them?"

"I don't know what I believe. I've been sterile all my life. Why would that suddenly change? Yet like you said, that device is real. Could the rest be just as real?"

She picked up the scanner and rolled it on her hand. "You first."

He picked up the scanner and ran it over himself. "You ready?"

"No, but it's never stopped me before." They moved to the main screen.

He dropped it into the slot on the terminal on the center table and pulled up the data. "My heart, you are still my world, no matter what this says."

She touched his heart. "I'm frightened and excited at the same time."

Storm's DNA loaded, showing the strand in multiple colors. His stats loaded next. There, on the bottom, was a small symbol that would tell them if he was fertile or not. He let out a pent-up breath before opening the symbol. "I never thought this would happen."

He hugged her. "Now you."

"But what if they are wrong?"

"My heart, if I'm fertile, I'm sure you are too and the only reason it wouldn't show up is because of the device." He pulled up the scan his uncle did back at Streya's home. "Ready?"

She nodded. She wasn't but knew that wouldn't stop him. Her DNA strand filled the screen, waivered for a moment, then snapped back into place. "What was that?"

"I believe that was the device protecting you." He worked on the computer for a few moments, fighting with the data there. "I'm trying to get the original image to come back up so we can see what it says, but I'm having trouble."

"It doesn't matter, does it? It's all true." She walked away from the screen. "This is my home, always has been. We were destined for each other, no matter what planet we're on or from."

He watched her as she worked her way through all the information they learned. "You do realize that it's about to happen, don't you?"

"You're not going to bring up that stupid dream again, are you?"

"I have to." She touched the screen. "Everything he said is right here. My dreams have never lied to me. I trust them and they are telling me there is more coming."

"And you fear for my life."

"As you fear for mine." She touched his face. "Each time I've had these dreams, they have saved my life. I'd like to think now that you're my mate it will do the same for you, but you have to listen to them."

"But I don't want to have you in danger."

She went into their bedroom. "Storm, you're not listening to me. My life wasn't threatened. Yours was." She handed him the handheld she had put what she remembered of the dream on. "Your uncle knows more than what I loaded here, but between the two of you, someone should be able to figure out what to do."

"I don't believe we can't keep you protected. We need to see my mother." He took her hand and headed for the door. "She should be able to help us."

"Storm, you can't stop the dream. It's going to happen whether you like it or not." Heather found herself running to keep up with his long legs once again.

"What do you mean?" He slowed down when he realized how fast he was moving.

"I've tried every tactic I could think of to stop what ever happened in past dreams to no avail. They always happened and when I tried to manipulate them I sometimes made it worse." She was grateful he slowed down.

"So you want me to let you be kidnapped? Put your life in danger because of a dream?" His face grew angry. "I'm not going to let that happen, so stop talking like that."

"Storm." He ignored her and continued to his mother's rooms. "My heart." That he couldn't ignore. He stopped and looked at her, not happy with the way their conversation had been going. "I mean you no disrespect, but I have dealt with these dreams all my life."

"I can't let you get hurt."

"I won't be hurt as long as you don't try to force changes that will affect the outcome. Please, Storm."

He didn't knock, just pushed the doors open. "Mother."

"Oh, no." Heather looked around. Anseri's room had been destroyed. It looked like a huge fight had happened there. Pulling out her weapon, she stepped over shattered glass. She used as much caution as possible as she searched the room for his mother.

"Where the hell is she?" asked Storm, his voice laced with concern.

"Storm, she's over here." Heather knelt beside her mate's mother. Setting her weapon down, she touched her wrist and the side of her neck for a pulse.

Her eyes fluttered open. "No."

Heather looked at her. "No?"

"Trap." She closed her eyes and licked her lips.

An ice-cold finger of fear ran up her spine. They hadn't had time to do anything more than talk about what could happen, and now the time had come. She looked up and saw three men behind Storm. Words wouldn't leave her mouth as she tried to warn him. One of them hit him from behind with a hypo.

He went down fast, head striking the edge of a short table to his right. Heather jumped up to go to him and found herself surrounded by seven men.

One spoke. "Take him out."

Heather moved, grabbing the closest man to her and breaking his neck in seconds. The body slid lifelessly to the ground. "You touch him and I will kill every one of you just like that. If you leave Storm alone, I will come willingly. Those are my conditions."

The man she assumed was the leader nodded and gestured for her to walk in front of him. She wanted to check on Storm, make sure he was okay, but knew if she faltered at all they could change their minds. Her engagement ring caught the light. In her vision, she never had the ring on, so in one quick movement, she pulled the ring off and let it drop to the floor.

She looked at Storm's still form once more before allowing the men to lead her out. What would happen now was up for grabs.

SIXTEEN

Storm came to in the medlab. He found himself surrounded by security as well as medical people. He growled at them to get away so he could figure out what had happened. His head hammered. Touching his forehead, he found a horrendous bump and realized it was tender.

"I'm still working on that." The doctor pulled his hand down. "You took a hard fall and a heavy dose of a neurolizer. I'm surprised you survived it."

It took a second before he realized where he was and what had happened before he fell unconscious earlier. "Heather."

"Gone." His mother answered him. She had been moved to another medical bed nearby. Her color was off. He had never noticed how pale his mother looked before this. "She offered herself when they threatened your life."

"Why didn't she fight?" He couldn't understand why she would give herself up so easily.

"To protect you." His mother waved off one of the doctor's assistants when they tried to inject her with something. "You see that body there? She killed him to keep them

238

from ending your life. I took care of the other one when he circled around to finish the deed, anyway."

"Where is she?"

"We don't know."

Heather's heart pounded in her chest. How was she going to get out of this? She hadn't thought past keeping Storm alive. Now she had to figure a way to escape.

"Welcome."

"Send me home."

"To your mate? The man who has slept with more women than the years you have been alive?"

"He is my world." She didn't know the voice, but it had to be someone who knew Storm well. Heather knew of his sexual exploits. She had read his file.

She felt something cold against her neck before her world turned upside down.

Heather opened her eyes to find Storm sitting on the bed beside her.

"You okay?"

She looked around to find herself back at the medlab. "I think so. What happened?"

"My mother's apartment was attacked." He took her hand in his. "They tried to take you, but I was able to stop them."

She didn't remember it that way. She had sacrificed herself to keep him alive. Yet here he sat. How could that be? Storm smiled at her but didn't seem himself either. Something was wrong. She just wasn't sure what it was.

"Problem?"

"No." She wasn't sure what to do. Everything seemed backward. Storm had been knocked out and she had been taken, so how was he sitting on her bed? Did he rescue her that fast? It didn't make sense.

"It's okay, my love."

My love? Storm never used that term of endearment. They talked about that. My love was an Earth phrase, not a Vespian one. This couldn't be real. She tried to distance herself from the image of Storm without causing any type of reaction.

"Something is wrong." He smiled at her but seemed to sense she wasn't happy.

"Since when did you use a human endearment? You told me you were above that." Not exactly what he said, but it was a test to see what Storm said next.

"True, but I thought that was what you wanted to hear."

She smiled. No matter what the man said, now she knew who he wasn't. "You're not Storm."

"How can you say that?" He acted indignant, but she could see a touch of fear in his eyes. He didn't think she would see through his disguise so fast.

"I know my mate better than you think."

She found herself feeling woozy again. Her mind started to wander, and she lost touch with reality.

"How the hell am I supposed to find her, Mother? I have nothing to go on."

She sat on the couch, watching her son pace like a predator. "My brother has a theory, if you'd bother to listen to him."

"He speaks in riddles. How am I to interpret that?"

"It would help if you would listen to me from time to time instead of blowing me off." He walked into the room. "At least your mate was honest in her feelings toward me."

"She called you creepy."

"She did." He grinned as he sat next to his sister. "And I can see her viewpoint, but I also believe I proved my abilities."

"You pushed her to believe in her dreams."

"Was I wrong?"

"She allowed herself to be kidnapped because you walked through her dreams. What do you feel you can do that no one else can?" Storm knew his anger over her kidnapping closed his judgment.

"How well do you know your mate?"

"Better than you."

"Are you sure about that?" He looked at Storm. "Your mate would know you. Of that I am sure, but I'm not sure about the other way around."

"What are you saying?"

"You are selfish. You refused to listen to her when she tried to make you see the future that could be. Now you need to believe in the power of fate. The one thing you have never believed in."

Heather woke up and found herself sitting in the main room of the elder's hall. It didn't make sense for her to be there. She saw no one else in the room. Strange.

Storm stood on the other side of the room. She could tell by his silhouette. Then the room changed. It filled with people. So many she couldn't see him anymore. Her mind couldn't handle the overload. Everything shut down.

She opened her eyes once again and found herself back at the medlab on Earth. Looking around, she couldn't figure out how she got there so quickly.

The head doctor smiled at her. "Good to see you awake."

"What happened?"

"You took a hard blow to the head when those men attacked the embassy. You've been in a coma for several weeks."

Coma? Nothing made sense to her. "What about the ambassador?"

"He's fine. Heading back to Vespia tomorrow."

She wanted to ask so many questions but decided against it. Her mind felt like it was filled with fuzz. "What happened?"

"You don't remember?"

"Sorry."

"You were assigned to protect the ambassador. On your first evening, you found the embassy under attack and you stopped them. In the process, you were hurt, which landed you in here for the last few weeks."

"What about the treaty?"

"It's still being worked out. You putting your life on the line really helped move it forward."

She slid her legs to the edge of the bed.

"Oh, no you don't." He pushed her legs back onto the bed. "You are still under my control until I clear you. You've been unconscious for over two weeks. There is no way you're getting out of this bed."

"Yes, sir." She leaned back against the pillows on her bed. Now what?

"She's been gone for twenty hours now. We have to find her now or we'll never find her." Storm felt trapped. He didn't know what to do and had very little to go on.

His uncle sat in a chair opposite him. "You have no faith."

"What should I have faith in? My mate is gone, just like

you predicted. Yet you can't tell me where she is. What sort of faith should I have?"

"Your ability to find her." One of the servants sat a glass in front of him. "I know she would be able to find you if the situation was reversed."

"Are you saying I'm not as strong as my mate?" Storm stood in anger.

"Heather believed in her dreams. She understood what fate is. Are you saying you aren't as strong a believer as your mate?" He watched Storm's anger come to a boil. "That is your decision."

"I don't know how to find her without help."

"And that was what I was waiting for." Hynna got up and moved to the area where his sister had been found. He picked up Heather's diamond ring and set it on the table. "Just how close did you and your mate get in your time together?"

"Why?"

"It's the only way to find her."

"You're not making any sense."

Heather had finally been released from the medcenter. She never knew true boredom until now. Her conversations with the head doctor and the psychiatrists had her questioning everything. According to them, none of what she remembered happening was real. She never went to Vespia, or married Storm. Yet to her it was.

She sat in her room, trying to figure out what was real and what wasn't.

The door chimed, and she hit the button to allow whoever was at the entrance. Admiral Barrington walked in.

"How are you feeling?" He sat on the edge of her couch.

"Not sure, sir."

"You sound back to normal. The doctor has cleared you to get back to work."

"Thank you." She was happy to hear that. Maybe she could get her life back to normal. Figure out where she got the crazy idea that she married the man. Marriage wasn't something she ever thought would happen to her, so why would she fantasize about it?

"You can start back whenever you're ready. Should I expect you in the morning?"

"Yes, sir."

He nodded and left the room. She stood and walked to her closet. Pulling out her uniform, she set it out for the next day. It had been too long since she had worn it.

Storm sat at the table his uncle had directed him to. "What do you want from me?"

"I want you to admit that there is more to this than what you can see and touch."

"Right now I can't see or touch my mate, so that is a hard question to answer." He wanted to take his uncle and shake him. What did the man want?

"How intimate have you and your mate been?"

"What kind of question was that? As intimate as any couple would get."

"No, no." He shook his head, acting like he was searching for the right words. He wanted to ask something beyond what he had. "Have you and your mate shared intimacy beyond that of a normal couple?"

Storm looked at his mother. "Do you understand what he's asking because I'm just not getting it."

"He wants to know how deeply entwined you and Heather are. Has anything happened that goes beyond the bond of mates?"

"Like what?" He looked from his mother to his uncle. "I'm not sure what you're asking."

"Have you and Heather shared thoughts?"

"No, but we have shared other things."

The man just stared at him, waiting for more info.

"Fine. The last few times we've had sex, we've shared each other's orgasms." He didn't like revealing something so intimate.

"Then there is hope. You need to connect with her. Find her through her mind."

"And how am I to do that?"

He placed the ring she'd dropped on the floor on the table. "This will give you something of hers to use to find her, and you will have to go through some rituals that will help you bond to her once you do. Understand we don't know what is going on where she is, so the first time or two you will only see what she sees."

"No wonder why my mate thinks you're crazy."

"If I help you save her, I don't care what anyone thinks of me." He stood and headed toward the door. "Coming?"

Storm stood. He was willing to do anything to get his mate back.

SEVENTEEN

Heather stared at the computer screen and pinched her nose. This was by far the dullest thing she had done in her entire career. So far they had her cataloging all the new files that had been streaming in from the Vespian society so it could be analyzed. The weird part was when she went to read it, she already knew it. This was information she had learned from Storm's sister. Yet that hadn't really happened so how did she know all of this? Could she have read this before her injury and forgot?

The more she thought about it, the more confused she became.

Admiral Barrington walked into her office to check on her.

"Sir?" She stood, knowing her next request could be denied without a blink of an eye. "I wish to be put back on active duty. Working behind a desk is not what I feel I should be doing."

"The doctors felt you needed it to recuperate totally."

"And I feel I have done that." She stood at attention. "The doctors have said as much too."

"I know. I received a clean bill of health from them about

an hour ago." He leaned a hip against the desk she had been sitting at. "So you want a new assignment?"

"Yes, sir." She let go of a mental sigh of relief.

"Alright." He handed her a hand-written note. Not something normally used nowadays. "The ambassador from Vespia will be marrying the human diplomat assigned to him, and we have been told we are to attend."

She looked at the invitation and felt a little sick to her stomach but showed no reaction. "Of course."

"You feel up to it?" He studied her face.

"Yes, sir." She couldn't tell him how confused she was. How she was having problems keeping this reality and the one she thought was real apart. If she did that, they'd probably want to keep her for more observation. Something she wanted to avoid at all costs.

"Good." He nodded as he filled out paperwork. "I will see you here at eighteen hundred hours."

She nodded.

Storm held her engagement ring, wondering why she had taken it off. "So what do you want me to do?"

"Drink this." His uncle pushed a drink in front of him. "It tastes horrible but will help you clear your mind so you can find hers."

Storm downed the contents. The bitter bile threatened to come back up. He gagged a little before he could speak. "Now what?"

"Focus on the ring and her essence. Have it take you to her."

Storm rubbed his head. He wasn't sure if he could do as his uncle asked, but if it would bring her home, he was willing to try anything.

He cleared his mind, not really knowing how he was

going to find her. It just didn't make sense. He found the drug taking control of him, guiding him through many dream states. He felt pulled toward one in particular and as he entered it, he found it familiar.

He saw himself standing up at the altar, saying his vows, except this time it wasn't Heather up there with him. She stood in the back with other Earth officers. The woman he stood with he didn't recognize at all.

He felt disembodied, floating amongst the guests, but not really there. Heather watched the ceremony with a detachment he didn't know she was capable of.

Didn't she understand this was all fake?

She stood with her commanding officers, her face devoid of emotion as she watched the proceedings. When the Storm at the wedding took his bride in his arms and gave her a knee-weakening kiss, he saw the lack of emotion from Heather crack just a little. One tear slipped down her cheek. She wiped it away before anyone else noticed.

Storm did. Her reaction told him she still hadn't accepted this reality one hundred percent yet. He had a chance. He hovered nearby, waiting and watching for any hint on who created this fake world.

Watching the ambassador marry affected her oddly. Heather blamed it on the coma. She had been married to the man in that dream and watching him marry another hurt her deeper than she thought possible. A tear slipped down her cheek, but she was able to remove it before anyone else saw it.

What she needed was a drink. Too bad she could drink all night long and not feel any effects. Once the ceremony was over, they were allowed to mingle while the governments set up a receiving line. Something Heather wasn't looking forward to. It was hard enough just standing in the back of the room. How was she going to remain professional that close to him?

The line started, and they were one of the first groups after the Vespian high council. Heather kept her eyes averted so she wouldn't accidentally catch the gaze of Storm's mother or the people who told her she was their daughter.

Her head started to swirl. This was a lot harder than she thought it would be. Claiming to have a headache and begging permission to seek medical attention for it she raced out of the reception and leaned against the wall. Why was she having such a hard time trying to keep reality and her dreams straight?

Everything she had been through seemed so real. Now she knew it was all in her head, so she should be relieved. Why wasn't she?

Heather did go to the med center. She knew the admiral would be checking up on her if she didn't.

"Lieutenant? What brings you here?"

"Got a slight headache at the reception."

"I told the admiral I didn't think it was a good idea for you to attend that thing. You've just started working again and knowing about your fantasies it would be hard on you." He took a scanner and ran it over her.

She didn't like the fact he called her alternate reality a fantasy, but she took the shot he gave her and headed back to the reception. On her way she heard her name being paged and went to the nearest communication panel to answer it.

"Lieutenant, I have a new assistant looking for you."

"Assistant? I didn't ask for an assistant." She rubbed her head. Was there something she had seen on this, long before the coma?

"I believe you were to pick one before you were hurt and declined. Since you're better, the admiral has assigned someone to you to start immediately," a female voice informed her. "I'm sending him to you now. Be nice."

249

"Great. Make sure he's in his formal uniform." She shut off the communication and walked back into the reception.

"Feeling better?" asked the admiral.

"I was until I found out I had to babysit someone." She nodded to a young man, looking all flustered. "My new assistant?"

"Yes, Ma'am." He was all smiles as he settled himself beside them.

"You finally picked one?"

"No, sir. I was told you did. I was told I tried to get out of it before my accident, but it looks like I have to train him, anyway."

"I must have signed off on it with some other things." Barrington touched her arm. "You still need to pay your respects to the ambassador. He did ask about you."

"Yes, sir." She swallowed hard and tugged on the jacket of her uniform. Heather headed to the now dwindling line, new assistant in tow. "You don't have to follow me everywhere."

"Yes, Ma'am, I know, but after everything you've been through, I thought you'd like the company."

Heather looked at him. Young, handsome, he was going to turn a lot of heads. What caught her attention the most was his eyes. A vivid gold with an amber ring. Just like Storm's.

She needed to get a grip on herself. They reached the ambassador pretty quickly.

"Lieutenant, I'm glad to see you back on your feet." He smiled at her and she smiled back.

"Thank you, sir." She shook his hand, confused by the sensations when she touched him. There was no thrill she had felt before and when she looked him in the eyes, she only saw the gold of his eyes. The amber ring was missing. It was like he wasn't really the ambassador, but some imposter. She puzzled over this as she headed back to the table they had been assigned. Heather thought about asking if the ambassador had a stand-in this evening, but decided it was probably her, not the ambassador. That was wrong and her question would only raise more questions about her sanity.

Everyone took their seats with one vacant one next to Heather.

The admiral picked up the place card. "Who is Myh Eart?"

"I am, sir." Her assistant responded as he sat down beside her. "I guess my name had been added to the invitation list when your secretary realized I'd be here by the wedding."

Heather shot him a look to quiet him down. He smiled at her but remembered his rank.

Small talk was the conversation at the table as the meal arrived. People let her know how happy they were to see her back at work. She nodded and thanked them, hoping they would let it go pretty quickly. She wanted the night to end as fast as possible, but it just dragged on.

Most of the questions after that were aimed at her new assistant, so keeping him quiet so he wouldn't get into trouble wasn't working out in her favor. She found his answers to their questions vague, but it didn't seem to bother anyone else.

It just didn't feel right.

———

"Well? Did it work?"

Storm kept hearing his uncle, but he was trying to ignore him and focus on the scene in front of him. He had to excuse himself so he could focus on the voice in his ear. "Yes, uncle, it worked. She believes I'm her assistant. Now, can I get back? I don't want to have her suspect anything out of the ordinary. She already seems to have problems with some of the things I say and do."

251

"Just remember, you are an Earth officer and not her mate. You step over that line too soon and you will give yourself away to whoever is doing this to her. Have you seen anything out of the ordinary?"

"No. Her admiral is there, but I saw images of him and it looks like the same man. Other than that, she's surrounded by the same people as when I met her. If there is someone manipulating this whole thing, then they haven't shown up in this created world yet."

"True. They could be waiting for her to truly accept this fake reality before they enter. Be very careful." His uncle patted him on the hand. "I'll be here when you need me."

Storm closed his eyes once again and entered Heather's mind. He never thought to do this, even though the doctor recommended it. What did the doctor know before he had his mind wiped?

Heather sat in the chair, not really eating anything put in front of her. She pushed the food around on the plate a little, but nothing appealed to her. No one else had that problem.

"Lieutenant, eat or I'll have you sent back to the medical center."

"Just not hungry, sir." She pushed her plate away and stood up. "If you don't mind, I'd like some fresh air."

Storm watched her retreating back, wondering what to do. "Perhaps I should go with her."

He stood up as well and started after her. He heard one of the men there say *you know we should stop him*, and the other said *let him learn this one on his own. Our lieutenant knows how to put people in their place.* So he knew to tread carefully.

He kept her in view but didn't approach her.

"Ensign, why are you here?" She didn't look at him.

"I was told to be your shadow, ma'am." He waited for her to turn toward him, hoping he hadn't overstepped any personal boundary.

"So the only way I'm going to get rid of you is to duck

into the ladies room?" She turned to look at him, confusion filling her eyes.

"If you feel you must run from me." He wanted to take her into his arms so bad. "I read your file before I came here, so I know what you've been through."

"No one knows what I have been through." She turned her back to him.

"You're having problems figuring out which reality is right. This one feels like it should be right, yet there is a part of you that knows your other reality was right." He smiled when she turned back around and looked at him.

"Problem, Lieutenant?" The admiral had stepped out onto the terrace with them. Storm wondered how much he had heard.

"No, sir. Just trying to explain to the ensign that I need time to myself every once in a while."

"Well, the couple is beginning their first dance and you've been requested to join them on the dance floor with the family."

"Excuse me, sir?"

"I know it's a bit unorthodox, but they want to honor you for saving the ambassador's life. You'll dance with his best man." He turned and went back inside, expecting her to follow him.

"This is crazy." She rubbed her head, her voice soft, like she was talking to herself. "There was no best man. There was no reception on Earth."

She had totally ignored Storm's presence, which he found as a good sign. That had to mean she felt comfortable with him.

Heather headed back into the main ballroom, awaiting her fate. A man, definitely Vespian, approached her once the rest of the family started dancing. Storm didn't recognize him. Could he be the one orchestrating all of this?

Storm wished he could get closer to hear what was being

said. The fact that the man brought a smile to her face worried him. They only danced the one dance, then Heather joined him on the sidelines.

He wanted to know what was said so badly but pumping Heather for information just made her quieter. She headed back to the table. Several of the officers had already left because of their schedules the next day. "Sir, have I fulfilled all my duties?"

"Yes, why?"

"I was due at the security center about fifteen minutes ago."

"I thought you asked to be relieved of that duty?"

"Yes, sir, but I still had a few days on the books and it would have messed up the rotation if I asked to be relieved, so I kept them. Besides, it will be good for my assistant to see what happens there as well."

"Let him see the boring as well as the exciting?"

"Yes, sir." She smiled. "Am I dismissed?"

"You are."

She saluted and headed out of the reception.

He was happy to be away from there as well. Maybe now he could get a chance to talk to her. "You seemed to enjoy his company."

"Who?" Heather walked toward her office. She nodded to the young woman behind the desk before walking into security.

The young woman stopped him and asked for proper id. He pulled out something from his pocket and presented it to her. Once he was cleared, he followed Heather. She saluted another officer.

"You are relieved."

"Thank you, Lieutenant. Did you enjoy your evening?"

"I'm glad it's over. That's all." She took her jacket off and loosened her collar. "My uniform's still here?" She hadn't used her locker since she came back.

"Yes, ma'am. No one touched your locker while you were gone." He punched a few keys on the keyboard then stood back so she could do the same thing. Storm couldn't keep his eyes averted when she bent over and swore he caught a flash of red when she signed in. "See you in the morning."

Heather nodded and walked to a row of doors. Opening one, she pulled out a uniform. She stepped into a darkened office to change. "You plan on wearing that getup all night?"

He looked down at the formal uniform. "No, Ma'am, but the rest of my uniforms are in my room."

"I'm sure the world won't disintegrate while you go change." Fully dressed, she pulled up data on the screen, giving leave by ignoring him.

He had no clue how everything was laid out in her mind, so he ducked into a small alcove and willed his clothes to change. The uniform was strange to him, but he found it comfortable. Hoping he had allowed enough time to pass, he walked back into security.

Heather found Myh a little strange, yet there was something comforting about him. She stared at the data on the screen without really focusing on it. And the best man. Very charming, but there was something about him that didn't sit right.

And Storm. He seemed so different from the man she had known. The beautiful golden eyes that smiled at her were gone. If she didn't know better, she'd swear her new assistant had them. Each day got more confusing instead of settling down and making sense.

Myh came into the room with a smile on his face. She smiled back. She liked efficiency and his quick change said volumes on that.

"You need to sign in." She pointed to the screen. After

pulling up his information so he could sign in for the first time. "Um, interesting."

"What?" He followed the instructions then turned to look at her.

"If you merge the letters of your first and last name, it spells my heart." She felt just a little twinge. That was Storm's endearment for her.

"How about that?" He gave her a smile that reminded her of those heart-melting ones Storm gave her.

She needed to get a grip.

"Is that the file we're working on?" He brought her attention to the file she had on the screen.

"Yes." That was what she needed. Something to distract her from her thoughts.

"What language is that?" he asked her quietly. Like he didn't want anyone to hear him.

She looked at the screen. Her eyes saw English there. His question confused her. "What do you see?"

"I don't know. I'm versed in fifteen different languages, but I don't recognize that one. It looks ancient, though. Like it's some sort of dead language."

Heather rubbed her forehead again. The ancient language was probably something she made up in her dream, which was why she could read it, so why would it appear here? Her mind fought the conflicting information racing through her head.

Storm watched the confusion spread across her face. She didn't understand what was going on. The world they stood in became unfocused for a moment before she seemed to find her center and everything solidified again.

He knew, though. Her mind was trying to tell her this wasn't real by bringing up things that were. Unfortunately, it was being a little too subtle about it. Perhaps he needed to help it out a bit.

He found the work her mind had them doing boring, but he did see patterns emerging. It put her on a task to solve an ancient Vespian proverb. She saw it as a security issue. Until she saw it for what it was, the two of them would be stuck in her mind.

The woman at the desk called for Heather. Storm looked up to see the best man standing there.

"Oh, no. I don't need this right now." She said it softly. Rubbing her hands against the material of her uniform, she stepped out of the office to where the other man stood.

"I thought I would visit?" He didn't seem to be comfortable here in her world.

"Sorry. I'm on duty right now and can't leave." She looked at the young woman who was caught staring at her guest. "Thought you were leaving with the rest of the Vespian party."

"I was allowed to stay behind to help finish up the treaty. Perhaps we can see each other when you are off duty."

"Perhaps." Heather didn't want to commit to anything with this man. Storm wished she would call him by the name he might have told her so he could start a search for that person when he spoke to his uncle. "I'm sorry, but I must get back to work."

She walked right past Storm, so he stayed by the door and listened a little more. "That didn't go well."

"The lieutenant is very work orientated. It takes a lot to get her to notice anything else. They don't call her ice princess for nothing."

"Then I'll just have to keep trying." The man left then, and Storm went back to work with Heather.

"Who was that?"

"You saw him earlier." She gave him a mind your own business look.

"I meant his name. I wasn't aware that the ambassador traveled with anyone other than his basic staff."

"I was a bit surprised, too. He said his name was Ialog. Been friends with St—the ambassador for years."

"Interesting." It had to be the one who took her. He didn't know anyone by that name. At least he had a name to work with. He only hoped it was the man's real name and there was some record of him somewhere. "He seems to be attracted to you."

"Ensign, I think you are overstepping your boundaries."

"Sorry, Lieutenant." He might have pushed a little too hard there. Time to change tactics. "I have a twin sister at home, and our relationship allowed me to say whatever I feel."

"Really? A twin?" It hit a cord in her. "What is it like to have a sibling?"

"A pain." He laughed. "But she was also my best friend as we grew up. She'd tell me things she couldn't tell anyone else."

"Must have been nice." She started to sound drowsy and he noticed the image around him started to blur. They must have given her a sedative.

Storm opened his eyes. "She is very stubborn."

"Which is why she is such a good match for you. Did you learn anything of value?" He handed Storm a drink.

"I have a name, which I need to give to the team so they can find out if the person exists." Storm took a sip of the drink and winced. "What is that?"

"Something to help you maintain the mind link." His uncle pulled the glass away. "Each time you go in, it will get harder if you aren't careful. You need to keep yourself separate so she can see that the world she is trapped in is fake. If you lose sight of that, how will she ever see the difference?"

"Fine." He walked to the computer station and contacted

one of the men. "I have a name for you. Find out whatever you can."

"Yes, sir."

Storm transmitted the data and turned back to his uncle. "There seems to be a new man coming into the picture."

"Then you got to her just in time." He crossed to a small cabinet. "You must gain her confidence quickly before he can seduce her."

"Then I'll seduce her and she'll remember."

"No." He gripped Storm's wrist hard. "That's not the way this works. She has to want you to break the spell. If you seduce her, then she will end up pushing you out. Right now, she is your superior, and it's against her rules to fraternize with some who works for her of lower rank."

"Now what?"

"You have to become her equal in her eyes."

Storm rested for a few hours, keeping in contact with her mind. As long as she didn't go back into the world created for her he could rest. His uncle pumped all kinds of vile liquids into him to help keep the link and his mental stamina up.

Heather was suddenly in the restaurant next to the security center. He wasn't sure why yet so he remained with her without becoming solid in her world.

The best man showed up. Storm didn't like this.

"Thank you for meeting me, Heather." He slid into the booth she had been seated at.

"I'm not sure why you wanted to meet with me." She moved over a little when he moved a little too close.

"Lieutenant, do you mind if I call you Heather?" She shrugged. "I find you fascinating and wish to get to know you better."

That was smooth. Storm hovered nearby, wishing he could run interference, but knew he shouldn't reveal his presence to this man. He didn't seem to know Storm had infiltrated her mind.

Heather didn't seem to be thrilled at the man's attention, either. "I'm not sure that is a good idea."

"Why?" He moved a little closer.

"I was wounded when the ambassador was attacked." She looked at him. Her hesitation surprised Storm. Maybe she knew who he was deep inside. "I was in a coma for a while and am not quite back to normal. I need time to learn to be myself again. Until then, I feel I need to keep to myself."

"I don't wish to harm you."

"Harm me?" She moved away from him. "Why would you say that?"

"I'm sorry. Your human language is hard for me." He smiled and sat back.

That seemed to mollify her.

"How do human males woo your females?"

That brought a smile to Heather's lips. "Woo. Haven't heard that one in a long time. Just be yourself and try not to push me so hard."

"I can do that." The waitress came and took their orders. The rest of the evening went too well by Storm's standards. He didn't like the man so close to his mate. They walked back to her room, talking quietly. She stopped them by her door.

"Well, thank you for a wonderful evening." She hesitated again, allowing the man to take her into his arms and press his lips to hers. Heather did nothing for a moment, probably shocked by it all, then she started to fight him.

"No!" and the world dissolved around him.

The next time he entered her mind, he found himself in a gym. Heather worked out nearby. This time, Storm took on his persona and walked up to her. What time of day was it in her mind? There was no real way to tell.

She spotted him. "Morning, Ensign."

"Morning, Ma'am." He smiled. "Didn't expect to see you here."

"I work out every morning." She continued through her routine. Moving in small segments to a beat only she could hear.

He went to the weights and started to lift them. Why did she bring up this scene? The last three had the best man in them, but unless he showed up to work out with her, this was her mind creating something new. Did the man know it? Would he try to manipulate this to his advantage?

Should Storm?

He decided to let Heather control this scene. Let her make the first move.

She continued to work out in her corner while he kept to the spot he had picked. Storm watched her the whole time but didn't try to get in her way. Once she was done with her workout, she approached him. "Let's see what you got."

"Excuse me?" That could be taken so many ways and his libido was the first one to respond.

"You're fresh out of the academy, right?"

He nodded.

"Then let's see what you've been taught." She took a defensive stance and signaled him to attack.

"All right, but I might just surprise you." He thought about acting like a man from her planet and use those tactics but he wanted her to see him for who he really was. He used a maneuver she wasn't ready for and had her pinned to the mat in about thirty seconds.

She looked up at him in shock. He smiled down at her.

"You couldn't do that again."

"Oh, but I can." He hadn't let her up, enjoying the feel of her body pressed against his.

"Ensign, you will not be able to pull that one again. I promise you."

"Okay." He helped her to her feet. "And what do I get if I can?"

"What?" She looked frightened.

"You don't believe I can pin you like that again and I believe I can." He couldn't help the joy that raced through him. Maybe he could make this work in his favor.

"You want to make a bet?"

"Wouldn't you?" He smiled at her, knowing if she went along he might just be able to break the spell she was under.

"Alright." She didn't look convinced. "What do you wish for?"

"Well, you seem so sure I can't do that again, what do you want from me?" He didn't know what she would say to that, but he wanted to know what she desired and hoped she would take this time to tell him what she wanted.

"I—I don't know."

"Sure you do, Heather. You've never had a problem telling me what you want from me." He made sure his lips were next to her ear as he said, "Ever."

A slight shiver flowed through her, but she didn't have an answer.

"I know what I want from you." He kept his lips close to her ear. The room had emptied as he spoke, her mind cleared the room at the promise his voice held. "Something simple. Just a kiss."

"Ensign."

"Forget our ranks for just a moment." He walked in front of her so she would look him in the eyes. "I'm not asking for anything more than a kiss. How could that be too much? You give your friends a kiss when you see them right? Relatives get them too."

She looked at him but didn't answer. Did he push too far? The reality flickered for a moment before she agreed. "There is no way you're going to be able to do that again."

"Yes, Ma'am." He took his stance and waited. She made the first move and he had her pinned beneath him in about twenty seconds.

She looked up at him, a mixture of emotions in her eyes. Shock he could do it a second time, then excitement and fear which fought each other. Storm took her face into his hands, if he didn't he feared his hands would have a mind of their own.

His heart beat harder at the thought of being able to kiss his mate. He lowered his face to hers, capturing her lips before using his tongue to sweep into her mouth. Her body responded the way he hoped, he could feel her tongue dancing with his, giving as much as she was taking. He got lost in the sensations of the kiss.

Then just as fast as the scene became real he watched as it disintegrated and he was back with his uncle.

"What happened?" His uncle seemed concerned that he had been released so fast.

"Just what I wanted." No matter what his uncle thought, Storm didn't feel he made a mistake pushing her a little. Now he had to see how that would affect the rest of the times they were together.

***

Hynna sat across from Storm. Heather's mind only took a few moments before she had created another scene to this fake reality. Storm took it as a good sign.

"Ready to go back in?" his uncle asked him.

"Yes." He closed his eyes once again and found himself just outside her door. He rang the buzzer and the door slid open. She stood there wearing the same shift she had worn when they first kissed. Part of her mind remembered. He went hard in seconds. "Lieutenant?"

She didn't think twice about what she had on. "Come in and let the door close."

He did as she asked. Praying his body's reaction didn't show in her dream world but by the smile that spread across her face he knew he was just as hard here as he was sitting in the chair with his uncle watching. Instead of getting upset with him she laughed and pulled a uniform on. His being screamed for him to pounce on her as he saw flashes of her skin while she changed. It took every ounce of willpower to stay rooted to the spot.

Her lack of modesty confused him. This wasn't the same woman who was embarrassed by their mating ceremony. She did it to see how he would react and his reaction made her happy. What was going on inside her mind now? Did the kiss do this? He needed to know more before he could be sure.

"Ready?"

"I need a minute." Storm swallowed hard, working to keep his hands from reaching for her.

"What is the matter, Ensign? Not used to seeing an officer change in front of you?"

"Not one so desirable." He couldn't lie to her.

"You find me desirable?" Her features softened.

"Very much." He placed his hand over her heart. "Remember, my heart?" He hoped she did.

Heather stepped back from him. "We're due to speak to the ambassador's best man in a few minutes."

"About what?"

She tilted her head then called him along, not answering his question. Sometimes he found these scenarios a bit confusing. They walked down several corridors before they stood in front of large white doors. They opened to reveal an opulent room.

"Heather, thank you so much for coming. I was afraid I wouldn't be able to see you before I got called back to Vespia."

She smiled and took the hand he offered her. She ignored her assistant as she spoke to the man. "You needed to speak to me?"

"Yes," said Ialog.

Storm could see her reaction wasn't what the man wanted.

"You and I have spoken about you coming home with me. I came to see if you were ready."

"No." Her words came out forceful. "I can't go with you. I have told you that before."

"Why not? What is holding you here now? The ambassador is gone. You've outstayed your usefulness here. It's time."

"No!" She took off in a run, trying to get to the doors before he could overpower her.

Storm moved with her, blocking the man from reaching her and helping Heather get out the door before she could be stopped. She ran down a corridor. One he recognized. He took her hand and led her to the nearest alcove. It was the one from her memory. He pulled her into the small dark room and closed the door.

Now there was nothing but the two of them. Once again he placed his hand over her heart, hoping she would remember. The darkened interior wrapped them in a gentle cocoon. He hoped this time she would remember because they were running out of time.

"Storm?"

His heart sang. "Yes, my heart."

"Where have you been?"

"Looking for you. It hasn't been easy." He pulled her into his embrace. "But I have found you now."

"I don't understand." Her voice filled with sadness.

"What?" he brushed his fingers down her throat.

"I saw you marry another."

"Only you. Three times I believe." He needed her so badly but heeded his uncle's words. "Everything else has been a nightmare."

"How do I know it's really you?" She touched his face.

"You tell me." Just a touch aroused her. The steady beat of his heart calmed her. Even now he could feel the rapid tempo of her heart slow to match his.

Her hand covered his heart as they stood together. She pressed her lips to his shirt, then the collar of his uniform. When he felt her tongue lick along the length of his neck, he felt it all the way to his toes.

Heather continued her exploration. He wasn't sure what to do. His desire wanted him to grab her and have his way with her, but after all he had been through, he knew he needed to listen to what his uncle recommended. But keeping his hands to himself was torturous.

"Storm?"

"Yes, my heart." He touched her face the way he had in the past.

"I don't know how to get home."

"Yes you do. First you need to break the hold of this dream reality."

"How?"

"What is the one thing that you know is real?"

"Us." She pulled him down into a deep kiss. One that shattered the room. Now it was just the two of them. They stood in a brightly lit area devoid of anything but them. Her hands worked against the seals of his uniform, fighting with the cloth as she forced the uniform off his shoulders.

He could only mimic her movements, releasing her uniform in the same places she released his.

"Why do I feel like I'm moving through water to remove your clothing?"

"Because you're trying to use your hands when you should be doing this with your mind." He suddenly stood before her naked.

She closed her eyes for a moment and she stood before him devoid of clothing. "You should have told me that a long time ago." She touched his face. "I need to feel you inside me again, please."

He lifted her and pushed himself deep inside. Closing his eyes, he was home. Heather moved against him, their minds as one. She would shift to increase the sensations and he felt it just as strong. They shared everything.

Storm gripped her hard as he felt her orgasm start. "Together, my heart. We have to do this together."

"I'm not sure I can wait." Her head dropped back as she felt everything tighten. "Is that you or me?"

"You." He pulled out and then surged back in. They both felt his shudder. "That was me."

He found her throat and nibbled. Every time he slid in and out he could feel her get closer. When she tightened against him, they both felt it. She tightened her hold on him. "Now, Storm."

He couldn't agree more. Everything shifted when he picked up the pace. Heather moved with him. Racing for an invisible goal. Her body tightened against him, squeezing him so he was reaching his orgasm with her. As their world exploded the device keeping Heather locked from him shattered, exposing all she was to them. He felt the strength of her mind, how it protected her. He could see everything she did. His mate belonged to him and only him, no matter what someone else wanted.

Storm recognized where she was being kept. He opened his eyes. "I know where she is."

EIGHTEEN

Heather's release was so powerful. Only Storm could give her this. The desire that raced through her paled in comparison to the joy of knowing she hadn't been dreaming all along. The world where Storm was her mate was real.

Another sensation took over. One she had never felt before. It started in the back of her head. It was slightly painful, but it felt like a veil tore in her brain. Energy flowed through her, more powerful than she had ever felt. The darkness around her disappeared, and she found herself secured to a metal bed. Where was she?

"How did you overcome the medication?" the voice asked her.

"Let me go." She pulled against her restraints.

"Sorry, Heather. You're not going anywhere."

She looked around, trying to figure out where she was. The images she had seen in her vision were very close to what she saw now. The ceiling was dark because the lights hung so low. The row of cabinets she had seen were old lockers lined up. If she could get a chance, she'd wanted to find a weapon to protect herself. But how could she get off the table?

"It has happened, hasn't it?" She could hear the excitement in the voice. Was whatever he wanted from her at hand?

Changes continued inside her. She felt a second heartbeat and just a hint of a thought. A baby? Now? How was she going to protect it?

"What are you talking about?" Her head swam with all the new sensations floating through her mind. Heather found it hard to think straight.

"Your gift, my dear. I wanted to see it for myself."

"You know what my gift is?" Her head filled with so many things. She wished she could release some of the pressure. Her head felt like it would explode.

"I had an idea."

A strange noise filled the air as a weird contraption came above her and scanned her body.

"Your mind had been going through a lot of changes. It was hard to create a world for you to believe in. But I found one close to your reality, and it was starting to work. I should have known your mind would break any creation my computer could make the moment your body absorbed the remnants of your device."

"Why have you been after me?" He didn't know Storm had helped her break its hold and she wasn't about to tell him.

"You're not the only one with ancient blood in them. And not the only one who gets visions. I knew you would find your mate and that you would come to your full potential. My goal in all of this has been a simple one, Heather. Has from the beginning. I want your child."

Heat filled her as something sliced into her.

She wanted to fight it but didn't know how. Her main thought was to protect her child. She now understood why her parents did what they did to protect her. It was up to her to do the same thing. "I won't let you take my baby from me. If I can't have it, you can't either."

Her mind stretched and pushed, forcing her to do something she never wanted to do but she was able to protect her child at least for a little while. Now she had to get out of there before the voice knew what she had done.

The chains that bound her were easy to break. They snapped like a child's toy. Finding herself free, she slid off the bed and onto the floor.

She didn't know how long she had been there, but her legs gave out when she tried to put weight on them. She struggled to move. There wasn't much time. She could hear the footfalls of people running toward the room.

Her heart beat hard in her chest when she realized there was no escape for her. She didn't want it to end this way.

Light blared into the room, illuminating everything around her. She found herself swept up in a warm embrace. One she recognized. Tears ran down her cheeks when she knew she was safe at last.

She opened her eyes once again. Was this real? Or was she still trapped inside some nightmare? "Storm?"

"I'm here." He sat on her bed and took her hand in his. "You're safe now."

"You sure?"

He laughed as he touched her face. "Yes, my heart. You're now home where you belong."

She rested her head back against the pillows behind her. "Did you catch him? Ialog?"

"No." He rested his hand against her heart. "He was gone before we arrived."

"He won't stop until he has what he came for." She touched her stomach.

"So you know what he is after?"

"Yes." She sat up and took his hand. Pressing it against her stomach, she said just two words. "Our child."

"What?" He wasn't the only one who said that. Heather looked around to find immediate family all around her.

"I'm pregnant." Heather smiled. Joy filled her when she realized she could now celebrate this with her mate. They made a child together. "She made me aware of her presence the moment my mind broke free."

Storm just stared at her in awe. "A baby?"

"Yes." The joy she felt was contagious. He looked at her before hesitantly touching her stomach. The knowledge lit his face up.

"Wait." Storm removed his hand. Concern filled his voice. "You said the baby was what he was after."

"He was. All he said was she was the reason he went through everything he did. It was never me he wanted."

"But what about all those times he tried to kidnap you?"

"Look back at those events now. What was the one thing it did? Bring us closer together. He knew our relationship wouldn't grow if we weren't united against a common foe. He needed us to bond quickly because of my device. He wanted to kidnap our child before we had the means to stop him and knew once that moment was gone, he wouldn't be able to get to her. He seemed to know when the device would be completely absorbed and he was ready the moment it happened."

"If he wanted her." Storm touched her stomach again. "Is she safe?"

"Yes, but I didn't have a lot of time and didn't know how to stop him, so I tricked him into doing the only thing I could think of. Make him take the wrong egg." She placed her hand on top of his. "He still got away with one and can still do whatever he had originally planned with it. We have to get it back."

"And we will." Storm pressed his other hand against her heart. "But you have been through a lot and need to rest. Mate's orders."

She smiled at him and lay back against the pillows. Happy to be safe and home.

He walked to his uncle. "You have anything to say?"

"Why would I? I'm just some crazy old man, remember?"

"I think you proved that isn't true." Storm wanted to throttle the man, but without his help, he never would have found Heather. "Is this over?"

"No."

"You said she was the key." He kept his voice down so he wouldn't be heard.

"And she was, but she is right, too. Your children will be targets as well. I need to meditate more and maybe I can have a better answer for you." He walked off, leaving Storm to stand by himself. He turned to look back at his nephew. "You did good, Storm."

He gave him a nod, grateful it had worked out.

Heather's parents came to him next. "Do you think she'll ever forgive us for sending her away like that?"

"That's a question I can't answer. She's the only one who can." He looked over to find her watching them. "Why don't you go and talk to her?"

They weren't sure what to do but after a few more tries Storm was able to get them moving to her side. He felt like he was in some sort of congratulatory line because people were waiting to speak to him. Next was one of the young men he had assigned to check out the name Heather had given him. "Sir, the search is done."

"And what did you find?"

"Very rare name. Comes from a very old family that

doesn't seem to exist anymore." He handed Storm a computer chip that had all the data they could find.

"Thank you."

"Glad to see her safely home, sir."

"Me too." He shook his hand. "Go on home to your family. I'll contact everyone when we're ready to get back to work."

"Yes, sir." He saluted and moved on.

"And how are you feeling today, Mother?"

"Much better." She walked a little slow, but he had been informed she would make a full recovery. "I wanted to tell you that I wasn't aware of the injections. It wouldn't have happened if I did."

"Heather's parents believed it was for her and my protection. We might not like being manipulated like that, but who knows how different my life might have been if they hadn't."

"You're scaring me a little. That is the most mature thing I think I have ever heard you say."

"Haven't you heard? I'm going to be a father."

"The other scary thing I heard. You were bad enough, but your child? We are in trouble. She or he will be spoiled to death. Like their father, they will get away with too much, and their grandparents will dote on them too much." His mother kissed him on the cheek before moving to her rooms.

The doctor came to check on Heather, and Storm stood at her side.

"You look wonderful, my dear." He sat on the edge of the bed and ran a scanner over her. "Glad to see you back and in one piece."

"Glad to be back, Doctor. How are you feeling? I understand you've been a bit under the weather yourself."

"I'm fine, now." He smiled at her. "And you seem to be as well." He closed the scanner and put it back in his bag.

A slight nod from Heather had Storm putting an arm

around the doctor so he could take the scanner undetected. He brought it back to her. "Now, why did you want this?"

"I didn't mean anything by it. Just trying a few things." She held out her hand. "Can I see it?"

He dropped it into her open palm. "What are you looking for?"

She checked the readings and sat back. "How prevalent are twins in our race?"

Storm found the question a little strange. "Why?"

"Because we're going to have twins, too. Just like both our parents." Her face held joy and fear over the news. "I went from not being able to get pregnant to carrying twins so quickly. It's a lot to accept."

"You'll do fine. By the time they're born next year."

"Year? How long do Vespian pregnancies last?"

"Eighteen months."

Her eyes got very wide.

"How long did they last on Earth?" Did he frighten her with that?

"Nine months. Women on Earth got very cranky toward the end of their pregnancy because they wanted it over and that was for only nine months. How evil will I get when I start feeling like I'm pregnant forever?"

He laughed and kissed her forehead. "I will make sure you have all the information on a Vespian pregnancy available to you. It is nothing to be afraid of. Women have been going through it for a millennia."

"One of these times I'd like to meet a race where the male of the species carried the offspring." Then she grinned. "Or perhaps just gets to feel what women go through to carry a child."

He didn't like the look she gave him. "And what are you plotting now?"

"You'll see."

He grew tired of the parade of people who came to see

Heather. He didn't realize how far the news of her kidnapping had gotten until all these people came to see her. Her parents said their goodbyes, promising to visit again later.

The room finally emptied out, and he locked the door before someone else could enter.

"Now." He climbed on the bed next to her and cradled her in his arms. "There was a definite threat in your words earlier, and I'd like to know what is going on in that glorious head of yours."

"Understand I'm still new to my abilities." She closed her eyes for a moment.

He felt her thoughts brush against his. Gentle, slightly seductive. Then she was there in his mind. He found the intimacy beyond anything he had ever experienced. Her thoughts mingled with his. Then he sensed something else. Her joy filled him as he focused on it. Another thought joined them, then a second one. There wasn't a lot to the thoughts yet. Their presence in the world still so new but he felt them.

"Is it like that for you all the time?" he was in awe over what he just experienced.

"Sort of. I know there is another presence but wasn't sure about the second one until we saw the scanner. I got fleeting touches, but it would have taken another month or two before I was sure."

"Will they be with us every time we're intimate?" Knowing their children would know when they were having sex with his mate might deter him a little.

"I can block them out right now. Don't want to over stimulate them while they're this young, but I'm not sure about the future when they are stronger."

"And are you going to deny me my favorite play area because of them for the next eighteen months? That's a very long time for me to do without."

"I know." She planted a soft kiss on his lips. "Normally I

would say of course not, but I know as time goes on I'm going to need leverage."

"What sort of leverage?" He closed his eyes when her gentle fingers slipped under his shirt to brush along his abdomen.

"I don't want to be trapped at home for eighteen months because my mate has this archaic belief that I'm too fragile to work. Would you pull that one on me?" She opened his shirt and started pressing little kisses to his chest.

"You're my mate, and I need to protect you and our children." She wasn't fighting fair, so the moment she pulled up to glare at him, he took advantage and rolled her over. Pinning her with his body, he gave his wicked smile. "Although you have proven time and again, you can take care of yourself, I still feel it is my duty to keep you safe. If I say you can return to work, will you do as I say?"

She looked up at him, her beautiful violet eyes sparkling. "Do I get to fight you tooth and nail on any overprotective maneuver you might pull?"

He lowered his lips to hers for a deep, sensual bone-melting kiss. She could have anything she wanted if she kept kissing him like this. "Are you going to argue with me in front of any of my men?"

He captured her lips for a second time. Their tongues dance their favorite dance together.

She sighed when he broke the kiss for a second time. "I know better. But I might pout if I don't get my way."

"Noted." He opened the gown the medics had put on her, exposing her body to his touch. "You are so beautiful."

She opened her mind to him so he could feel the tingles his fingertips brought to her as he drew circles around her nipples. He felt her nipples harden and silently beg for his hot mouth. When he swirled his tongue against the tender flesh, they both groaned.

"I may never want to get out of bed again," he murmured against her skin.

She laughed and pushed him over. Having released him from his trousers earlier, she smiled a wanton smile. "You think that was good? You haven't felt anything yet." In one move, she straddled him and impaled them both. She squeezed him on the way down, making them shake with need.

His hands moved to her hips, helping her set a tempo that aroused them more. At her mental urging, he slid his fingers into her folds and found the small nub he knew she liked to have him caress. Waves of overwhelming need flooded them. Her body clenched tight and sent them over the edge. The freefall experience left them a little breathless.

He rolled them over and brushed a few stray hairs out of her face. "Access to multiple orgasms? Now I know I never want to get out of bed."

Storm moved inside of her, the tightness of her walls hugging him, causing delicious sensations to roll through him. He slid in and out, building the friction higher and higher. Heather wrapped her legs around his waist to give him better access.

The bond between them had merged their individual sensations into one. There was no his versus her, just theirs. It transcended the physical. White hot energy shot through them both. The faster he moved, the stronger it got. The release they craved was there in front of them. Storm reached it first, feeling the explosion in his soul. Heather came right behind him. Once again, they had the sensation of free falling.

It was so delicious he wanted to do it over and over again.

Um, excuse me. Could you two stop sharing this with me? Almost had an accident because of it.

"Who the hell was that?" He stared at Heather, who looked just as shocked as he felt.

"I believe that was my brother."

THE END

———

Coming Winter 2023
Passionate Desire, The Desire Series, Book 2

———

Don't miss out on your next favorite book!

Join the Satin Romance mailing list
www.satinromance.com/mail.html

THANK YOU FOR READING

Did you enjoy this book?

We invite you to leave a review at your favorite book site, such as Goodreads, Amazon, Barnes & Noble, etc.

DID YOU KNOW THAT LEAVING A REVIEW...

- Helps other readers find books they may enjoy.
- Gives you a chance to let your voice be heard.
- Gives authors recognition for their hard work.
- Doesn't have to be long. A sentence or two about why you liked the book will do.

ABOUT THE AUTHOR

Writing for Barbara Donlon Bradley started innocently enough, like most she kept diaries, journals, and wrote an occasional letter but she also had a vivid imagination and wrote scenes and short stories adding characters to her favorite shows and comic books.

As time went on, she found the passion for writing to be a strong drive for her. Humor is also very strong in her life. No matter how hard she tries to write something deep and dark, it will never happen. That humor bleeds into her writing. Since she can't beat it, she has learned to use it to her advantage.

Now she lives in Tidewater Virginia with a cat who thinks he owns everything, her husband and daughter.

www.barbaradonlonbradley.com

ALSO AVAILABLE

Novels

Love Is…

A Portrait in Time

Love on the Run

Love's Quest Series

A Quest For Love

Magical Quest